ANGELS OF MERCY

ANGELS OF MERCY

A MERCY ALLCUTT MYSTERY, BOOK 4

ALICE DUNCAN

Without limiting the rights under copyright(s) reserved below, no part of this publication may be reproduced, stored in or introduced into a retrieval system, or transmitted, in any form, or by any means (electronic, mechanical, photocopying, recording, or otherwise) without the prior permission of the publisher and the copyright owner.

This is a work of fiction. Names, characters, places, and incidents either are the product of the author's imagination or are used fictitiously, and any resemblance to actual persons, living or dead, business establishments, events or locales is entirely coincidental.

The scanning, uploading, and distributing of this book via the internet or via any other means without the permission of the publisher and copyright owner is illegal and punishable by law. Please purchase only authorized copies, and do not participate in or encourage piracy of copyrighted materials. Your support of the author's rights is appreciated.

Copyright © 2012, 2019 by Alice Duncan.. All rights reserved.

Book and cover design by eBook Prep
www.ebookprep.com

January, 2020
ISBN: 978-1-64457-109-5

ePublishing Works!
644 Shrewsbury Commons Ave
Ste 249
Shrewsbury PA 17361
United States of America

www.epublishingworks.com
Phone: 866-846-5123

ONE

My goodness, but things move fast in Los Angeles. I'd barely begun to think about purchasing my sister and brother-in-law's lovely home on Bunker Hill—the name of which my parents deplored because it had been borrowed from a revered eastern landmark—when the deed was done!

Oh, very well…things didn't happen *quite* that quickly, but almost. Chloe, my sister, and Harvey Nash, her husband, had intended to build their own home, probably in Beverly Hills, in anticipation of a family to come, the first infant member of which was already on its way to being born. Then Velma Blackwood and Stanley Hastings, two huge names in the motion-picture business, divorced. Their gigantic home in Beverly Hills, complete with swimming pool, acres of gorgeous gardens and huge iron privacy fences, went on the market. Harvey said the deal was too good to pass up, and Chloe liked anything that didn't require her to work hard—Chloe had suffered from morning sickness for a couple of months by then—and *voila*! I owned a house.

I already lived in the house, Chloe having kindly offered me a haven from our parents when I dared leave the nest, which was in Boston, almost three thousand happy miles away. It was thus I ended up buying the Nash home, only a couple of blocks away from Angels Flight, the almost vertical funicular railroad running the steep block from Olive to Hill, and which I took to work every day.

I loved that railroad. I also loved my job. I'd had to endure gobs of pressure from my parents and assorted other relations to get it, what's more. You see, I was born and bred in the upper echelons of Boston society, and the women in the Allcutt clan did *not* work for their bread. It was baked for them by cooks and served to them by various maids, butlers and house boys. In leaving home and securing employment clear across the country, I had bucked centuries of proper Allcutt heritage. Phooey on heritage, say I.

What I wanted was experience of the real world, and there wasn't much of it to be found in my parents' Beacon Hill estate in Boston. But I was getting plenty of valuable experience as secretarial assistant to Ernest Templeton, P.I. By the way, P.I stands for Private Investigator. I only mention it because I didn't know what the initials stood for until Ernie told me.

I didn't have to go to a real-estate agent or an attorney to purchase the Nash place. Harvey sent his own personal representatives to me at the Bunker Hill house, so I was able to secure the property with ease and in comfort. I'll admit it here, but I'd never tell Ernie, that having scads of money does make one's life easier. This didn't mean I took grievous advantage of the legacy my great-aunt, Agatha, left me; I only used her money for emergencies, and it didn't look as if it would be running out any time soon. The principal was invested in secure bonds and so forth, according to my odious brother George, his nose wrinkling the while. Both George and my father are bankers. Banking is a fine profession for them, but I had tired of my ivory tower in Boston eons earlier. Therefore, I'd made my way to Los Angeles, where I was jolly well enjoying myself.

No one in the Allcutt family except Chloe and me approved of people enjoying themselves. The women in my family are supposed to take tea with friends, shop, go to the theater occasionally, do "good works" at their assorted churches and deplore everything else. Our church was Episcopalian. I think being an Episcopalian is *de rigueur* in Boston for some reason. My mother almost suffered a spasm when she learned I'd gone to services at the Angelica Gospel Hall a month or so ago and enjoyed a couple of rip-roaring sermons delivered by the church's charismatic female preacher, Adelaide Burkhard Emmanuel.

Anyhow, now that I owned the property on Bunker Hill, my next plan was to rent out rooms. The house had suites of rooms, any of which would serve as a wonderful apartment for a working woman like me. My first tenant would be Lulu LaBelle, receptionist at the Figueroa Building, where I worked for Ernie on the third floor. Lulu was also a good friend of mine.

On this, the third Monday in September, I'd come to work in a sunny mood. This, in spite of the shocking news of another celebrity death published in the newspaper just that morning. As I read the paper over breakfast, I shook my head, thinking Los Angeles was quite a violent place. Much more violent than staid old Boston.

Anyhow, Chloe and Harvey had sent in a swarm of people to pack and move them and their belongings to their newly acquired mansion in Beverly Hills, and I'd spent a good deal of time and a tiny bit of Great-Aunt Agatha's money in furnishing the former Nash residence. Chloe and Harvey had left most of their furniture, Harvey claiming it would be easier to buy new stuff than move the old. See what I mean about money? I only had to make a few purchases to round out my household furnishings.

Because I'd planned the acquisition of my home and what I aimed to do with it carefully, I'd already hired Mr. and Mrs. Emerald Buck to be my housekeeper/cook (Mrs. Buck) and caretaker (Mr. Buck). Mr. Buck also worked as the custodian at the Figueroa Building, but he said he didn't mind keeping things running in my home, as well as doing his regular job. The man was a positive fountain of energy. I also provided them with their own apartment, which sweetened the deal for them.

But that's not the point. The point was: I was in a great mood when Ernie Templeton strolled into the office about nine-thirty on that hot Monday morning. According to Chloe, the month of September is always hot in Los Angeles, although in Boston it's generally beginning to cool off a bit by then. However, for my independence from my overbearing mother, I could endure months of hot weather. Already had, come to think of it.

"Good morning, Ernie," said I, beaming at him with genuine pleasure. I liked Ernie. He was a trifle nonchalant and definitely not cut of the same upright cloth as my social "equals" in Boston, but this characteristic only made him more appealing to me. He was a good, honest man—a shade too honest sometimes—and an overall good egg.

He frowned at me. This was his habitual greeting, so I didn't take umbrage. "What the devil are you so happy about?"

"It's Monday, I love my job, and I now have a home of my very own."

He grunted. "Oh, yeah. You bought Chloe's house, didn't you?"

"Indeed I did. Now I intend to stock it with girls like me who hold jobs in the neighborhood."

"Huh. Must be nice to have money."

He was always saying things like that. As a matter of fact, he'd pegged me as a rich girl the moment he saw me. I'd chalked up his astute perception to long years in his profession. He was good at this detectival business. Before he became a P.I., he'd belonged to the Los Angeles Police Department, but he couldn't stand the corruption therein and had quit. I was almost accustomed to his snide references to my upper-crust roots by then.

Ergo, I only said, "Yes, it is."

With a characteristic roll of his startlingly blue, almost turquoise, eyes, he moved toward his office door. I, you see, sat in the outer office, where I had my own desk, my own telephone, and a good deal of my own property, which I'd bought here and there to spiff the place up some. The office—nay; the entire building—had been a run-down, dirty mess when I'd first begun working for Ernie in July. Some of the run-downedness had been the result of an inefficient, not to mention mentally disturbed, custodian, but this problem had been fixed by the hiring of Mr. Buck, who kept the place shiny and clean.

Figuring Ernie's words were it as far as morning greetings that day would go, I went back to work. Well…

To tell the truth, there wasn't much work to do in Ernie's office at the time. Ernie and I had solved a terrible murder the preceding month, but business had been rather slow since then. A couple of wives wanting Ernie to spy on their husbands; a couple of husbands wanting Ernie to spy on their wives. That was it. The business side of a private investigator's life can be, all things considered, a bit on the sordid side in between murder cases. I'd never tell my mother so. Actually, I didn't have to. She told me how sordid it was every time she wrote me a letter.

On this morning, however, before Ernie shoved his office door open, entered, flung his hat and coat at the rack set there to receive them—he often missed, but that's neither here nor there—and plunked himself in his swivel chair to read the *Los Angeles Times*, he hesitated. Then he stopped. Then he turned around and spoke to me again.

"Who are you going to rent rooms to?"

"Lulu, of course. But I suppose I'll have to place an advertisement in the *Times* in order to find other working girls who need a place of refuge from the rigors of Los Angeles life."

"Huh. You're going to get yourself into trouble, Mercy. You know that, don't you?"

Ernie and I'd had similar conversations earlier in our association. He considered me too innocent for words. I agreed with him, which had been the whole point of my moving west and getting a job. I wanted experience of the real world in order to write the novels I had within me begging to get out. Gritty stuff. You know what I mean. How can a girl write gritty stuff when she has no understanding of grit? The answer to this question is: she can't.

"I will not," I said hotly. "You think I'm an idiot, don't you, Ernie Templeton?"

He heaved a deep sigh. "No, I don't think you're an idiot. I think you have no experience, and maybe you'll find yourself in trouble because of it. How do you plan to select these so-called working girls of yours?"

"Well...um, actually, I haven't given the matter much thought yet." Golly, I hated admitting the truth.

"Figures." Ernie slouched over to me and sat in the chair beside my desk. "Tell you what, Mercy. You place your ad in the *Times*, and when people begin responding, I'll sit in on the first interview to show you how it's done."

"Interview?" I blinked blankly at him.

Another eye-roll. "How the heck else do you expect to choose which people you want gracing your grand home? You're not going to let in any old Tom, Dick or Harry, are you?"

"Heavens, no! I'll allow no men at all above the first floor."

He covered his face with his hands for a second and his shoulders shook slightly. I think he was laughing at me, and I resented it. "Good God, Mercy," he said in a voice hinting of both amusement and exasperation. "I'm not talking about allowing men in your house. I'm talking about finding suitable tenants. You can't just let in anybody, you know, or you'll end up with a house full of riffraff."

Deciding it would behoove me not to chastise Ernie for his amusement at my expense, I said stiffly, "Very well. I shall interview the women desiring accommodations."

"Do you know how to interview anyone?" he asked, his tone laced with doubt.

I bridled instantly. "I certainly can't do any worse than you did when you interviewed me!"

He grinned. He would. "Yeah, that was something, wasn't it? I knew you'd do the minute I saw you."

I sniffed significantly. "There. You see?"

"But you don't have my experience."

"I've learned a lot—"

"Yeah, yeah, yeah. I know. You fancy yourself a real detective by this time. But you're not. Tell you what. You show me the ad before you take it to the *Times*. I want to make sure you word it properly. Then, as I said, I'll sit in on the first interview with you. In fact, I'll conduct your first interview. Show you how to go about it. Then you'll know what questions to ask of these working girls of yours."

"Hmm."

"You'd better take my offer, Mercy, or you're liable to end up in the soup."

I hated to admit it, but he might well be right. My judgment concerning people hadn't always been the best of late, although I chalk up this circumstance merely to having been reared in the confines of the aforementioned ivory tower. I was learning and learning fast. Therefore, rather than refuse Ernie's proposal and perhaps make a huge mistake, I said graciously, "Very well. Thank you for your kind offer."

"You're welcome." And he rose and slumped to his office. Shortly thereafter I heard his hat hit the floor, Ernie's soft ensuing "Damn," and the workday began.

About the only interesting thing to occur during the rest of the day was that I composed what I considered a nice ad to run in the *Times*:

Rooms to let to employed, single young ladies.
Telephone Miss Allcutt at Hollywood 3-7265.

As much as I didn't want to, I showed the ad to Ernie before I took it to the *Times* to place it. He was correct in that he was the one with the experience in the office, after all.

"You're giving them your home telephone number?" he asked, squinting at me.

As I sat in the chair across from his desk, I'd been wringing my hands in anticipation of what I expected from Ernie, which was criticism. It looked as if I wasn't going to be disappointed in my expectation. "Well…yes. If I'm at work, Mrs. Buck will answer the telephone. Why? Don't you think it's a good idea?"

"I think the idea stinks. I also think you shouldn't say, 'Telephone Miss Allcutt.' Hell, Mercy, if you write that, you're announcing to the world you're a single woman alone in the world."

I goggled at him for a moment, confused. "I don't see how it announces anything of the sort. It's only my name."

"Just leave out the 'Miss Allcutt' business altogether, all right? It's safer that way. You don't want any madmen showing up at your door looking for single women, do you?" He tapped the side of his head. "Think about it, Mercy."

I thought about it. Again, I regretted the conclusion I came to, which was that Ernie was, as usual, right. I sighed. "But what should I say then?" I was losing a good deal of my confidence along with some of my happy mood.

"Just give the telephone exchange. Don't mention your name,

and definitely don't let on you're a young, unmarried woman living alone in that huge house."

"I'm not living alone!" I cried, because it was the truth, and because his words stung. Darn it, you'd think I hadn't learned a single, solitary thing about life on the mean streets of Los Angeles in the months I'd lived here, and that wasn't accurate. "The Bucks have already taken up accommodations in the suite of rooms downstairs. And I'm not stupid, either, Ernie Templeton! You're acting as if I don't have a lick of common sense."

Ernie sucked in about a gallon of air. His voice, when he used it again, was measured. "I didn't mean to imply you have no common sense, Mercy, and I know you're not stupid. You're... still a trifle innocent of the world, is all."

I sniffed.

"What I propose," he said, in the same measured tone, "is that you leave out a name, any name. Just have the *Times* print the telephone exchange, only make it the one here at the office. That way, nobody you don't want hanging around will know your home telephone number, and if an undesirable person *does* happen to show up, it'll be here, and there will be lots of people in lots of other offices—primarily me—to hear you holler for help or kick the rotter out. Doesn't that make good sense?"

He didn't sound sarcastic as he asked the last question, so I didn't get mad at him. Rather, I said, "But wouldn't you mind having my prospective tenants calling here at the office?"

He shrugged. "Hell, why not? Nobody else ever calls."

He had a point there, unfortunately. "Well..."

"It's fine, Mercy. I'll be happy to hear the telephone ringing. Anyhow, when it comes to interviewing tenants, this will be a good place to do it. If you conduct interviews here, I won't have to go out of my way and neither will you. It'll be neutral territory. Besides which, if anyone really unsavory shows up, he or she won't know where you live."

Darn it, he had another good point there. "All right," I said, feeling humble. "Thank you, Ernie."

"You've already enlisted Lulu and the Bucks, right?"

"Yes," I said. "Lulu will be moving in over the upcoming weekend. And I consider both Lulu and the Bucks a very good start in what I believe will be a noble enterprise. Why should young women who have to work for a living be any different from young men who have to secure employment?" My feminist sensibilities were another thing my parents deplored. Sometimes I wondered what they'd have to deplore if I weren't around.

"No reason I can think of," Ernie said with casual indifference, curse him. "Mrs. Buck is going to feed the herd of nubile young ladies?"

Frowning, I said, "I wouldn't put it *that* way. But yes. I aim to set up a sort of boarding house. Lulu's told me there are a lot of boarding houses in Los Angeles, some for men and some for women. The ones for women give young women a safe refuge away from work and healthy meals. For the proper recompense, of course."

"Of course."

Approximately three weeks earlier, Ernie had sat me down and explained to me the appropriate rent I should expect to get from my prospective tenants. I'd been going to give Lulu a big break on the rent, but he'd pointed out to me that if I did so, Lulu would have felt she owed me something and she'd end up resenting me. This notion hadn't once occurred to me, but after thinking about it, I realized he was correct. In other words, he'd been a big help to me then, but his attitude now niggled at me.

"Darn you, Ernie, I'm learning! Quit disparaging me, will you? It was I, don't forget, who saved you from a murder charge not long ago!"

"How could I ever forget?" He rubbed his behind, which had been badly bruised in the incident mentioned.

"Ernest Templeton, if you aren't the most—"

He held up a hand, stopping me in mid-rant. "You're right. I appreciate you helping with that case."

"*Helping?*" I arched my eyebrows at him.

"All right. I appreciate you saving my neck."

"That's better." I sniffed again. This was becoming a bad habit of mine when in Ernie's company, and I resolved to stop doing it.

"Even though you almost got yourself killed in the process."

"It wasn't my fault!" I cried, stung.

He shrugged, a gesture as characteristic of him as my sniff was of me. "And I'm not disparaging you. I'm only trying to get you to understand you need…I mean to say, you might benefit from a little help from a man who's been loose in the big, bad world for many years now. Until you moved out here to live with Chloe and Harvey, you'd never seen hide or hair of the seamier side of life. Admit it, Mercy."

"I admit it readily," I said smartly. "Which is why I showed you my ad before I went to the *Times* to place it. However, I *won't* be ridiculed."

"I'm not ridiculing you," Ernie said, sounding world-weary and as if he thought I were sorely abusing him. Nuts. "I only want to assist you. Detecting is my business, after all. Has been for years and years. I'm good at it. I expect I'll be able to spot a…" He paused, pursing his lips as if searching for the right word. He settled on *objectionable*. "I expect I'll be able to spot an objectionable tenant a little better than you can. Because of my experience with the criminal element."

"Heavens! You don't really think criminals will answer my ad, do you?" The possibility had not occurred to me, thereby, I regret to say, justifying Ernie's doubts about my interviewing abilities. Darn it. "I mean, I certainly don't want any of…those types of women renting rooms in my house."

"Exactly my point. So you'll leave out your name and use the office telephone number, right?"

I thought about it for a moment or two, wishing I could see a flaw in Ernie's plan. I couldn't. "Right," I said.

And just in time, too, because Ernie's best friend and, according to Ernie, the only honest copper in the entire Los Angeles Police Department, shoved open the outer door just then, and I rose to go do my duty as Ernie's assistant. I mean his secretary.

"'Lo, Mercy," said Phil Bigelow, removing his hat like a true gentleman, unlike some other men I could mention. Phil and I had been on a first-name basis for months by then.

"Good morning, Phil. Ernie's not busy, so you may walk right in."

Phil chuckled. "When is he ever busy?"

"Not often, I fear," I said ruefully.

"Well, maybe that's about to change."

Brightening, I said, "Oh! Do you have a case for him to work on?"

He shook his head at me. "You know I can't talk about my work with you, Mercy."

"Phooey. You talk about your work all the time with Ernie. I'm his private secretary, so I should be in the know, too."

He gave me a big grin. "Well, I'll let Ernie tell you about this case then, if he thinks you can help."

Oh, great. Phil knew good and well Ernie *never* wanted me involved in any of his cases. Which was silly, considering I'd been of great assistance to him quite often since I'd come to work for him.

Men. As Chloe sometimes says, there's no doing anything with them.

This being the case, and since it was lunchtime, I said farewell to my aggravating employer and his almost-equally aggravating best friend and took the stairs down to the lobby, where I approached Lulu's reception desk.

"Want to go to the *Times* office with me, Lulu? I'm placing an advertisement for young ladies to take rooms in my house."

Lulu, who looked rather like a pansy that day, in a vivid yellow dress with brown accessories, and with her lips and fingernails painted a bright, startling red, rose from her desk as if she'd been shot from a gun. "You betcha!" Then she reached into her drawer, drew out a mind-bogglingly yellow hat and pinned it to her bottle-blond curls. Lulu, you see, was aiming to be "discovered" by a motion-picture producer, who would then make her a star, and she dressed accordingly.

I had my doubts about the way she was going about trying to be "discovered." I mean, I should think such an agenda would require a trifle more positive action on a girl's part than sitting behind the reception desk at the Figueroa Building on Seventh and Hill and waiting for a picture producer to stroll in, but what did I know?

According to Ernie, nothing at all.

Upon this lowering thought, Lulu and I left the building and headed to the *Times*.

TWO

As much as it pains me to admit it, Ernie was right. He taught me a whole lot about interviewing prospective tenants. In fact, I was at the point of thinking of "my" women as being angels of Mercy. I suppose that sounds egotistical, but I was honestly attempting to do some good in the world, a concept as alien to my family as the concept of a woman working to pay for the space she took up on this earth. As far as I was concerned, my family was about as divorced from reality as a family could be. However, my family's not the point.

The first person to telephone the office in response to my advert in the *Times* said her name was Miss Caroline Terry. Her call came in a day after the *Times* ran my ad for the first time. Therefore, this was on the Wednesday of the same week. Miss Terry seemed relieved to know I was the person to whom the boarding house (her term, although I pretty much agreed with her) belonged.

"Oh, I'm so glad!" cried she. "I…well, you know, a girl alone in the big city can't be too careful."

Exactly what Ernie had told me not two days earlier. I said, "So true."

"Um, I suppose you'd like to meet me before I take up residence in your home," Caroline said, still sounding shy.

"Yes, please. I'd like to set up an interview with you at a time convenient to both of us. I, too, am a working woman," I said with perhaps too much pride. I had a sneaking hunch Miss Caroline Terry would be more than grateful if she discovered a rich great-aunt had left her a substantial competence upon which to live so she didn't have to earn her keep. Sometimes I think life is incredibly unfair.

"Oh, I'm so glad!" she repeated. "I was afraid I'd have to ask for time off from work, and I hate to do that. My supervisor expects us girls to be here every day, on time, and in trim order."

"Indeed? Where do you work?"

"I'm a clerk in the hosiery department at the Broadway Department Store."

"My goodness! My sister and I take luncheon there every now and then," I said, happy to have a point in common with Miss Terry already.

"Oh," said Miss Terry. "How nice."

She didn't sound ecstatic to know I was in the habit of dining at the Broadway's lunchroom with my sister. I guess I could understand that. According to Ernie, most working women can't afford to dine out except at taco stands and such. I hoped I hadn't made a mistake before I'd even met Miss Terry, who sounded—over the telephone wire at least—to be a nice girl.

"The Broadway is also close to my place of employment, which is on the third floor of the Figueroa Building on Seventh and Hill."

"Yes, I know the building. It's right there near Angels Flight."

My railroad. I felt my heart warming toward Miss Terry.

"Um, could you come at lunchtime? Or after you get off work? Of course, I don't know your working schedule."

"On Fridays, I work from one o'clock until nine in the evening," she said.

"So late?" I was mildly shocked, believing in my innocence that young women should be safe at home after dark.

"The rest of the week, the Broadway closes at six p.m.," she explained. "But on Fridays, we stay open late so other people who work during the day have an opportunity to do their shopping."

"Of course. That makes sense." I thought for a moment. "Well, then, can you come to the Figueroa Building on Seventh and Hill at, say, ten o'clock on Friday morning?" This would give Ernie plenty of time to get to the office. Unless, of course, he was working on a case—and even after Phil's visit and some subtle probing on my part, I didn't know if he was or wasn't, curse it.

"That would be perfect," she said, sounding happy. I guess she'd expected to be put to more bother in order to apply to live in my home.

My sympathies were stirred. When I went to tell Ernie he had an appointment to interview a young lady at ten o'clock on Friday morning, I didn't tell him about my sympathies, since he'd have sneered at me. I'd known for some time by then Ernie saved his sympathies for bigger things than ladies who had to work for a living.

He glanced up from the *Times*. I noticed he'd been working the crossword puzzle. Crossword puzzles were quite the rage at the time. I enjoyed working them myself sometimes.

"Yeah? The time should be all right. God knows I don't have anything else to do."

This gave me an opening, and I leaped into it. "You aren't working on a case with Phil?"

With a slight uplift of his left eyebrow—or perhaps it was his right—Ernie said, "You'd love it if I were, wouldn't you?"

I decided to tell the truth. "It would certainly be more interesting than practicing my shorthand. Which, by the way, I never use anyway. Why don't you write more letters, Ernie? Transcribing shorthand letters would be a more productive use of my time than doing exercises out of the book."

"Hell, if I had any clients, I might send them a bill every once in a while, but I seldom need to write letters. If you want to practice your shorthand, you should go work for an attorney."

My fists went to my hips and I glared at him. "Are you trying to get rid of me, Ernest Templeton?"

He held his hands up in a warding-off gesture. "Lord, no! Just saying, is all."

"Hmph. Well, I happen to like working for a private investigator, and I think both you and Phil are mean to keep secrets from me. It's not as if I'm going to go haring off to do any investigating of a serious crime on my own."

His other eyebrow rose until both nearly got lost in his hairline. I noticed he needed a haircut. "Right. Like you've never gone off investigating on your own before."

Lifting my chin, I replied with dignity. "Last month, when you were accused of a crime you didn't commit, I did my best to find the real culprit." Then I changed my stance until I stood glowering at my boss. "Nobody else was doing anything to clear you, don't forget!"

"How could I ever forget? I was right there when you almost got yourself murdered."

I think he actually shuddered, although it must have been my imagination because my casual, take-it-easy employer didn't do things like shudder at the notion of another person in peril.

"Perhaps that was a mistake," I grumbled. "I had no idea the person in question would try to murder me."

"Well, that's nice to know." He was being snide again, drat the man.

Our discussion, if you could call it a discussion, was interrupted just then by the outer office door opening. I turned on my heel and left my irritating boss, only to find Mr. Emerald Buck standing in front of my desk nearly strangling the cloth hat he held in both hands. He appeared upset. I rushed up to him and held out my hands.

"Mr. Buck! Whatever is the matter?"

"Miss Mercy, I needs to talk to Mr. Templeton. It's important, or I wouldn't be botherin' him with it."

Ernie, who had evidently detected the distress in Mr. Buck's voice, rose from his desk chair and came to stand in his office door. "What's the matter, Buck? I'm game to help if I can."

Interesting. Ernest Templeton had flatly refused to assist a friend of Chloe's and mine when said friend's mother was in trouble. Yet Mr. Buck didn't even have to tell Ernie what his problem was in order for Ernie to offer his assistance. I don't believe I'll ever understand the man as long as I live—which might be a good thing.

"Thank you, Mr. Ernie," said Mr. Buck, who was a gentleman of the Negro persuasion.

Here's another unfair thing about life. I knew for a fact Mr. and Mrs. Buck's daughter was attending college, on a scholarship mind you, in a southern state at an all-Negro college. According to Lulu, none of the colleges in Southern California would admit a Negro woman student, even one who clearly had the brains to win a scholarship.

It grieved me to see Mr. Buck so upset. I'd never before known him to be in anything but a genial, happy frame of mind. Unless, of course, he adopted his happy pose because we white folks expected it of him. I'd have liked to question him about the subtleties of race relations, but I wasn't quite sure how to go about it.

Anyhow, none of that mattered. Ernie said, "Come on in, Buck." He must have seen me frown at him, because he sighed gently and said, "Why don't you join us, Mercy? You can take notes in shorthand while Mr. Buck tells us his story."

"Thank you, Mr. Templeton. I shall be happy to take notes." So I went to my desk and grabbed a lined green stenographer's pad and two of the pencils I kept sharpened and standing at attention in a cunning little cup I'd bought in Chinatown. They pretty much stayed sharp all the time, too, unless I used them for practice.

Mr. Buck stood to one side so I could enter Ernie's office ahead of him, a considerate gesture that would have sat well upon any gentleman, black or white. I smiled at him as I went in and took a seat as far from Ernie's desk as I could get, wanting to remain inconspicuous. This was my own idea, by the way. I didn't want Mr. Buck to feel he needed to curtail any explanations or censor his words because he feared offending my pink and shell-like ears.

Ernie said, "Pull up to the desk, Mercy. Don't you want to have a hard surface to write on?"

So much for my considerate intentions. Giving Ernie a sour look, I said, "I am accustomed to holding my pad in my hand and writing with the other hand, thank you, Mr. Templeton."

"What's with this 'Mr. Templeton' stuff?" Ernie asked as if he really wanted to know. "Buck here knows we're all friends."

We were, were we? Well, we'd just see about that. I said, "Very well, *Ernie*."

He grinned at me and waved Mr. Buck into the chair directly opposite his on the other side of his desk. "All right, give it to me straight, Buck. What's the matter?"

Mr. Buck swallowed a couple of times, as if he were fighting strong emotions. After getting them under control, he said softly, "It's my son. Calvin."

"What about Calvin, Mr. Buck?" I found myself saying. Then I snapped a glance at Ernie, realizing I wasn't there to conduct an interview but to take notes. I murmured, "Sorry."

Darn it, I *really* wanted more responsibility in the firm. But I'd have to earn it and so far, even though I'd saved Ernie's life and solved a couple of big crimes, I hadn't yet, according to Ernie. I think he was being too fussy, but I resolved to keep my mouth shut, especially since Ernie met my glance with one of his own that clearly exhibited exasperation.

"So," said Ernie, taking over, "what about Calvin, Buck?"

Mr. Buck swallowed again. "He...he..." He pulled out a handkerchief and wiped his eyes. "The police have arrested him for murder!"

I know my eyes went round. I didn't drop my pencil, but it was hard to keep my mouth shut. Under the circumstances, I'm sure you can hardly blame me.

Ernie, cool as the proverbial cucumber, said, "Who's he accused of killing?"

"Mr. Milton Halsey Gossett."

I gasped. I couldn't help myself, in spite of the furious look Ernie shot me. But...Mr. Milton Halsey Gossett, for heaven's sake! I was pretty sure it was the Gossett murder about which Phil Bigelow had visited Ernie on Monday. Mr. Milton Halsey Gossett was a gigantic name in the moving-picture industry, and his murder had shocked the entire world, rather as the murder of Mr. William Desmond Taylor had four years earlier. The Taylor murder had never been solved. It was the lousy job the L.A. Police Department had done on the Taylor case, in fact, that had disgusted Ernie so much, he'd quit the force.

Ernie leaned back in his chair. After one quick glance at me, he focused his attention on Mr. Buck. Thinning his eyes slightly, he said, "What did your son Calvin have to do with Mr. Gossett, if anything, and why do the police suspect him of the killing?"

Mr. Buck sucked in a deep breath. "Calvin worked for Mr. Gossett as a houseboy. He's a student, but he needs to earn money for his books and stuff. Mrs. Buck and me don't make a lot of money, and we have a girl in college in Mississippi. Even though she's there on a scholarship," he said with obvious pride, "we still needs to pay for her housing and so forth. So Calvin, he's always worked hard. He's a good boy, Mr. Ernie. He's a *good* boy. He'd no more kill Mr. Gossett than he'd fly to the moon!"

"But he did work for Gossett?" Ernie didn't allow himself to be sidetracked by irrelevancies like the relative goodness of individual murder suspects.

Perhaps this was what made him a good detective: his dogged, single-minded determination to get to the bottom of things. I filed this bit of information in my brain to bring out and study later.

"Yes, he worked for Mr. Gossett. He worked from four to eight o'clock in the evenings and all day on Saturdays. He tidied up and served dinner and things like that. Mr. Gossett has…had him a cook-housekeeper, but Calvin served the meals. Mr. Gossett paid him pretty good, and Calvin said he was a nice man."

"Was Calvin there when the cook found Gossett's body?" Ernie asked.

According to the articles I'd read in various newspapers, Mr. Gossett had been murdered Sunday night in the living room of his home on Carroll Street in Los Angeles. I'd visited another home on Carroll not long before, and it was a lovely street with beautiful homes. The articles didn't mention a time of death, but they did say the cook-housekeeper who discovered the body when she went to work on Monday, about mid-day, was hysterical when she ran screaming from the house. Mr. Gossett had been shot at point-blank range, much as Mr. Taylor had been. It occurred to me perhaps there was a maniac in Los Angeles killing motion-picture directors, but I abandoned the notion almost as soon as it flickered through my brain. It seemed highly unlikely a homicidal maniac would wait four years between murders. If you know what I mean.

Mr. Buck shook his head.

"How'd the police find out your son worked for Mr. Gossett?"

"I reckon the cook told 'em. I think she suspected Calvin done Mr. Gossett in. In fact, she said so to the police." Mr. Buck's voice contained a note of bitterness for which I couldn't fault him.

"Why would she suspect Calvin?" asked Ernie, as if cooks suspecting houseboys of murder was an everyday kind of thing.

Mr. Buck looked from Ernie to me and back again, as if undecided whether or not we could handle what he was going to say.

Ernie saved him the trouble. "The cook's white? Therefore, she told the police your son, who's black, must have killed Gossett?"

After a moment, Mr. Buck nodded. "You gots it about right, Mr. Ernie. But Calvin didn't do it! He didn't even work for Mr. Gossett on Sundays, and that's when the man was killed. Hell... sorry, Miss Mercy."

"Think nothing of it," I murmured, figuring I shouldn't mention I heard lots worse than that from my boss on a daily basis.

"Anyhow, Calvin, he's studying to get into college just like Loretta—she's our daughter—and he spends all day on Sunday studying, after we gets home from church in the morning."

"What church do you attend?" asked Ernie.

"First AME on Harvard."

The First AME Church. Hmm. I'd ask Ernie what an AME Church was later. I'd never heard of an AME church before.

"What time does church start?"

I didn't see what this had to do with anything, but I dutifully wrote the question on my secretarial pad.

"Nine in the morning. We gets out about noon and have dinner at the church. Then we goes home to Miss Mercy's house, and Calvin does his studying until bedtime."

Golly, I didn't know that!

Ernie glanced my way. "Did you see Calvin on Sunday, Mercy?"

I shook my head. "No. Sorry." I wished I could have supplied an alibi for poor Calvin, but I didn't believe I should lie about the matter, either.

Mr. Buck hung his head. "I'm right sorry, Miss Mercy, but we didn't know what you'd think about having a young man like Calvin in your house, so we...well, we didn't tell you about him. I'm sorry, Miss Mercy. But, honest, he's a good boy."

"I'm sure he is, Mr. Buck, and I don't mind at all. He's welcome to study in...your rooms any time he wants."

Which just goes to show how even the best of us—not that I consider myself the best of us—have prejudices that leap to the fore at the most inconvenient times. I'd been going to say that Calvin could study in my house any old time he wanted to, but I'd changed my wording at the last minute. The truth was, if I'd seen a young Negro man lurking around my home, I might have been suspicious of his motives for being there. It's a wicked, unfair world, but I think I've mentioned that before.

Ernie gave me an enigmatical glance before continuing his questioning of Mr. Buck. "Did the police give you or Calvin any indication as to why they might suspect him except for the fact that he worked for Mr. Gossett and is a Negro?"

"Nobody told me nothin'," said Mr. Buck. "They ain't told

Calvin nothin', either. Poor Calvin's about to lose his mind, locked up in that jail. And Lottie and me can't bail him out because it's a murder charge, and we don't have money for bribes and suchlike."

Don't ask me why, but his words shocked me. Honestly, I knew better than to be surprised, since about the first lesson I'd learned after coming to work for Ernie was that money could buy pretty much anything in the City of Angels, from liquor to freedom from criminal charges. Angels, my foot.

"Nobody saw Calvin near the Gossett home on Sunday?" Ernie asked. As I said before, Ernie was not easily distracted from gathering information once he started.

Mr. Buck shook his head. "I don't know, Mr. Ernie. Like I say, nobody's telling me nothing."

"I'll look into the matter for you, Buck. Try not to worry."

A short gust of air was all the benefit Ernie got from his suggestion. How could the Bucks not worry? What Mr. Buck had said about Calvin being arrested because of his race was probably darned close to the truth. And—I knew this from experience—once the police had a likely, or even an unlikely, suspect in their sights, they didn't generally bother to look for anyone else who might have committed the crime.

Rising from my chair, I shuffled my pencil into my pad hand and held out my empty hand to Mr. Buck. "I'm so sorry, Mr. Buck, but if anyone can clear your son's name, it's Ernie. He's the best in the business, you know."

Mr. Buck took my hand, shook it, and nodded. "Thanks, Miss Mercy. That's what I've heard, too."

I noticed his eyes were red, as if he'd either been crying or trying not to cry. My heart went out to him, and I wanted to rush home right then and comfort Mrs. Buck. But I had a job and the only bad thing about having a job—well, there might be more than one thing bad about some jobs, but not mine—was that, from eight in the morning until five in the evening, my time belonged to Mr. Ernest Templeton, P.I. Except for the hour I got for lunch, of course.

"Please remember it. I know you can't help but worry about your son, but Ernie will fix everything. You'll see." I was putting a lot of emphasis on Ernie being a top-notch investigator. I hoped I was telling the truth.

"Thanks, Miss Mercy," Mr. Buck said again.

Ernie and I watched as he shambled, stoop-shouldered, from the office. Then Ernie turned to me.

"So I'm the best there is, eh?"

"The poor man needs all the encouragement he can get, Ernie. I figured it wouldn't hurt to lie a little." My last comment was meant as a joke.

Ernie must have taken it as such, because he grinned. "But I do mean to do my best for the poor guy."

Just then the outer office door opened again, and Mr. Buck reappeared. Both Ernie and I looked at him expectantly. Personally, I was hoping he'd say he'd forgotten to mention that a well-known hoodlum had been seen lurking around the Gossett home on Sunday night, but he didn't.

"I forgot all about money, Mr. Ernie. I'm sorry." He stuck his hand in his pocket and hauled out a handful of bills. "I ain't got no idea how much you charge, but—"

Ernie cut him off. "Put your money away, Buck. I'll send you a bill later."

Mr. Buck squinted at him quizzically. "I don't want you to do nothin' for me for nothin', Mr. Ernie. I pays my way, and so does Calvin."

"I know it. But we'll talk about it later. Right now I want to do some investigating. I'll talk to you later about the money."

After hesitating, his hand full of cash, Mr. Buck said, "Well…"

"I'm not taking your money right now," said Ernie more firmly. "We'll discuss it later, after I learn more about the case."

Reluctantly, Mr. Buck stuffed the money back into his pocket. "You be sure to bill me, Mr. Ernie. I don't take nothin' for free."

"Don't worry. I never give away my services," Ernie said with one of his more insouciant grins.

Mr. Buck didn't look as if he believed him, but he left the office again.

At once, I turned upon Ernie. "You humiliated the poor man, Ernest Templeton! How could you do such a thing?"

Holding up a hand, Ernie said, "Take it easy, Mercy. I want to talk to Phil about this before I waste any of my time on the case. For all you know—hell, for all *I* know—Calvin is guilty as sin of murdering Milton Halsey Gossett."

I stiffened. "I don't believe it."

"Huh. You're a hell of a lot nicer than I am then. Or more gullible. That's probably it."

There it was again, rather like an elephant standing in the office: my plaguey innocence of the world. I sniffed, offended, and said, "Well, I'm going to take luncheon now."

"You do that. I'm going to visit Phil."

Hopping from my high horse in an instant, I said, "Will you tell me what Phil says about the matter?" Before he could object, I reminded him, "I have a personal interest in this case, don't forget. The Bucks work for me. Therefore, it's important for me to know what's going on."

With one of his characteristic eye-rolls, Ernie said, "We'll see."

Drat the man!

THREE

Lulu and I took our lunch around noonish at the counter of a drug store not far from the Figueroa Building. Lulu was all agog about Calvin Buck having been arrested for the murder of Milton Halsey Gossett.

"Golly, Mercy, do you think he did it? Wouldn't that be something? The Bucks live right there in your house! What if it runs in the family or something?"

I gave Lulu a repressive frown. On this particular day, she wore a low-waisted red flowered number with short sleeves matching her violently red fingernails and lipstick. "Don't be ridiculous, Lulu. The Bucks are good, upstanding citizens, and I'm sure their children are, too."

"Well...you're probably right. And I do know that once the coppers get their hands on somebody, they hate to let him go."

Lulu and I both had good reason to know this. In fact, the police had arrested Lulu's brother, Rupert, for murder once, and it had been like prying fighting dogs apart to get them to release the poor fellow. Fortunately for all, I, Mercedes Louise Allcutt, had discovered the real killer before poor Rupert had been hanged. Actually, I think California uses the electrical chair, but that's neither here nor there."

"Exactly, and the fact that Calvin is a Negro is a strike against him to begin with. Plus, he worked for Mr. Gossett."

Lulu's eyes went round. She had pretty blue eyes, although she plastered too much mascara on her lashes for my taste. "He *worked* for the man? Wow, that puts a different light on things, doesn't it?"

"Does it?" My voice took on an icy crispness.

"Well...yes, it does. I know you want to believe he didn't do it, Mercy, but if he worked for the man. Well..."

"But Mr. Gossett was killed on Sunday, and Calvin Buck didn't work for him on Sundays."

"He might have gone there for some reason or other," said Lulu, taking a small bite of her tuna-fish sandwich.

My choice that day was corned beef on rye. With mustard. I'd taken to eating corned-beef sandwiches as often as possible because my mother condemned them as remnants of the so-called "dirty" Irish who cluttered up Boston. Of course, the Irish in Boston did all the work people like my mother didn't want to do, but she saw things in her own way and couldn't be brought to understand she and people like her *needed* the worker proletariat. Probably a whole lot more than the worker proletariat needed her, as a matter of fact. I told her so once, and she called me a Socialist, which I'm not. She wears blinders, my mother, kind of like the horses pulling vegetable carts back east. If I ever got mad enough at her to tell her so, she'd probably disinherit me.

Hmm. I'd have to think about my possible disinheritance further when I had more free time. Right then, we were discussing Calvin Buck and his false imprisonment.

"Nonsense. Mr. Buck told Ernie and me"—I know I made it sound as if Ernie had included me in the discussion, which was perhaps wrong of me, but at least I'd been there at the time

—"Calvin spends all day Sunday after church studying. He wants to get into college like his sister Loretta," I explained.

"Yeah? He must be pretty smart. I wonder what he aims to do with a college education. Sweep floors?" Lulu bit into a carrot stick, which, along with a pickle spear, came with her sandwich.

I swallowed a bite of corned beef. "Sweep floors? What do you mean? Why would a college-educated man want to sweep floors for a living?"

Lifting a heavily penciled eyebrow, Lulu gave me a pitying gaze. "Mercy, this is nineteen twenty-six. What the heck else can a Negro boy do for work, college education or no college education?"

After staring at her for a moment, I pondered her words. They made me sad. "But…surely there are opportunities for anyone with a college degree, Lulu. Why, maybe he could teach or—"

"Where's he gonna teach?" Lulu interrupted with persistent logic.

"Well…I don't know. Do you mean to tell me, if a Negro man has as good an education as a white man, he can't get the same kind of job the white man can?"

Even I, in my naiveté, knew this to be a stupid question. How incredibly depressing. Before Lulu could enlighten me, I muttered, "You're right, of course."

With a shrug, Lulu said, "I bet there are Negro schools and stuff where educated black people can teach. Heck, Calvin's sister is going to college somewhere in the south, isn't she? Maybe Calvin will go there and then teach in that college after he gets his degree."

"Maybe," I said, thinking that, while women were considered second-class citizens, at least we white women could get jobs as something other than cooks and housekeepers. There's nothing wrong with being a cook or a housekeeper, I know, but I've noticed more than once that male cooks are called chefs, and they earn a heck of a lot more money than female cooks, who are called cooks and earn maybe a third as much as their male counterparts.

Every once in a while, I felt like taking a soap box to Pershing Square and hollering my frustration at the masses, like so many of the nutty folks in Los Angeles did. Only if *I* did it, right would be on my side, darn it.

I took another bite of my sandwich along with a nibble of my own pickle spear and thought about the inequalities rife in the world. Then something Mr. Buck had said at the office returned to me, and after I swallowed, I asked, "Say, Lulu, have you ever heard of an AME Church?"

She sipped her water and thought. "I don't think so. Why?"

"Oh, nothing. Mr. Buck said he and his family attend the First AME Church on...I don't remember the street. I just wondered what AME stood for, is all."

With a shrug, Lulu said, "Beats me."

"I'll ask Ernie when I get back to the office." Providing Ernie had returned from his visit with Phil.

"Let me know when you find out. I wonder if it's anything like the Angelica Gospel Hall."

"I don't know."

About a month earlier, Lulu and I had attended services at the Angelica Gospel Hall and heard the famed, acclaimed (and often reviled) leader thereof, Sister Adelaide Burkhard Emmanuel, preach. The experience had been interesting for me, but Lulu had been swept away by the glory of it all. She'd returned quite often to services there, according to her own reports, but eventually she'd tired of all the noise and rah-de-dah and quit.

After downing the last of her sandwich, Lulu said with a shrug, "My family are all Baptists, but the Baptists aren't any fun.

I kind of liked the Angelica Gospel Hall, but all that shouting got to me."

"I was reared in the Episcopal Church myself, but it's kind of formal. The word 'fun' doesn't apply to Episcopalians either. I enjoyed our visits to the Angelica Gospel Hall, too. Well, except for my last one." I couldn't repress a shudder as I recalled my encounter with a crazed person at the Hall.

"I guess not," agreed Lulu. "You looked really bad after your last visit, too."

She would have to remind me, wouldn't she? Well, it didn't matter. The bruises had faded eventually. Heck, even the worst of them were now only a faintish green.

"But I sure loved our dinner at the Ambassador," Lulu said with a rapturous sigh. "And meeting John Gilbert! Oh, Mercy, what I wouldn't give if he'd only offer me a part in his next picture."

I didn't bother to tell her John Gilbert, although a wonderful actor and a fine gentleman—although I understood from Chloe he drank quite a bit—didn't have a whole lot of say in the casting of the pictures he graced with his talent. Lulu had her own ideas, and if they didn't always correlate with reality, she didn't care. But there you go. As I've already said, I had my own doubts about Lulu's ambitions and how she aimed to achieve them.

We walked back to the Figueroa Building after lunch, and I took the stairs to the third floor to commence my afternoon's work, if there was any of it to do. Ernie hadn't returned yet, which figured. Sometimes, when I was in a grumpy mood, I thought Ernie spent more time out of the office than in it. I felt grouchy. Thinking about the inequities rampant in the world always turns me surly.

So that the afternoon wouldn't be a complete waste of time, I decided to type out the notes I'd taken during Ernie's discussion with Mr. Buck. I had just finished the last page when

ALICE DUNCAN

Ernie strolled in, looking as casual and nonchalant as ever. Although I was in a not-very-sunny mood, I did my best to smile at him.

"I typed out the notes of your interview with Mr. Buck, Ernie."

"Yeah? Enterprising of you."

I gritted my teeth. "What did you learn from Phil?"

"Not much."

"Darn you, Ernie Templeton! I want to know what you learned! Mr. and Mrs. Buck work for me, and I *know* their son didn't commit Mr. Gossett's murder!"

"Yeah? How do you know that?" Ernie strolled over to my desk and plunked himself down in the chair next to it. He took off his hat, scratched his ear, and settled his hat on his lap. "You know a lot more than the police know."

"I...Oh, curse you, Ernie, I don't know. I just don't want him to be guilty." The admission was a tough one to make, but at least I was being honest.

"I don't want him to be guilty, either. Phil let me talk to the boy for a few minutes, and I don't think he did it. God knows how anybody's going to prove his innocence, though."

"But he isn't supposed to prove he's innocent! It's the prosecution's job to prove he's guilty!"

With a wry grin, Ernie said, "That's your pie-in-the-sky innocence talking, Mercy. You know it."

I gave him a hot scowl, which bounced off him the way all my hot scowls did. He grinned some more, blast the man. "You drive me crazy," I said under my breath. Then something almost pertinent occurred to me. "By the way, what is an AME Church?"

"African Methodist-Episcopal," said Ernie. "They're basically Methodists, but the Methodists won't allow Negroes to sully their lily-white doors, so they formed their own church. Anyhow, the

Methodist Church is still called the Methodist-Episcopal Church in most places."

"Huh." More inequality. And this time in the very church established by the man who preached we're all God's children and should love one another. Life really upsets me sometimes. "I see," said I.

"Anyhow, poor Calvin is scared to death, and I don't blame him, but I also don't think he did the deed. The problem, as I see it, is to find the real culprit, since the coppers aren't likely to let him loose unless someone more probable turns up, and they're not looking."

"Oh, Ernie! How discouraging. Doesn't *Phil* care that Calvin's not the murderer? I thought he was an honest copper."

"He is, but he's about the only one on the force. Your run-of-the-mill L.A. policeman is happy to slap a shade in the clink and leave him there. It's quick, easy, and over, and that's the way they like it."

"A shade?"

"A Negro," Ernie explained as if to an infant who knew nothing, which, I lament to say, was pretty much the case. "A 'person of color,' as somebody I knew once put it."

"Oh." Thinking dark—indeed, shady—thoughts, I said, "I'm glad you left the force, Ernie. I don't know how Phil can stand it."

"Sometimes he can't."

"But he *is* going to search more deeply into the Gossett case, isn't he? He isn't going to allow Calvin to suffer for a crime he didn't commit, is he?"

"Phil is subject to direction from his superiors, Mercy. He'll do what he can, but it isn't going to be much."

"I see," said I, who saw perfectly. Nobody was going to do anything except Ernie and me, and I wasn't sure about Ernie. "Then it's you and me, right? We're going to get to the bottom of the matter."

"Hold on there a minute," said Ernie sternly. "You're not going to get mixed up in the Gossett mess. And you're definitely not going to go off investigating anything on your own."

I sniffed.

"I mean it, Mercy. We're talking cold-blooded murder here. You might think you know what you're doing, but if your past escapades haven't taught you anything, they've taught me you're a babe in the woods here in L.A. I swear to God, I'll tie you to your chair if I have to in order to keep you out of the Gossett case."

"I'll stay out of it if *you*, Ernest Templeton, stay in it. If you refuse to help Calvin, I'll have no choice but to investigate on my own." Never mind that I had absolutely no idea how to do that or where to start.

"Right. I suppose you'll do what you did last time and go to services at the First AME Church. You'll be pretty conspicuous there, don't you think?"

I'm fairly certain steam had begun puffing out of my ears by then. I was *so* angry with my infuriating employer. "If I have to," I said, "I'll go there and anywhere else I deem necessary. I doubt the good folks at the First AME Church will chuck me out once they learn my purpose." I'm usually not given to making such emotional statements. But Ernie was so exasperating, what with his refusal to give me an answer about the Calvin Buck matter and his total disregard of my overall usefulness, I couldn't seem to help myself.

Evidently Ernie believed my statement, however, because he said in something of a bellow, "I'll investigate the case, for God's sake! Just you stay out of it."

Lifting my chin, I said, "Very well. Thank you, Ernie."

"You're welcome," he grumbled in about the least gracious tone of voice I'd ever heard, even from him.

So much for that. I went back to my duties, which meant I

sat at my desk and read a book. What the heck, why not? I didn't have anything else to do since I'd already transcribed Mr. Buck's interview, and Ernie wasn't giving me any notes to type about his jailhouse visit with Calvin Buck, blast him. Ernie, not Calvin.

When I returned to my home in the evening, I entered with a feeling of mild trepidation, because I wasn't sure what to expect on the Buck front. I knew Mr. Buck was upset; I could only imagine what Mrs. Buck must be feeling. The notion of having a child of my own arrested for a brutal, not to mention widely publicized, murder made my skin crawl.

But I found Mrs. Buck in the kitchen, slicing cooked potatoes for something she called Potatoes Lyonnais. She'd learned her fancy cooking skills at her former jobs, which were all for rich people. Come to think of it, her present job was working for a rich person. Nuts. I did so like to think of myself as an average working girl, as silly as it sounds.

I approached her tentatively when she turned to see who'd invaded her kitchen. "I'm so very sorry about your son, Mrs. Buck."

She kind of crumpled, leaving her potatoes, the knife and the cutting board where they were and sitting with a thump in a nearby chair where she started crying. "Oh, Miss Mercy, Calvin didn't do it. I know my son, and I know he didn't do it! Besides, he was right here studying when that man was killed."

Hurrying to her and putting my arms around her, I said, "I know it, Mrs. Buck. Mr. Templeton went to speak to your son today at the jail, and he told me he'll discover who the real killer is. He promised, Mrs. Buck, and Mr. Templeton keeps his promises."

I got the feeling she wasn't accustomed to her white employers hugging her, because she kind of stiffened for a minute. I released her, hoping I hadn't offended her dignity.

"I know it, Miss Mercy. Thank you. Mr. Buck, he told me Mr. Templeton—and you, too—were aiming to help free Calvin."

I think she only added the *and you, too* part because she didn't want to offend *my* dignity. Boy, human relationships can sure be complicated sometimes, can't they? Nevertheless, I asked, "Are you sure you're up to cooking this evening, Mrs. Buck? If you need some time off—"

"No!" she all but shouted. Then she sobbed again, wiped her tears on her apron, and said, "I'm sorry, Miss Mercy, but I have to keep busy. I truly do. Otherwise, I'll go right 'round the bend."

I eyed her sternly, trying to discern the truth in her statement. Since I'm lousy at reading truths in people's faces, I had no luck. Darn it, people are always reading things in other people's eyes and facial expressions in novels. How come I couldn't do it? Perhaps this was yet another skill I needed to practice under Ernie's tutelage. If he'd agree to tutor me. So far, everything I'd learned about detecting had been gleaned behind his back and sometimes at great pain to me, because he never wanted me involved in his cases. "Are you sure, Mrs. Buck? Because I don't want you to ruin your health by doing housework and cooking if you need rest."

"Ruin my health? Mercy, Miss Mercy, I'm no fragile flower, you know. Why, girl, I been working all my whole life long. Working's all I know. I don't think you white…um…I mean…" She looked downright guilty.

With a sigh, I said, "I know what you mean, and you're right. I grew up in a rich man's house as his daughter. We had cooks and maids and people like that to wait on us hand and foot, so I know exactly what you mean. My mother would pitch a fit if one of the maids ever got sick or had a family emergency. But I want you to know I'm not like my mother. I may not know much about the real world, but I have enough sense to realize we're all equal in God's eyes, even if we don't treat each other as equals. Please let me know if there's anything at all I can do to help you or Mr. Buck in this time of great distress for you."

I think she was as surprised as I was when she reached for my hand and squeezed it. "You're a good girl, Miss Mercy. You've already done more than anybody else could have. You've got Mr. Templeton helpin' our child."

Returning her squeeze, I said, "Well, maybe. But please let me know if there's anything else you need. If you require time off or anything in order to…I don't know. But you might need time off to take care of business downtown or go to the police station or the jail or wherever."

"Thank you, child. You've got a generous heart, and I'll keep your kind offer in mind and you in my prayers." She sniffled, took a hankie out of her apron pocket, and did a better job of wiping the tears from her cheeks than she'd done with her apron. "Now I gots to get back to them potatoes. They won't slice themselves. I'm fixing ham slices to go with 'em, and lots of greens. And I got you a Charlotte Russe for dessert."

"Goodness. You don't need to go to so much trouble for me, Mrs. Buck. Once I stock the house with tenants, though, I'm sure all the girls will appreciate your fine cooking. I know I do." Which was nothing but the truth. In fact, I was having to watch my waistline. Mrs. Buck was a *very* good cook. In fact, if she were a man she'd be a chef, by golly.

The rest of the week passed boringly enough, until Friday morning rolled around. I was excited to be conducting my very first interview with a prospective tenant. Or sitting in on my very first interview with a prospective tenant, Ernie not having wavered from his stance in regard to the interviewing thing.

However, this morning's practice would serve me in good stead, because I had another interview scheduled in the afternoon with a girl named Peggy Wickstrom, who'd told me over the 'phone she worked at an all-night diner in Los Angeles. I'd been a trifle startled when she'd told me she worked nights, but then good sense tackled me and reminded me that not every girl in the world had the education or training to be a professional secretary like me or, like Caroline Terry, clerk at the hosiery counter at the Broadway Department Store.

Miss Terry showed up early for her appointment by two or three minutes. I took this as a good sign, punctuality being important to me. I often wished it was as important to Ernie, but this Friday morning he'd strolled into the office at a little past nine as usual, never mind that the office opened promptly at eight. Promptly because *I*, unlike my employer, was efficiency itself in matters such as timeliness and so forth.

I smiled at Miss Terry, who smiled tentatively back at me. "Miss Terry?"

"Y-yes. Are you, um, the party whose house has rooms to let?"

"I am indeed." I rose and walked over to her, holding out my hand for her to shake. "My name is Mercy Allcutt, and I am looking for tenants to occupy the apartments in my house. Please," I added, sweeping a hand at the two chairs I'd placed in front of my desk, "take a seat, and I'll fetch Mr. Templeton, my employer."

"Mr. Templeton?" she said with some trepidation. "I didn't..."

"He's offered to conduct this interview for me," I told her, feeling a combination of emotions. Did I really want to admit to this young woman that Ernie didn't believe me capable of conducting an interview on my own? Deciding to soft-pedal my own incompetence, I said, "He's had lots of experience with interviewing people, you see. He's a private investigator, after all. I'm his secretary." I said the latter with a touch of pride.

"I see." She hesitated for only a moment before taking the seat I'd indicated.

ANGELS OF MERCY

So I went to get Ernie, who was leaning back in his chair, his feet on his desk, shooting rubber bands at the wastebasket. What a productive use of his time. I almost said he might spend his time more usefully by attempting to discover who'd killed Mr. Milton Halsey Gossett, but I didn't. Perhaps he'd given up his morning of investigative efforts for my benefit because he'd offered to conduct this interview. I wished I believed it.

Nevertheless, Ernie, roused from his amusement, put on his coat, straightened his tie and joined Miss Terry and me in the outer office. I introduced the two of them, and then Ernie started the interview.

Fascinated, I took notes. I wanted to be fully prepared for my own interview with Miss Wickstrom in the afternoon.

I got the impression Miss Terry was surprised to learn so young a person as I owned a home on Bunker Hill, a relatively exclusive neighborhood in Los Angeles, but she didn't ask any questions, probably assuming correctly that it was none of her business. I aimed to fill her in later if she worked out. After all, my aim wasn't merely to make money from the girls who tenanted my home. I hoped to make friends, as well.

At the end of the interview, it was decided Miss Terry would move in the following weekend. Ernie had demanded and received a full month's rent in advance, as well as another month's rent, just in case. He called it the "first and last months'" in advance. I was almost shocked enough to intervene, but a quelling glance from him stopped me. I guess he'd anticipated something of the sort from me.

After Miss Terry left us, however, I did ask him about it. "Did you have to have the money right this minute?"

"You're too soft-hearted for your own good, Mercy. You know that, don't you?"

"Well..." Was I? I didn't think I was, but perhaps Ernie knew best.

39

"You need to collect the first and last months' rent in advance, so if a tenant skips—"

"Skips? What does that mean?"

Ernie sighed. "It has been known to occur that a tenant will leave in the middle of the night, owing the landlord—or, in your case, the landlady—money."

"Miss Terry won't do such a thing!" I cried, horrified by the mere thought. "Why, Miss Terry is as honest as the day is long!"

"As far as you know. Don't forget: if all the crooks in the world looked like crooks, there'd be far less criminal activity, because we could spot the perpetrators before they perpetrated anything."

He had me there. "Hmm. I guess you're right. Still, I don't believe Miss Terry has evil intentions."

His gaze paid a visit to the ceiling, but he didn't reproach me further. Instead he said, "Probably not. But in case *another* of your tenants, one who isn't of the same fine moral fiber as Miss Terry, skips out on you, you'll have the money to renovate the room she lived in."

"Renovate it?" Good heavens, this was so confusing.

"Generally," he explained with what was for him great patience, "an apartment will need, say, a new coat of paint or something of the sort after one tenant leaves and another moves in. The month's rent in advance will supply the need, should the need arrive."

"Oh," I said, trying to grasp this concept of high finance.

"What you're going to do now," he continued without waiting for any more stupid questions from me, "is open a bank account solely for household expenses. In it you will deposit all rental moneys from your various tenants. *Only* from this account, you will repair any problems that might occur. You will deposit your tenants' *entire* rent moneys in the account, don't forget, and use it for nothing but maintaining the house."

"But—"

He held out a hand, and I shut up. "You may pay the Bucks out of that account after you build it up some, but you won't use it for another single thing. Got it?"

"But—"

"Damn it, Mercy! I'm trying to teach you how to get along in the world. That's what you claim to want, isn't it?"

"There's no need to swear at me, Ernie," I said, feeling miffed, but also knowing he was probably right. Darn it, he usually was.

"Sorry about the language, but I want to know you understand how to go about becoming a landlady. Do you think you understand the money angle now? I know you have money of your own, but the point of this present endeavor of yours is to learn how to live like the common folk. Right? That's what you're always telling me, anyhow."

I took a deep breath and wanted to scorch him with it, but I didn't. Rather, I said humbly, "Yes, Ernie. I understand the money angle and your point. Thank you."

He grinned. "Good. Then let's go to lunch. I'm game for Chinese. How about you?"

I glanced at the clock on my desk. "But it's only eleven-thirty. It's too early for lunch, isn't it?"

"Hell no. Let's go."

So we went. Who was I to argue with the boss?

FOUR

Margaret "Peggy" Wickstrom arrived at the office at two-thirty, as arranged over the telephone. She was precisely on time, which pleased me.

I have to admit to being a little nervous about the impending interview. I had read over the notes I'd taken when Ernie'd interviewed Caroline Terry, but I was on my own now and only hoped my perception of Miss Wickstrom and her answers would be valid.

She entered the office with the same tentativeness Miss Terry had exhibited, and I began to relax some. After all, I was in charge here, right?

Smiling cheerily, I said, "Miss Wickstrom?"

"Yes." She eyed me with doubt writ large on her face for a moment. "Um, are you the person with the rooms to rent?"

"Indeed I am. Won't you please take a chair?" I indicated one of the chairs in front of my desk.

"Um...sure." She seemed to inspect me closely as she neared the chair.

To be fair, I inspected her, too. She wore a simple brown day dress of a lightweight material, cut at a smart "flapperish" length at mid-calf. Her hair, too, had been cut and shingled and gleamed with hair tonic. She had a spit curl in the middle of her forehead, which seemed rather silly to me, but who was I to cavil at current fashion? According to my sister Chloe, my own clothing choices were dull as dirt. Besides, this young woman, unlike I, had to work as a waitress. I figured she probably wore a uniform for her job and enjoyed playing the flapper in her off hours. Therefore, I decided not to hold her spit curl—and what a disgusting name for it—against her.

Not that her appearance was in any way off-putting. She had dark hair, which seemed to be molded to her head in a glossy cap, brown eyes that went well with her dress, and neat brown shoes and handbag. She did not wear a hat, but I didn't hold the lack of a hat against her, either. Neither a waitress nor a clerk at the Broadway made a whole lot of money, after all. Although I'd never tell him so, I would be eternally grateful to Ernie for telling me the going rate for room and board at a boarding house.

For some reason, I didn't feel as comfortable with Miss Wickstrom as I had with Miss Terry. I chalked up my attitude to nervousness on my part. Therefore, I adopted a serene pose and folded my hands on my desk. "So, Miss Wickstrom, you say you work at an all-night restaurant downtown?"

"Yes."

"What is the name of the place? I wasn't aware Los Angeles had all-night restaurants."

Her eyes went round, as if in surprise. "Oh, my, yes. There are lots of them. They're mainly for the movie folks, you see."

"Oh. Because they work odd hours?" Actually, because Harvey Nash was a bigwig in the pictures, I knew very well they often worked odd hours, especially the staff and crew who had to build the sets, run the cameras, scout for locations, and those sorts of things.

"Exactly," she said, seeming satisfied by my understanding. "And I work at Clapton's Cafeteria."

"Ah." I'd actually been to Clapton's with Chloe and knew it to be a respectable cafeteria, so I felt the tiny bit of apprehension I'd had about Miss Wickstrom evaporate. Don't ask me why I'd had that initial reaction to her, because I don't know. As I've said, I'm not an expert at judging people.

"We get all sorts of folks from the pictures at Clapton's. The late shift people often come in there. Why, I've even seen some of the big stars."

I eyed her closely, attempting to discern some of Lulu LaBelle's fervor for stardom glinting in Miss Wickstrom's eyes, but I couldn't find any. A dud: that's what I was at discerning folks' ulterior motives. How discouraging.

"I see. How long have you been employed at Clapton's?"

"Seven months," she answered promptly.

I checked off that item in my notebook. "And do you have transportation to and from Clapton's? My home is on Bunker Hill. Do you consider Bunker Hill too far away?"

"Oh, gee, no. I take the bus. Or…"

Was that a blush I saw staining her cheeks? I leaned forward, trying to decide, and came to the conclusion I was imagining things. I prompted, "Or?"

"Or…well, sometimes the fellow I'm walking out with will drive me in his Runabout."

Perhaps it *had* been a blush! For some reason, the notion pleased me, probably because it meant I wasn't as much of an idiot as I'd believed myself to be when it came to judging people. However, this brought up a pertinent point I figured I'd best get out into the open right then.

"It's nice to know you have a gentleman friend, Miss Wickstrom. However, I need to tell you gentlemen aren't allowed upstairs in my home. There's a nice living room in which you may entertain callers, and of course you may use the yard on warm summer—or autumn—evenings, if you wish. But otherwise, gentlemen are to be confined to the downstairs rooms, and they must leave before nine p.m."

"Of course," she said, as if this stricture was a given. "That's the way it always is."

I was happy to hear it.

"But it don't matter, since I work nights."

I grieve to report that her grammatical error gave me pause. Yet again I reminded myself not every young woman in the world had been given my opportunities and instantly forgave her the lapse. Heck, Lulu's grammar wasn't always stellar, and we were great pals.

The rest of the interview went well, and I was rather more pleased than not when Miss Wickstrom said she'd drop by the following Monday with the first and last months' rent money. "You can give me the address then," she said, which I considered thoughtful of her. I guess she didn't want me to think she might come over in the middle of the night and rob me blind.

Not that she could. Buttercup, my intrepid apricot-colored toy poodle, was better than a gang of doorbells at announcing guests, invited or otherwise.

"That will do nicely." I rose from my desk chair in an effort to look professional and efficient—which I was, in the secretarial sense. This landlady business was new to me. "Thank you for coming today, Miss Wickstrom. I hope you will enjoy your new accommodations."

"I'm sure I will," she said. "Bunker Hill is a swell area."

My mother would drop dead if she heard that. Ever since Chloe had told her she and Harvey lived on Bunker Hill in Los Angeles, she's never entirely recovered.

Speaking of my mother, whom her friends called Honoria and Chloe and I called the Wrath of God, I'd assumed I was safe from her dictates and interference when I moved from Boston to Los Angeles. Alas and alack, I discovered my mistake when she visited Chloe a month or so back, decided she enjoyed the weather in Southern California, and she and our father bought a mansion in Pasadena where they intended to spend their winter months. Chloe and I offered each other such consolation as we could, but the fact was that the devil was going to be loose in Southern California for three or four months out of every year, and we'd just have to endure. Fortunately for both of us, Pasadena was several miles from Bunker Hill in Los Angeles and even farther away from the Nashes' new Beverly Hills home, so I expected we'd both survive.

Ernie was skeptical when he returned to the office and I told him I'd accepted Peggy Wickstrom as another tenant in my home.

"You sure about her?" he asked. "You sure you got all the information you need about her?"

"Yes," I said positively. "I'm sure. I think she'll work out just fine."

"Well...I hope to God you're right. I probably should have stayed here this afternoon and supervised the interview, but I had to check out something on the Gossett case."

As you might imagine, this snippet of information made Peggy Wickstrom and Caroline Terry both fly from my thoughts. "Oh? And did you find out anything of import?"

"Not really."

My exasperating boss strolled toward his office. Well! I wasn't going to put up with *that* nonsense. I followed him and plunked myself down in the chair in front of his desk even before he'd thrown his hat and coat at the rack. When he turned around and saw me, he frowned. I'd expected this reaction.

"What?" he said. As if he didn't already know.

"Exactly what did you check out, and what did you learn?" I demanded.

"Dammit, Mercy, I'm not going to involve you in this case!" He even thumped his fist on his desk for emphasis before he sat in his swivel chair.

I, being an expert in the care and feeding of Mr. Ernest Templeton, P.I., by this time, didn't even flinch.

"I'm not involved in any way whatsoever. I am, however, intensely interested. It won't cost you even a moment's anxiety if you tell me what you discovered during this afternoon's investigation. I've already promised I won't become involved. However, I do believe I'm entitled to information as you discover it."

"You do, eh?" He clearly didn't share my sentiment.

"Yes. Don't forget the accused man's parents are employed by me in my own home."

After heaving a gigantic sigh, he said, "I didn't learn a whole hell of a lot, to tell the truth. Calvin Buck worked for Mr. Gossett, just as Buck told us. He worked in the afternoons and on Saturdays and did a competent job. I talked to Mr. Gossett's cook, who doubled as his housekeeper. She's still pretty upset. She's the one who nailed Calvin as the culprit and, as I suspected, it was for no better reason than because Calvin's a Negro. She admitted she didn't see him at the Gossett place on Sunday."

"How deplorable," I said.

"Yeah. Probably. But that's the way it goes. I also talked to the gardener. He told me a little more about Gossett, who wasn't the sterling character his cook thought he was."

I'm sure my eyes widened in eager anticipation, because Ernie gave me an evil smile. "No, he didn't smuggle liquor or drugs, and he didn't run a pimping ring."

I blushed at those words, curse it. Ernie only gave me another wicked grin.

"He did know some pretty crooked characters, though, and he laid out a lot of dough on the gee-gees."

"The gee-gees?" I think I blinked at him.

"The horses." Ernie rubbed the fingers of his right hand against his right thumb. "You know. He played the ponies."

I must have still appeared blank, because Ernie did one of his patented eye-rolls and said, "He played the horses, Mercy. He was a gambling man."

"Oh!" It all suddenly became clear to me. "He bet money on horse races!"

"Right."

"Do you think he owed money to his…what do you call those fellows who take bets and then have people's kneecaps crushed when they don't pay up?"

"Bookies." Ernie gave me a pitying look. "Bookmakers. But they generally don't kill the folks who owe them money. What would be the percentage in that?"

"But…well, I've read a lot of…" My voice petered out when I saw the expression on Ernie's face.

"You've read a lot of mystery novels," he finished for me.

"Well…yes. But they can't *all* be fiction."

"What are they filed under in the library?" he asked sweetly.

"Oh, very well, they are fiction. But it still doesn't make any sense that a…whatever you called it—"

"Bookie," Ernie said helpfully. "Short for bookmaker. And as I said, they don't kill the folks who owe them money, because then they'd never get their money back again."

"Yes. But wait a minute!" I'd just thought of something pertinent. "What if they wanted to make Mr. Gossett an example of what might happen to a person who doesn't pay his debts? Something of the sort might happen, might it not?"

"I suppose it might. I suspect those guys don't consider

murdering a deadbeat anything more than a reminder to their other clients that they mean business."

"There." I felt proud of myself for a second or two. "But... still, I suppose they can't kill *all* their clients who don't pay promptly. Who'd be left?"

"Of course they can't kill 'em all, but a murder like Gossett's would send a pretty strong message. *If* that's what happened, and I don't think it did."

"Wouldn't he just give Gossett more time to pay the money back?"

Ernie shrugged. "Maybe Gossett couldn't pay and the bookie knew it. Maybe Gossett was in too deep and there was no way he could ever repay his debt. Maybe he owed other people? Hell, Mercy, *I* don't know. I've only just begun my investigations. I don't have any of the answers yet. All I have at this point is more questions."

"Hmm. But you do intend to follow up this gambling lead, don't you?"

"Of course."

"Do you know the name of his bookie?" Even saying the word made me feel as if I were experienced in the dark dealings of Los Angeles's bleak underworld. That sounds stupid, doesn't it? But it's the truth.

"Not yet, but I expect I'll be able to find out fairly quickly."

"Are you going to tell Phil about this discovery of yours?"

"Sure. He'll probably be the one who'll supply me with the bookie's name."

"Do you mean the Los Angeles Police Department knows the names of those criminals?" The notion astonished me.

"Sure."

"Why don't they go out and arrest them all, then?" I asked, furious that such fell businesses should be known by the authorities and allowed to flourish.

"They can't arrest anyone without proof of wrongdoing, Mercy. These guys—the bookies—they know their stuff. When I was on the force, we raided plenty of places where we *knew* either bootleggers or bookies—or both—were operating, only to rush in to find a squeaky-clean room. There are folks all over the place who tip these guys off to the cops' plans."

"You mean snitches?" I was proud of knowing that word. "Who squeal to the coppers?" That one, too. Squeal, I mean.

With a shrug, Ernie said, "Hell, there are probably plenty of cops who use bookies and bootleggers themselves."

I think my mouth sagged open for a moment. It shut with a click of teeth, and I asked furiously, "Do you mean to tell me there are customers for these despicable characters in the police department itself?"

Ernie shook his head as if, even though he knew the level of my inexperience, this question had astounded him. "Mercy Allcutt, where have you been for the last two or three months? Didn't I tell you the first time I met you that I left the force because of all the corruption there? What the devil did you think I meant?"

Good question. "You're right," I said, chastened. "How silly of me not to understand the depth of the depravity in the department. I guess I just...I don't know. It's shocking to me to know people who are supposed to be public servants are so vile."

"Not all of them are," he reminded me.

"No. I guess there's always Phil." I'd even had my doubts about Phil once or twice, although I hadn't told Ernie so. But it seemed unlikely to me that one man alone could withstand the temptations of an entire force of men with whom he worked.

"To be fair," said Ernie, "Phil's not the only one who isn't corrupt. In fact, most of the coppers on the force are as honest as they need to be. But there are a few stinkers in the midst who sully the nest, so to speak. You know, like that 'one bad apple' thing."

"I guess." The notion was still pretty darned depressing. "I'm glad you're going to continue to investigate the murder, though. I'm sure Calvin's innocent, and you're just the man to figure out who the real crook is." I spoke those words to placate Ernie, who looked as though he needed encouragement.

He said, "Yeah."

So much for encouragement. At least I had his word that he'd continue his investigation. Although I hadn't said as much either to Ernie or to the Bucks, if it came down to Ernie investigating the matter, I aimed to pay him myself to find the culprit and free poor Calvin Buck. I was positive the Bucks would be humiliated if I offered them money at this point, and I also knew good and well Ernie would pitch a fit. Therefore, I waited.

Oddly enough, the telephone rang just then. Oddly, because it so seldom rang. I hurried to answer it, leaving Ernie relieved, I'm sure.

Picking up the receiver, I said in my most professional secretarial voice, "Mr. Templeton's office. Miss Allcutt speaking."

"H'lo, Mercy."

"Chloe! How are you feeling?" I was always delighted to hear from my sister. I missed her a lot, even though she and Harvey had only been officially living in their new residence for about a week and a half by then.

"I think I'm getting better," she said.

"You still sound a little wan."

"Wan?" Chloe wasn't big on vocabulary words.

"Pale," I said.

"How can somebody sound pale?" she asked. Reasonably, I must admit.

"Well, you know. Pale and shaky and not in the pink of health is what I meant."

"Oh. Yes, I suppose I'm still a little wan. But I'm feeling better than I did only a week or so ago, so that's a good thing."

"A very good thing. I hope you're eating well and taking lots of fresh air and exercise."

"God, Mercy, you sound like my doctor."

"The doctor knows best, Chloe. I hope you're eating apples. I read in some article somewhere that the old saying 'an apple a day keeps the doctor away' really applies. Apples are supposed to be extremely healthy for ladies in your condition."

"Pregnant, you mean?" Chloe occasionally got peeved with me about what she called my prissiness. So did Ernie.

"Yes. Pregnant women."

"Don't worry. I'm eating tons of apples. I got really constipated, and the doc said to eat apples for it. I must have eaten ten pounds of apples in the last week."

Ick. I hadn't really wanted to know about Chloe's bowel problems, although I was pleased to know they were being solved, and by a remedy recommended by me, by golly. "Good. Glad to know you're feeling better."

"Hey, Mercy, Harvey and I are going to dinner tonight at the Ambassador, and I thought we'd stop by to see how you're getting along. You hired a cook and the guy who cleans at the Figueroa Building as handyman, right?"

"Yes. The Bucks. And so far they're working out really well. Mrs. Buck can cook better than anyone I've ever known."

"Even Mrs. Biddle?"

Mrs. Biddle was the Nashes' housekeeper and an excellent cook in her own right.

"Well, Mrs. Buck cooks as well as Mrs. Biddle, anyway."

"Glad to hear it. Is it okay if we stop by?"

"Of course! I miss you, Chloe."

"I miss you, too, Mercy. In fact, I wish you'd agreed to move to Beverly Hills with us. God knows the house is big enough for an army to live in, and I just keep rattling around in it and feeling sorry for myself."

"Aw, Chloe, don't feel sorry for yourself. In a few months, you'll have a brand new baby to love."

It was kind of flattering to know I was missed, but I didn't like the note of loneliness in Chloe's voice. What she needed to do was get a job. I was never lonely because I got to go to work every day and meet people. I sensed she wouldn't appreciate a suggestion along those lines, so I said only, "It'll be wonderful to see you and Harvey again."

"Want to go to dinner at the Ambassador with us?" I detected a hopeful lift in her voice.

"I'm sorry, Chloe. Mrs. Buck's already got dinner cooking, and I want to do a few things in the house. I'll show you when you get there. What's more, I have two more tenants! That makes three, counting Lulu."

"Wow, I'm impressed. You worked fast. Are you sure about these women? They *are* women, aren't they?"

"Of course, they are! I wouldn't rent rooms to a gentleman."

"It's the guys who aren't gentlemen you need to worry about," said my sister drily.

"I know, I know." Darn it, did Chloe, too, think I'd just come across the Atlantic on the boat that had transported the Puritans? Probably. What a lowering reflection.

"Just teasing," said Chloe, who might have meant it, although I know she tended toward Ernie's conviction about me being too naïve for my own good.

"Do you know what time you'll stop by?"

"Oh, I don't know. Probably somewhere around ten, if that's not too late. This stupid dinner is for some bigwigs on the picture Harvey's studio is going to produce next. All sorts of stars will be there. It's sort of an opening gesture, welcoming them all to the Nash Studio fold or something of the sort. Harvey told me, but I don't remember everything he said. All I know is that John Barrymore will be there, and so will his sister Ethel."

"I hope Mr. Barrymore behaves himself."

"He'll have to. The Ambassador honors Prohibition."

"Really? I'm surprised."

"They have to," said Chloe. "It's a public place. I'm sure lots of drinking goes on in the rooms they rent, but they can't overtly serve alcohol in their dining room."

"That makes sense. Sure, come on over at ten-nish. I don't have to work tomorrow, because tomorrow's Saturday."

"You don't have to work on days other than Saturdays, either," Chloe reminded me. She didn't disapprove of my working as our mother did, but she didn't see any point to it. After all, as she'd pointed out approximately seven hundred times before, I didn't need the money.

"I love—"

"I know," she said with the hint of a sigh. "You love your job. How's Ernie, by the way?"

"He's fine. He's…but I'll tell you all about it tonight."

"On a case, is he?"

"You betcha. It's a good one, too."

"All right, then. See you tonight, Mercy."

"Bye, Chloe."

Oh, boy. I wanted to know what Chloe thought about my plans for her former home. Besides, I honestly did miss her.

FIVE

I learned shortly after their arrival that Chloe and Harvey didn't merely want to see how their former house was getting along under my supervision.

"Your *Roadster!*" I all but bellowed. "I can't take your Roadster, Chloe!"

"Why not?" asked my sister, grinning like an imp. Chloe was a truly beautiful woman. She had lovely blond hair and perfectly regular features with an oval face and blue eyes and looked very much like a rather languid angel. To all these assets with which she was born, she also had a fabulous fashion sense, a great hairdresser, and always looked like a million bucks. Maybe more. She was lots prettier than I, but neither of us cared a hoot about that. We loved each other. "It's way past time you learned to drive, Mercy, and I'll pay for your instruction. If, of course, Ernie doesn't decide to teach you himself."

"Ernie?" I said, dumbfounded.

"Sure." Chloe gave me a sly wink. "I bet Ernie would love to teach you how to drive."

Chloe was positive there was more to Ernie's and my relationship than that of employer and employee. Besides, she liked him a lot, so I suspect she wished her suspicions were true, even though they weren't.

"But...but, Chloe, you need your machine."

"Not the Roadster, she doesn't," said Harvey, also grinning at me. "It's too small." He put his arm protectively around Chloe, who returned the favor. "Pretty soon, she's going to have a wee tyke to care for, and I want her and the child to be absolutely safe."

"You think the Roadster is unsafe?" I asked weakly.

"No, he doesn't," said Chloe, elbowing her husband in the ribs.

Harvey only grinned some more. He was *vastly* excited about his impending fatherhood. "But I want Chloe to have a big car with a chauffeur, so she won't have to divide her attention between the kid and the road, if you see what I mean."

"Oh," I said, still bewildered. "I guess I understand."

And just wait until I told Lulu Chloe'd given me her Roadster. She'd probably faint. The gap between the rich and the poor in what was supposed to be a nation of equals flashed through my mind, but I resolutely shoved it aside. It wasn't Chloe's fault she'd married a rich man, any more than it was my fault I'd been born to a rich family. Well, so had Chloe. But I just want you to know I understand how unequal everything was. Still is, for that matter. But there I go: wandering off the topic again.

"He bought me a brand new 1926 Rolls-Royce Silver Ghost," said Chloe, a touch of awe in her voice. "He had it shipped to Los Angeles all the way from Great Britain."

"Oh, my!" Inequities aside, boy, was I impressed. I'd seen pictures of the Rolls-Royce Silver Ghost, and it was some machine. Not that Chloe's Moon Roadster was any slouch in the automobile department. A 1924 model, it had been the latest thing until now, two years later. Shoot, the car was practically new. "But do you really want to *give* me the Roadster? Can't I buy it from you? It's such a…a huge gift. I mean, all I'm giving you guys for Christmas is a poodle."

Both Chloe and Harvey laughed at my comment, and I decided it had been a silly thing to say. But…my own automobile? Good Lord. And I couldn't even drive.

"Take it and learn to drive, Mercy," said Chloe. "Consider it a gift from me because I miss you so much, and now you'll be able to visit me more often."

I threw my arms around my sister. Since she and Harvey still encircled each other's waists, this meant poor Harvey got jostled a bit. Still, what a lovely gesture. In fact, I got a trifle teary.

"I don't know how to thank you," I said with a sniffle.

"You don't have to thank us," said Harvey, straightening his tie, which I guess I'd knocked askew when I'd knocked *him* askew.

"I'm sorry, Harvey," said I, contrite. "I didn't mean to shove you."

"It's perfectly all right," said the ever-genial Harvey. "I'm glad to see sisters who love each other. My own two sisters haven't spoken to each other in decades."

"Really? That's hard to imagine." I felt sorry for Harvey and his sisters.

Chloe tutted. "Honestly, Mercy, you sound like a Salvation Army lady. Would you speak to George if you didn't have to?"

As mentioned earlier, George was our awful brother. I felt my lip curl. "Right. If either of your sisters is as horrible as George, Harvey, I don't blame them for not speaking to each other."

"They're both horrible," said Harvey. "I don't like either one of 'em, so I don't talk to them, either."

Goodness. Small wonder Harvey was looking forward to creating a family of his own, since his birth family seemed to have failed him in the companionship department.

"Well," said Chloe, yawning. "I'm tired. So show me all these wonderful changes you've made, and then Harvey and I need to get home."

Home. Oh, my. Until a little more than a week ago, this had been Chloe's home. Feeling a trifle sad, I led her and Harvey through the house, pointing out pictures I'd put on the walls and rugs I'd bought for the tenants' rooms. I'd decided, while I was renting out apartments, the furnishings still belonged to me, so I'd chosen things I liked.

"Good Lord, is this a Bukhara?" Chloe stared at the carpet upon which she stood, and which graced the floor that would be, after tomorrow, Lulu LaBelle's sitting room.

"I think so," I said, squinting down at the rug. "I bought it because it's pretty. I'm not sure where it came from. Somewhere in Persia, I guess."

"I guess. It must have cost a fortune."

I shrugged. "Even though I'm renting apartments, this is still my home." I smiled at the thought. *My home.* All my own. No Mother to boss me around. No Father to look at me over his spectacles as if I were a worm he'd have squished if I didn't belong to him. Mine, all mine.

"Good taste," muttered Harvey, eyeing the rug with a connoisseur's taste. Harvey was the chief decorator in the Nash household, Chloe not much caring one way or another how her home was furnished as long as she didn't have to do it herself. Not that Chloe was lazy, exactly. She was, however, a trifle indolent, and if she didn't have to do something, she was happy. "I think this one's Caucasian," he continued. "I recognize the pattern. It's gorgeous."

"Caucasian? But it's not white," I mumbled, feeling as though I'd probably just made a fool of myself.

"Caucasian. As in: from the Caucasus."

"Oh. Where are the Caucasus?"

"Oh, Armenia, Azerbaijan, Georgia, Russia. Parts of those countries are in the Caucasus Mountain Range."

"Oh. Well, thanks, Harvey." I didn't know the difference between a Caucasian rug and a rug from Bukhara, but I was pleased to know Harvey approved.

"Where'd you get it?" he asked.

"At a little store in Chinatown."

His eyes opened wide. "Really? What's the name of the place? I'll have to pay them a visit."

"Chung Lo's," I said. "Um...I paid twenty-five dollars for it. Did I get taken for a sucker?"

"Twenty-five bucks for *this*?" Harvey's eye's popped wide open. They appeared huge behind his eyeglasses. "Good God, Mercy, if this is genuine, you got the deal of the century!"

I perked up. "My goodness, that's nice to know."

Harvey knelt on the floor, lifted up a corner of the rug and peered at it closely. He shook his head. "By God, you have an original antique Caucasian rug here, Mercy. I've got to visit that place. Let me write down the name." So he took a notebook from his breast pocket and wrote Chung Lo's name and approximate direction of his shop on it.

"Are you sure you want this to be in Lulu's room?" asked Chloe. "If the rug's worth so much, maybe you ought to move it to your room."

"That's not very nice," I said, although I'd been thinking the same thing.

"Nuts. You need to protect your investment," said my sister, who'd never had to worry about an investment in her life. Well, neither had I, but it seemed I'd actually purchased something worth a little money, and somehow knowing about it made a difference.

"Let's take a look at the rug in Mercy's room," said Harvey

reasonably. "If this rug is worth more than that one, we can switch them."

"Who's going to switch them?" asked Chloe doubtfully.

I looked at Harvey, who gazed back at me.

"Harvey and I can do it," I said with conviction. "Heck, Chloe, these rugs aren't all *that* heavy."

"I don't want Chloe helping," Harvey said firmly.

"Of course not," I agreed. "Not in her delicate condition."

"Delicate condition!" Chloe sniffed. But I knew good and well she wouldn't have helped lift anything as relatively un-heavy as a rug from the Caucasus even if she weren't pregnant.

So we inspected the rug in my own sitting room. The way the house worked was that there were suites of rooms all over the place. Two suites, each containing a sitting room, bedroom, another room and bathroom had been built on each wing of the house. Along the broad upstairs corridor was another suite of rooms, only this one consisted of two sitting room/bedroom combinations. Attached to each sitting room/bedroom was a dressing room with a huge closet for clothing. A bathroom resided between the dressing rooms, so Caroline Terry and Peggy Wickstrom would be sharing a bathroom. Lulu and I would each have a bathroom to ourselves.

Anyhow, I knew, because Lulu had told me, that this arrangement was much more luxurious than most boarding houses she'd lived in or seen. I hoped Miss Terry and Miss Wickstrom would agree, since they'd be the ones sharing the bathroom. I didn't think they would mind, because their work schedules were each opposite the other.

The Bucks shared a suite of rooms off the breakfast room downstairs. Their apartment consisted of a sitting room, a bathroom, a bedroom and a dressing room. They'd seemed pleased with their accommodations when I'd showed them where they'd live. I hadn't actually interviewed the Bucks, since I already knew

Mr. Buck (and so did Ernie). Well...to be honest, I didn't interview the Bucks because I didn't think of it.

Anyhow, all those words are just to explain the layout of the house. What we did was walk from Lulu's apartment in the west wing to mine in the east wing. Harvey took a good gander at my rug, and he and I ended up switching the rugs.

"Not that I don't trust your friend to be neat and tidy," said Harvey as we grunted, each holding one end of the rolled-up rug. "But there's no sense tempting fate."

"Lulu's a good kid," said Chloe, strolling behind us and yawning every now and then. "But can you imagine her dropping powder or lipstick all over that gorgeous rug? Or *nail* varnish? Makes one queasy."

Of course, according to Chloe, pretty much anything made her queasy these days. But she had a valid point, and so did Harvey. And Lulu did wear a whole lot of makeup.

"So tell me about your other two tenants," Chloe said as Harvey and I straightened the rug in Lulu's sitting room.

Pressing a hand to my back—the rug might not have weighed a whole lot compared to all the rest of the rugs in the world, but it had been plenty heavy enough for me—I told her about Caroline Terry and Peggy Wickstrom.

"Are you sure they're women of upstanding character?" asked Harvey, who was doing a little panting and back-holding of his own.

"Absolutely. In fact, Ernie interviewed Caroline in order to show me how to do it. I interviewed Peggy myself."

This explanation seemed to satisfy my sister and her husband, and they shortly thereafter took their leave. Only then did it occur to me I probably should have asked Mr. Buck to help Harvey move the rug. Oh, well. I'd learn how to handle this landlady business soon enough.

Lulu and her brother Rupert arrived early the next morning with Lulu's belongings. There weren't many of them.

"Golly, Miss Allcutt, this place is swell," said Rupert, gazing around in awe and admiration.

He wasn't as much of a hick as he sounded. In fact, he worked for a dear friend of mine, Mr. Francis Easthope, a costumier at Harvey's studio, and Mr. Easthope had a swell home of his own. However, Lulu and Rupert came from a small town in Oklahoma where, from what I'd been able to gather, the height of entertainment was tipping over outhouses on Halloween. Rupert definitely wasn't blasé about the splendors of Los Angeles at this point in his young life.

"Thanks, Rupert. I love it. I was so happy that Chloe and Harvey sold it to me. Although I miss Chloe a lot."

"Say," said Lulu, putting down a battered suitcase at the foot of the staircase, "isn't that Chloe's machine out there in the drive?"

"Oh! I forgot to tell you. Well, I haven't seen you, but I should have told you right off."

"Quit babbling, Mercy, and tell me what?" Lulu demanded.

This particular Saturday she wore subdued clothing. I guess not even Lulu LaBelle wanted to move to new lodgings in fancy clothes and get them all dirty. In fact, she wore a pair of trousers that would probably have served her well as she rode horses in Oklahoma. If she rode horses there, which I'm not sure about.

However, she was correct to remind me I was babbling. "Chloe gave me her Roadster!" I cried with glee.

"*Mercy!* She *didn't!*" Lulu's eyes nearly popped from their sockets.

"She did! Harvey bought her a brand-new 1926 Rolls-Royce Silver Ghost, and she gave me her 1924 Moon Roadster!"

"Oh, my God, that's the *berries!*" shrieked Lulu. She embraced me, and we both did a little happy hopping around at the foot of the stairs. I noticed Rupert whip Lulu's suitcase out from in front of us, which brought me back to my senses.

"But," I said, breathless, "we'd best get your stuff stored. If I knew how to drive, I'd take you for a spin, but I have to learn first."

"Mr. Easthope allowed me to borrow his Flivver so I could help Lulu move," said Rupert, his eyes twinkling with glee. "Want me to drive you around a bit in your new car? I can't be gone too long, but I'm sure he wouldn't mind."

Thinking fondly of Francis Easthope, who was not merely one of the most handsome men on the face of the earth, but one of the kindest, I said, "That would be fun, Rupert. Let's get Lulu's stuff stowed, and you can drive us around Bunker Hill a little bit."

"Oh, boy, a Roadster," Lulu said, her hands clasped at her bosom. "Your own car. Is Ernie going to teach you how to drive it?"

How come everybody instantly thought about Ernie when it came to me learning how to drive? I didn't ask, afraid Lulu, who was an honest girl, might tell me. "I haven't asked him yet. Chloe said she'd hire somebody to teach me."

Lulu gave my shoulder a little push. "Applesauce. Let Ernie do it. He'd love to."

I had my doubts, although I didn't voice them. "Let's get your stuff upstairs. Then we can go for a spin."

So we did, and it was a whole lot of fun. The spin part, not the arranging Lulu's stuff part. Rupert drove us all around Bunker Hill, and we got to see all the beautiful houses. Then he drove up Carroll Avenue and we saw more beautiful houses, including the one in which Mr. Milton Halsey Gossett had been killed. Then, at my request, he drove the Roadster to Mr. Easthope's bungalow on Alvarado Street—not far, in fact, from the bungalow court in which Mr. William Desmond Taylor had lived and in which he'd been murdered four years earlier.

"Are you sure he won't mind?" Rupert asked timidly.

"I'm sure he won't," I said with more emphasis than I felt. But my trust in the goodness of Mr. Francis Easthope proved not to be in vain.

At our knock, he opened his own door. After blinking at his houseboy—who would normally have opened the door for people knocking thereon—and Lulu, his glance landed on me, and his face seemed to light up. I appreciated that. "Mercy! Have you kidnapped my houseboy?"

We all laughed, Lulu and Rupert a trifle nervously. "Not at all. But Chloe gave me her Roadster." I swept my arm in a wide gesture, and Mr. Easthope glanced out at the curb where the shiny, almost-new Roadster sat. "And Rupert agreed to take us for a spin, since I don't know how to drive yet."

"I'll be darned," said Mr. Easthope. He sounded a shade puzzled, so I hurried on with my explanation.

"I know it seems stupid, but I thought you might like to know Chloe and Harvey are doing well, and Chloe gave me her Roadster because Harvey just bought her a brand-new 1926 Rolls-Royce Silver Ghost."

His eyes went round at that news. "My goodness! That's some machine your sister's going to be driving. It was nice of them to give you the Roadster."

"I think so, too, but Chloe won't be driving the Rolls. Harvey's going to make sure she and the baby are chauffeured everywhere she wants them to go."

Francis Easthope threw back his head and roared with laughter, and I think Lulu, Rupert and I all relaxed for the first time since we stepped onto his porch. After he stopped laughing, he said, "Well, show me this fancy new machine of yours, Mercy. I can't wait to see Chloe's Rolls."

"Me, neither," I said.

And, although I'm fairly certain Mr. Easthope had seen Chloe's automobile tons of times, he politely allowed me to show him all the Roadster's magnificent properties, from its gleaming blue outer coating to the rumble seat, the running board and even the pedals on the driver's side I didn't know how to use yet. Then we decided Rupert had better drive Lulu and me back home and return to work at Mr. Easthope's place.

Actually, the whole weekend was enjoyable. I'd already known I missed Chloe, but I hadn't known I didn't really like living all by myself—well, except for Buttercup, who was a darling, and the Bucks, but they were staff—until Lulu moved in. Mind you, we didn't spend every minute of the weekend together, but it was fun to sit in the living room and chat about this and that from time to time. We read the ads in the *Times* for the movies playing in town and decided we'd go see *Flesh and the Devil*, mainly because it starred John Gilbert, whom we'd both met. Well, it also starred Greta Garbo, but we didn't care about her. Also, I was very pleased that Lulu enjoyed Mrs. Buck's cooking.

Lulu spent most of Sunday puttering around her new apartment and exclaiming every now and then about how much she loved it.

"You can't even imagine the dumps I've lived in since I left Oklahoma," she said at one point. "I get a whole bathroom all to myself! Are you sure you're charging enough rent?"

If I charged her any more, she wouldn't be able to afford to live there. We both knew it. However, Ernie and I had discussed this precise thing when I'd first started thinking about buying Chloe's house, and I had an answer ready for Lulu.

"I'm charging the other girls a little more. That makes up for the little bit of a discount you're getting. Besides, Lulu, you're my friend, and I want you to live here!"

With dismay, I saw her eyes fill with tears. She made a quick swipe at them and said, "You're a real pal, Mercy. When I first met you, I wasn't sure about you, but you're a real pal."

Hmm. Interesting. "What did you think of me at first?"

Lulu scuffed her shoe on the rug, making me silently thank Harvey for suggesting the old rug switcheroo. "Aw, Mercy, I don't want you to take this the wrong way."

"I won't," I said, hoping I was right. "Heck, when Ernie first saw me, he pegged me for a rich girl from back east who aimed to play at having a job until the novelty wore off, and then I'd quit. But that's not true now any more than it was then. I *want* to work. I *want* experience."

"I know you do. Now," said Lulu, again making a quick wipe of her eyes and smudging her mascara. As she hadn't aimed to set foot out of the house that day, God alone knew why she'd decided to wear makeup, but I wasn't about to quibble. Lulu was Lulu, and I liked her as she was. "But I'm afraid I had about the same opinion when you first high-stepped it into the lobby of the Figueroa Building."

High-stepped it, had I? I tried hard not to resent Lulu's words. "Well, I'm glad we've got that settled. We both like each other." I grinned at Lulu, and she grinned back at me.

The following day it was swell to have a pal to walk with me the couple of blocks to Angels Flight. I, naturally, had on one of my professional-looking business suits, a blue number I wore with a white shirtwaist. The only hint of frivolity was the little ruffle of white at the neck of the shirtwaist. With it I wore black shoes, a black hat, and I carried a black handbag.

Lulu, as usual, wore much more eye-catching garb than I. This morning she'd elected to don a green-and-white dress with a low waist and a big bow in back. I feared for the bow, since

Lulu'd probably be sitting on it most of the day. Naturally, I said nothing about the possibility of squishage. I was too busy ignoring her bright green hat, shoes and bag. Her fingernails were, as ever, painted a brilliant red, and her dyed-blond hair had been finger-curled and waved to within an inch of its life.

When we got to Angels Flight, it didn't look to me as if Lulu wanted to pay the nickel fare, so I paid for both of us.

"You can't pay for me to take this thing every day, Mercy. I won't let you."

"But it's a steep walk from Olive to Hill. This is so much easier, and besides, I love this railroad."

"I love it too, but I can't afford to spend ten cents a day on transportation. Heck, ten cents can buy my lunch."

Shoot, I hadn't thought about the tiny railroad ride from Lulu's point of view before. This demonstrates yet one more difference between those with funds and those without funds. To me a dime a day was nothing. To Lulu, it might mean the difference between a new tube of lipstick and no new tube of lipstick. I ought to use a more dramatic indicator, but Lulu wasn't going to starve, no matter what she spent her money on, since Lottie Buck cooked breakfast and dinner for us.

"Tell you what," I said after thinking the matter over for a minute, which was all the time it took for the railway car to go from Olive down to Hill, where it let us off. "We'll split the difference. You pay another dollar per month rent, and I'll pay your way both ways on Angels Flight every day. That way we can still go out for lunch every now and then." I'd known, if I thought long enough, I'd be able to come up with a food angle to fit the situation.

Lulu's brow wrinkled. She wasn't anywhere near stupid, but she was also not a deep thinker. She didn't need to be. Well, heck, neither did I. But I knew I had money and she didn't and, while it wouldn't pinch my pocketbook an itsy-bitsy bit to pay her fare on Angels Flight every day, Lulu would end up resenting me for it if she couldn't somehow repay me for doing so. Ernie had taught me as much, and he'd been correct, even though the truth had initially come as a shock to me.

"Will a buck extra every month make it fair?" she asked, clearly not fancying doing the arithmetic in her head.

"Absolutely fair. Fair for the fare," I said, attempting humor.

Lulu eyed me oddly, so I guess she didn't get the joke. "Well…"

"Darn it, Lulu, I like taking Angels Flight! If you don't take it with me, I'll feel obliged to walk with you, and I don't want to walk that steep block, especially in hot weather, or if it ever rains. *Please* take my offer."

"Well, if you put it that way…"

"Good," I said, pouncing like a lioness on its prey. "You'll be doing me a favor, and it's settled."

"If you say so."

She didn't sound convinced, but she didn't argue any longer, so I considered the topic closed.

Silly me.

SIX

Ernie held up his hand to stop me in mid-ramble. "Hold on a minute. One thing at a time. Lulu's paying you another *dollar* in exchange for you paying her way, both ways, on Angels Flight every day?"

I huffed to a stop. I'd been spewing forth about the delights of my weekend, beginning with Chloe giving me her Roadster and rattling on to Lulu's moving in, Mrs. Buck's delicious cooking, and my bargain with Lulu about Angels Flight when he'd stopped my barrage of words with his darned lifted hand. I didn't like the way his eyebrows tilted. I took a deep breath and decided I had perhaps been going on at a rather rapid clip. I said, "Yes. It's fair." I left out the little play on words I'd used with Lulu, anticipating Ernie's disgusted eye-roll if I tried it on him.

"You know it's not fair, Mercy. You'll be paying, what? A dime a day for maybe twenty days? That's two bucks, easy."

"Yes, yes, I know. But Lulu will be doing me a favor, because I want to take Angels Flight, and so does she, but she can't afford to pay ten cents a day to do it. And I definitely don't want to walk the steep block from Hill to Olive in the afternoon after work when it's a hundred and ten degrees outside, or if it ever rains here. Does it?"

I got the eye-roll even without my play on words. Figures. "Yes. It occasionally rains here. In fact, it'll probably begin raining any second, and you can't change the topic so easily. Lulu agreed to this plan of yours?"

I chuffed out an irritated breath. "Yes, she did. Especially when I pointed out she'd be doing me a favor."

Ernie's sigh sounded as if it came from his very soul. "There's no doing anything with you, Mercy Allcutt. You know that, don't you?"

I sniffed. "I don't think Lulu will be able to resent me for this. Heck, we're splitting the difference. So we'll both only be out another dollar per month, and we'll both get to ride that adorable little railroad every day."

"Adorable little railroad," muttered Ernie under his breath. However, I guess he decided we'd spoken enough about the Angels Flight matter, because he then said, "And you say Chloe gave you her car? Her Roadster?"

It was about nine-thirty on that sultry Monday morning. The weather remained warm, but clouds lowered overhead, and the sky looked as if it aimed to begin spitting at us any second. Good thing I kept an umbrella in my desk drawer. In fact, I kept it in the same drawer in which I kept the files, only there were so few files, there was plenty of room for the umbrella. Melancholy thought.

"Yes. Chloe gave me her 1924 Moon Roadster, because Harvey bought her a new 1926 Rolls-Royce Silver Ghost. And a chauffeur to drive her wherever she wants to go. He did it because he doesn't want Chloe and the baby to ride around in a small automobile, and he hired the chauffeur because he doesn't want Chloe's attention to be diverted from the road to the baby, or vice-versa."

Ernie whistled through his teeth. "On the level?"

I knew this piece of slang, so I repeated it, only without the question mark or the whistle. "On the level."

"Wow. I saw one of those on Sunset once. A Rolls, not a Roadster. You see Roadsters everywhere."

"Well, now I can see one in my own driveway," I said, irked about him taking my status as automobile owner with such nonchalance.

"Do you know how to drive it?"

I huffed. "Not yet. Chloe said he'd send somebody over to teach me."

"Hell, I'll teach you how to drive, Mercy. I've been driving all my life, just about."

Ernie had an old, beat-up Studebaker, which had seen *much* better days. It still ran, however, and I understood from Mr. Buck that Ernie was quite the whiz at tinkering with it in order to keep it going.

I hesitated a shade too long.

Ernie gave me a sideways look and said, "Come on, Mercy. It'll be fun. I'm a good teacher, and I promise I won't try to make whoopee with you in the backseat."

"Ernie!" I was honestly shocked. I knew as soon as I uttered the exclamation, however, that he'd only been teasing me, because he grinned. I could feel myself blush. Darn and blast!

"You're so much fun to razz. Honest, Mercy, It'll be fun to teach you to drive, and I'd get to meet your new tenant. You know. The one I didn't interview."

"So that's it, is it? You still don't trust me."

He held up another hand. Or maybe it was the same one. It doesn't matter. "I do, too, trust you. But I'd still like to see what you've done with the place. Lulu sounded like she was about to bust when she told me she'd get a whole bathroom all for herself."

"Yes, the bathroom was a definite selling point with her," I admitted.

"The bathroom and the fact you're undercharging her."

Before I could blow up, he held up yet another hand. "Don't holler at me, Mercy. We've been over this territory before. I have no quarrel with you giving a friend a break. Just don't give her too many more breaks, or she'll end up—"

"Resenting me," I said, interrupting him. Boy, before I moved to L.A., I'd never have interrupted anyone. If I'd ever *dared* interrupt my mother, I'd have perished a ghastly death. "I know. That's why I'm making her pay me another dollar a month for taking Angels Flight."

Ernie's nose wrinkled. "I think we already decided a dollar doesn't add up quite right."

"Don't even try to figure it out. Lulu said it was fair, and I think it's fair, so it's fair."

"Whatever you say, Mercy."

I didn't trust the meek tone in his voice, but after squinting at him for a couple of seconds, I decided he wasn't going to lecture me further. Before he could think of anything else to irk me about, I said, "Have you learned any more about the Gossett case?"

"Only that Gossett played the horses, liked the ladies, went to the speaks and bought illegal liquor. He wasn't a very nice man, although he treated Calvin Buck all right. But I fear Calvin is a rather strait-laced boy. He disapproved of some of Gossett's doings and some of the people who frequented his home."

I plunked myself down on Ernie's chair. "You visited him in jail again over the weekend?"

"Yup. Got there just as his folks were leaving. They had nice things to say about you and Lulu. Mrs. Buck thinks you're a class act."

Whatever that meant. "I'm glad they aren't fed up with their employment yet. What kinds of bad characters visited Mr. Gossett?"

"I don't have all the particulars at this point, but I'm working on 'em." He gave me an evil eye. "Now let me read the newspaper. Later on we'll figure out a schedule for your driving lessons."

If that wasn't a dismissal, I didn't know one when I heard one. So I honored his wish to be left alone with the *Times* and went back out to my room.

Ernie's prediction came true. The sky opened up just about lunchtime, and rain came down in sheets. I'd never seen rain in Los Angeles before, and I stood at the window behind my desk and gazed upon it in awe and wonder. Speaking of wonder, I began to wonder where I'd take lunch that day, since it didn't appear to be walking weather out there. Even racing across the street from the Figueroa Building to the taco stand would be a soaking proposition. The notion of sitting at my desk all afternoon in soggy clothes didn't appeal one tiny bit.

A few minutes later, Ernie came out of his office, shrugging into his coat and with his hat on his head. "Come one, Mercy. Let's collect Lulu and go have lunch somewhere. You can't walk anywhere in this weather."

Exactly what I'd been thinking. "Thanks, Ernie. I hope Lulu hasn't left already."

"If she's got a brain in that bottle-blond head of hers, she won't stir out of the building, even if it means not eating lunch. Think of how all that makeup of hers would run."

I got my own suit jacket, handbag and hat and put them on, then grabbed my umbrella. "You're not very nice, Ernest Templeton," I said. My giggle as I said it robbed the words of the chastisement I'd meant to impart. Then I gossiped. Just a little bit. "She put on makeup yesterday, even though she didn't aim to leave the house all day long."

Ernie held the door open for me to pass through. He wasn't

always so gentlemanly. "Maybe she expected one of Harvey's picture-making friends to drop by and discover her."

"I suppose that makes about as much sense as her filing her fingernails in the Figueroa Building lobby and expecting to be discovered there."

"Just about."

Ernie didn't have my personal qualms about the elevator in the building—I'd had an unpleasant experience with that elevator shaft once—so we took the elevator from the third floor to the first. Sure enough, as soon as the car got to the ground floor and Ernie shoved the elevator latch up and the door opened, we saw Lulu standing at the door of the building, peering out at the rain as though she wished it would stop.

"Hey, Lulu," said Ernie, startling her into turning around. "Get your coat and hat, and let's lam it out of here. I'm taking you girls to lunch."

Lulu's eyes lit up. "Honest, Ernie? Gee, that's swell. I was wondering how I was gonna get lunch today. Usually I bring my lunch, but I was so busy over the weekend, I didn't think to get anything for sandwiches and stuff."

I opened my mouth to tell her she could take supplies from my kitchen if she wanted to make her own lunch to take to work, but Ernie's elbow caught me in the ribs before I could blurt out my offer. I glared up at him, he frowned down at me, and I understood his unspoken words. Lulu was an independent woman of the world, and she wouldn't appreciate having my good works shoved at her any more than I'd appreciated my mother dominating my life back in Boston. Nuts. I'd get this right someday.

Fortunately for all of us, my umbrella was big enough for both Lulu and me to huddle under, and Ernie's Studebaker was parked smack-dab in front of the Figueroa Building. After Lulu and I hurried ourselves into the back seat, I asked him about his prime parking space. "How the heck did you find a parking place right in front of the building?"

Ernie turned and gave us a wink from behind the wheel. "I bribed the custodian. Buck saves me a place right there by the front door every morning."

"You *bribed* him?" I asked, trying not to think of Ernie and Mr. Buck as having underhanded dealings.

Ernie must have known what I was thinking because he said, "Relax, Mercy. He's doing the deed out of kindness. He appreciates the fact that I'm investigating his son's case. It's a little favor. You, of all people, should know about favors."

He would have to say that, wouldn't he? "Well, I think it's very nice of him. And you are doing him a great service." I sniffed. "God knows, the police department won't bother investigating the matter."

"You got that right," said Lulu with a sniff of her own.

I believe I've mentioned her brother's legal problems already. In Rupert's case, it was I, and not Ernie, who'd solved the murder. Believing it would be ungracious to point out this fact at the moment and under the circumstances, I didn't. Instead, I said, "Where are we going?"

"How about Charlie Wu's? I'm in the mood for pork and noodles."

Lulu and I exchanged a glance, and Lulu nodded. "Sounds good," I said for both of us. Charlie Wu's joint was a small hole-in-the-wall place on the east side of Hill, off the plaza there in Chinatown. I don't know if Charlie Wu's was its real name, because its real name was spelled out in Chinese characters, but it's what Ernie called the place.

Whatever its name, Charlie did serve excellent pork and noodles. Also, by this time in my Los Angeles life, I'd become fairly proficient with chopsticks, so I wouldn't feel like an idiot slurping up the noodles, which came in a bowl along with the pork and a bunch of vegetables. After one ate most of one's noodles, pork and vegetables, one then picked up the bowl and drank the remaining broth and whatever other chunks of food matter remained therein. This practice had made my Bostonically decorous soul blench at first, but now I could pick up my bowl and slurp soup with the best of 'em. Yet one more reason for my mother to be horrified. Yet one more reason I loved eating at Charlie Wu's.

Our lunch was delicious, and Ernie and Charlie had a vigorous debate over whether the Hollywood Stars or the Los Angeles Angels was the better minor-league baseball team. I had no opinion on the matter and neither, evidently, did Lulu, because we discussed hats while Ernie and Charlie argued about baseball. All I knew about the two teams under discussion was that Ernie favored the Angels and Charlie liked the Stars. Personally, I liked the Stars' name. Well, I liked the Angels' name, too, because it fitted Los Angeles. But the Stars was a perfect name for a Hollywood baseball team and seemed a tiny bit more clever to me than the Angels. But what did I know?

Hats were much more to my taste. "I know you like to wear office-y clothes to work, Mercy, but I think you should try more color when you're just resting at home on the weekend."

Very well, by then the discussion had veered away from hats.

"You're probably right, Lulu. Chloe *knows* you're right, and she keeps telling me the same thing. Maybe we can go shopping this coming weekend and I can get something frivolous."

"I'd love to go shopping with you! I know some swell consignment shops!"

Before I could ask Lulu what a consignment shop was, Ernie spoke.

"What's this about Mercy becoming frivolous?" He leaned over—Lulu sat between him and me at the counter—and grinned at me. "I'd like to see you being frivolous."

"Well, if you're going to teach me how to drive my new car, you probably will," I said with something of a flirtatious air. "Because I plan on wearing frivolous clothes every weekend from now on."

"Ha. I promise I won't tell your mother," said Ernie.

With a little eye-rolling of my own, I said, "Thanks a lot."

Lulu giggled. She'd met my mother.

By the time we got back to the Figueroa Building after lunch, the rainstorm had begun to subside, so we didn't get too awfully wet dashing from Ernie's car—the space for which had been saved by Mr. Buck—to the building. Lulu and I both thanked Ernie for lunch, and then Ernie sloped off to do some investigative work. I'm giving him the benefit of the doubt here. I honestly don't know what he planned to do with his afternoon.

Miss Peggy Wickstrom arrived promptly at three o'clock carrying an envelope full of money for her first and last months' rent. I was pleased she seemed to be an honorable girl and gave her a big smile.

"Thank you very much, Miss Wickstrom. You may move in any time now."

"Thanks. Mind if I sit? My dogs are barking. I had to walk all the way from the bus stop. Glad it stopped raining."

She wore the same dress she'd worn the preceding Friday, if anyone cares. I only note it because it appeared to me she was a hardworking girl without a gigantic wardrobe to call her own. Exactly the type of woman whom I hoped to assist in my new endeavor.

"By all means," I said, gesturing to the chairs in front of my desk.

"It's really wet out there," she said, leaning over to do something—probably wipe off her shoes or straighten her stockings or what-not.

"It was pouring when we went to lunch today."

"Yeah. It's been a hard day. I hope it clears up before I have to go to work this evening."

"Ah, yes. You have to work at night." Although I longed to offer her sympathy, several of Ernie's lectures knocked around in my brain some, and I didn't.

"My friend will be able to drive me to work, though, so it'll be all right even if it starts raining again."

"Your gentleman caller?"

She looked at me as if I were a specimen out of an historical museum somewhere, and I chided myself. I ought to have said *boyfriend*. Boyfriend was what everyone said those days.

"Yeah. Johnny. He'll take me to work."

"His name is Johnny?" For some reason, I found conversation with Miss Wickstrom something of a strain, which didn't make any sense to me. Heck, I was able to talk to Lulu and Caroline Terry and just about everyone else I came across with ease. Perhaps there was something restrained in Miss Wickstrom's manner that made me feel she wouldn't appreciate probing questions from me. I could understand that. We didn't, after all, know one another.

"Johnny Autumn," said Miss Wickstrom with something of a wistful air.

"What a charming name!" I cried, darned near enchanted. But really: *Johnny Autumn*? I decided I'd write the name down in my notebook as soon as Miss Wickstrom left the office and use it in a book one day.

"You think so?" She eyed me again as if I'd said something silly.

I didn't appreciate her expression. "Well, yes." I made my tone businesslike. "Thank you for bringing in your rental money, Miss Wickstrom. Do you expect you and your, uh, boyfriend will bring your things this week, or will you wait until the weekend? Just so I'll know to tell the housekeeper."

"Housekeeper?" Her eyes opened wide.

"Yes. Mrs. Buck. She will prepare a morning and an evening meal for us. I thought I'd explained this during our interview." I tried to sound severe but don't know how well I succeeded.

"Oh, yeah. I remember. You did. Hmm. I expect Johnny will move me during the week sometime. Will that be all right with you?"

"Indeed. Just give me a specific day, so I can warn Mrs. Buck to expect you."

"Warn her?"

"Just an expression." I was beginning to get a funny feeling about Miss Wickstrom. Reminding myself that, one, I'd interviewed her; and two, Ernie would never let me live it down if it turned out I'd rented rooms in my house to an undesirable person, I quashed my feelings. "But yes, I will need to know when to tell Mrs. Buck to expect you."

She chewed on her lip for a second. "How about Wednesday? I work nights, but I can probably move my stuff and still get to work on time. I don't have much."

Giving her a gracious smile, I said, "Wednesday will be fine. I'm looking forward to our association, Miss Wickstrom."

"Likewise, I'm sure," she said. Then she stood, said, "Thanks," again and walked to the door.

In spite of a teensy—almost an invisible—qualm about Miss Wickstrom, my happiness could hardly be contained for the rest of the afternoon. I'd conquered two of my goals! I'd bought Chloe and Harvey's home, and I had already rented apartments to three deserving, hardworking women who, I aimed to make sure, would be happy there.

Lulu didn't complain about taking Angels Flight up to Olive in the evening after work. The sidewalks were still wet, rain yet dripped from time to time, but the car Sinai (the other one was called Olivet) was dry as dry could be.

Mrs. Buck had prepared a delicious roasted chicken with potatoes and gravy, and with green beans and a tomato and cucumber concoction served with it. To top it all off, she'd baked an apple pie with a crust so flakey, it needed its filling to keep it on the table. Otherwise, it would have drifted up to the ceiling, it was so light.

"Oh, boy," Lulu said with a sigh after she'd downed her last bite of pie—served with vanilla ice cream, by gum. "I'm really going to like living here. I've never eaten so well in my life."

Her words, as you can imagine, made me extremely happy.

SEVEN

By the time the weekend arrived, my house was full, and I was enjoying my new role as landlady to deserving women who had to keep employment in the City of Los Angeles.

Only Lulu and I took Angels Flight every day. Caroline Terry might have joined us, except she didn't need to be at the Broadway until an hour after our own workday commenced.

"Anyhow, I like the walk," said Caroline at breakfast on Saturday.

"It's a long way to walk," Lulu commented.

"It's refreshing, as long as the weather's nice."

"I suppose if we lived a hundred years ago, we all have to walk," I said. Then I felt stupid, since my comment had been totally irrelevant. "Of course, we wouldn't have jobs, either."

"Oh, we probably would have," said Lulu, grinning. "We'd be working for rich folks like you. I'd be the housemaid and Miss Terry would be the lady's maid. She's a lot more dignified than I am."

"Please call me Caroline," said she with a blush. "And I'm sure you're wrong about your lack of dignity."

Oh, boy. She'd spoken those words with a straight face, even though she sat directly across from Lulu at the breakfast table. Caroline wore a natty green housedress with a delicate collar and cuffs. I wore a blue skirt and white shirtwaist. Lulu wore a bright red Chinese silk robe embroidered all over with yellow and green dragons.

As for Peggy Wickstrom, she wore black, and she spoke only when spoken to, which wasn't often, since Lulu and I had known each other for a long time and had lots to talk about.

Lulu said, "I'll call you Caroline if you call me Lulu."

Another blush stained Caroline's cheeks. She was a pretty girl, although terribly shy. "Thank you. How very kind of you."

"And everybody, please call me Mercy," I said, looking at Peggy Wickstrom as I spoke.

I guess she figured she hadn't been holding up her end of the conversation, because she finally said something. "Everyone can call me Peggy."

And that was it from her.

Mrs. Buck had prepared a lovely repast for us, consisting of scrambled eggs, muffins and bacon. She also served us each a half of a grapefruit, upon which she'd sprinkled sugar; then she'd let sit it in the refrigerator overnight so it wouldn't taste sour. The woman was a genius in the kitchen.

Conversation lagged a bit after Peggy spoke, so I decided to renew it. "Would anyone like to go shopping with Lulu and me today? I aim to get myself some suitable lounging clothes. Lulu and my sister claim my taste is dull as dishwater, and I want to get something comfortable and casual. And colorful."

For some reason, all of our gazes flew to Lulu in her bright red with dragons. She grinned back at us. "Don't worry. Mercy will never be as colorful as me. But we might brighten her weekends some with a little work."

I think I saw Caroline heave a small sigh of relief. The

expression on Peggy's face didn't change an iota. She said, "No, thanks. I got stuff to do today."

"I think I'll go to the library," said Caroline, thus solidifying her in my mind as a serious and well-mannered girl. "I want to see if they have any new books by Agatha Christie." Then she blushed again, probably because she thought her reading taste deplorable. My mother would have agreed with her. I, however, did not.

"Oh, I *love* Agatha Christie!" I cried, perhaps too exuberantly. "I love most mystery stories, actually."

"Mercy wants to write 'em," said Lulu to the table at large. "That's why she's working for a private investigator."

"Exactly," I agreed happily.

"My goodness," said Caroline. "What an...interesting ambition."

"It's not easy," I said. "The writing, I mean. And from everything I've read about the business, getting published is even harder than writing the books themselves."

"You've got connections," said Lulu.

"Not in publishing, I don't. Not that I'd take advantage of a connection. I mean, if I ever am a published writer, I want it to be because my book is good enough to be published, not because I know someone in the industry."

Lulu shrugged. "I don't know why not. It's the only way to make it in Hollywood. You gotta know somebody."

Peggy appeared totally uninterested in our conversation, which was all right with me.

"Do you really wish to write a mystery novel, Mercy?" asked Caroline with flattering attention.

"Yup. I sure do. I've even started one. I've managed to kill off one victim. Now I have to figure out who did the deed and why."

This comment seemed to waken Peggy from her former

stupor. "Gee, really? My boyfriend, Johnny, he knew that guy named Gossett who got plugged the other day."

Plugged? I guess that was one word for having a bullet shot through one's heart. And her gentleman friend had actually *known* Mr. Gossett? I was, of course, all ears. "My goodness, Peggy! Has he been questioned by the police? How well did he know Mr. Gossett? The man in jail for the murder right is innocent, and I know my employer would like to talk to Mr. Autumn."

Now Peggy looked as if she wished she'd remained out of the conversation. "Naw. The police don't even know about Johnny. Besides, Johnny hasn't seen Gossett for weeks and weeks. He used to do little jobs for him."

"Really? What kinds of jobs?"

Clearly flustered and also clearly unwilling to share information about her beloved, Peggy said, "Oh, you know. Little things. Errands. Like, when Mr. Gossett wanted to go somewhere but didn't want to drive, sometimes he'd get Johnny to drive him. Stuff like that. He'd ask him to pick up stuff for him. You know. Stuff like that."

Pick up stuff for him? "Um, what kind of stuff did he need to have picked up?"

"Oh, I don't know. He didn't know Gossett very well. I only mentioned it because you said you were writing a book about somebody who got killed."

"I see." I sensed that pursuing the matter would only annoy Peggy, but I made a mental note to tell Ernie about this interesting state of affairs. He'd probably accuse me of allowing an undesirable tenant into my house, but I considered Peggy's information worth the tongue-lashing I'd get from him.

"After we go shopping, I'm going to try to figure out the rest of the plot for my book. It's not as easy for me as it seems to be for Agatha Christie. Maybe you all can give me some tips." I smiled genially at my new family of tenants.

"Don't look at me," said Lulu. "All I read are the movie mags."

"I think it would be fun to plot a murder mystery," said Caroline softly. "You'll have to tell me about your book so far, and maybe we can chat about it. I probably won't be able to help you, but it might be interesting to try."

"I'd love to collaborate with you. Maybe tomorrow? We've both got things to do today, and I'm having my first driving lesson this evening."

We left the breakfast table shortly thereafter.

By the way, lest you think the Bucks never had time off for themselves, I ought to spell out their work schedule. Both Bucks worked Monday and Tuesday, Thursday and Friday; Mr. Buck in the evenings and Mrs. Buck in the morning and the evening, when she fixed the meals. In between times on those days she'd keep the lower part of the house picked up and the rooms tidied upstairs. The Bucks' Wednesdays were their own. On Saturdays and Sundays, Mrs. Buck fixed breakfast, but we were on our own for dinners. The Sunday restriction didn't bother me, since I had lots of money and could dine out at a dozen different restaurants. I did, however, make sure Mrs. Buck left plenty of bread, meat and cheese for sandwiches for the other girls, and sufficient fruits and vegetables to round out a healthy diet. Never let it be said the angels of Mercy were left to starve on weekends.

Lulu and I had a grand time shopping, and I came home later that day loaded with leisure wear, including a daring (for me) pair of silk lounging pajamas in the Chinese style. Chloe wore pajamas around the house all the time, but this was a first for yours truly. I decided I'd wear them in the evening, when Ernie was scheduled to come over to give me my first driving lesson. I was looking forward to it with mixed emotions. I really wanted to learn to drive, and I was happy Ernie wanted to teach me; however, I knew he'd be annoyed about a new member of my household being acquainted with someone who'd worked, however nominally, for the late Mr. Gossett.

But I braced myself and decided to clue Ernie in on Peggy's revelation at the end of our lesson so I could plead exhaustion and run into the house if he got really mad at me.

He rang the doorbell promptly at six-thirty, the time scheduled for our lesson. To my knowledge, that was the first time Ernie had ever been on time for anything. Naturally, Buttercup set up a riot even before the doorbell rang. The pup had supernatural hearing, bless her, and she loved announcing visitors. I ran to the entryway, scooped her up and opened the door, beaming at my slouching boss.

"Come on in, Ernie! You can say hello to Caroline and Lulu. Peggy had to work tonight, so she's not here."

Carefully wiping his feet on the pretty doormat provided for the purpose, Ernie grunted something I didn't catch, then strolled into my—*my*—home. He looked around the beautifully tiled entryway and cast his gaze toward the living room, which could be entered through an archway. "Looks about the same to me."

Blast the man! "Chloe and Harvey left most of their furniture. It wouldn't have fit into their new home. Besides, Harvey said it's easier to buy new furnishings than move the old ones."

"Makes it good for you, too." Ernie had removed his hat and put it on the shelf provided for the purpose beside the coat rack, where he deposited his overcoat.

I squinted at the latter garment with curiosity. "Yes, it does. They've both been extremely kind to me. Is it cold outside?"

"Cool," he said. "And we'll be out in the open air in the Roadster." He eyed me up and down and then up again. "You look different." He frowned as he said it.

If Ernest Templeton, P.I., wasn't the most frustrating human male in the universe, I don't know who was. I could feel the heat rise to stain my cheeks. "Lulu and I went shopping. This is one of my new, casual weekend outfits." Because I didn't want him to know how embarrassed I felt about his close scrutiny, I did a little twirl in front of him. My pretty blue pajama outfit fluttered as I turned. The garment wasn't garish, although it was definitely a departure for me. No dragons decorated my own personal silk pajamas. On the contrary, flowers and butterflies had been embroidered here and there upon it. *I* thought it was a gorgeous set, and I didn't appreciate Ernie's insouciant, "You look different." Darn it, I was trying to look *good*!

When I stopped twirling and glanced up at him, I noticed him nod. "Looks good, kiddo."

That was better, although I wasn't particularly fond of being called *kiddo*. Ernie called me *kiddo* all the time. Made me feel like his little sister or something.

But enough of that. "Come into the living room and say hello to Lulu and Caroline."

"Right. Then we'd better get going. It's getting dark already, and it's easier to teach someone how to drive when the sun's out."

"I'm sure that's true, so maybe we can have another lesson during the day someday."

"Tomorrow, in fact. I'm not going to let you loose on the streets of Los Angeles until I'm sure you know what you're doing."

"Darn you, Ernie Templeton! There you go, treating me like an idiot again!"

He patted me on the shoulder. "I don't think you're an idiot. I think you have a…um, healthy sense of self-confidence. I only want to make sure it's not misplaced before you begin driving on your own."

"Hmm." But we'd entered the living room by then, so I didn't continue ragging my boss.

"Hey, Ernie," said Lulu, who sat in a cozy chair with her feet on an ottoman and reading—what else?—a movie magazine.

"Evening, Lulu. Like your new quarters?"

"You betcha!" Lulu's smile was as wide a one as I'd ever seen on her face, and it made me glad.

"How do you do, Miss Terry?" Ernie said, politely turning to Caroline, who sat on the sofa, knitting.

The radio was turned on low, and music from a dance band somewhere filled the room with "Tea for Two," a catchy little tune from the play *No, No, Nanette*. The only thing I missed about living in Boston was its proximity to New York City, where one could go to see the newest plays and musicals when they came out. But Chloe had assured me such things would soon be commonplace in Los Angeles, and I saw no reason to doubt her. After all, Los Angeles had become the entertainment capital of the world. This assessment was according to Harvey, and I saw no reason to doubt him, either.

"Good evening, Mr. Templeton," said Caroline, her cheeks pinkening slightly.

The poor thing was *so* shy. I guess she didn't get much of a chance to chat with gentlemen behind the hosiery counter at the Broadway. Not that Ernie was particularly gentlemanly. However, he gave her a slight bow, surprising me. I guess he could act the gent when he wanted to. He never seemed to want to around me.

"You going to teach Mercy how not to run into things, Ern?" asked Lulu saucily.

She and Ernie were great friends. They'd known each other for about three years by then. And during all those years Lulu had been filing her nails behind the reception desk in the lobby of the Figueroa Building, hoping to be discovered. Maybe she was a slow learner or something.

"I'm going to try," said Ernie, sending a prayerful glance ceiling-wards.

I smacked him on the arm. "I'm not going to run into anything!"

With a chuckle, Ernie said, "Well, you'd better get a sweater or something, because it's going to be chilly out there. I'm taking you to the Chavez Ravine, where there's not much to hit if you do step on the gas instead of the brake or rip out the clutch."

Lulu laughed. Caroline smiled. I did neither of those things. Rather, I flounced up the stairs, got a black sweater that wouldn't look too awful with my beautiful new pajama outfit, and tripped downstairs again. At least Buttercup seemed to be on my side. She followed me up the stairs and down as if she wanted to go with us.

I knelt and petted her, and then gave her a hug. "Don't worry, precious. One of these days, Mommy will be able to give you rides in the car."

Ernie said, "Huh."

Scowling at him to let him know what I thought about his confidence in me—me, who was an extraordinarily efficient secretary, after all—I headed toward the door.

"Bye, gals," he said with a wave as he followed me out of the room.

Lulu held on to Buttercup. "Have fun, you two."

"Yes," said Caroline. "Have fun."

"I'll try," said Ernie. "I think Mercy's mad at me for some reason."

"For some reason," I grumbled as I opened the door.

"Hey, Mercy, I was only kidding."

"A likely story."

He only laughed some more, and I decided to contain my annoyance for the time being. He was doing me a favor, after all. Besides, I should be accustomed to his teasing by this time.

"You got the key?" he asked as we headed to the Roadster.

"Right here in my bag," I said, handing the key to him. My bag, by the way, went beautifully with my pajamas.

"Gotcha. All right. You get in the passenger side, and I'll show you how to start the thing."

He went so far as to open the door for me, so I forgave him a tiny bit of his teasing. "Thank you." My voice was relatively frigid as I stepped onto the running board and entered the machine—which, by the way, was approximately the same blue as my new outfit. Not to mention my eyes. He only laughed again.

Striving for patience, I sat with my hands folded in my lap. Ernie eased into the Roadster and sat behind the wheel for a moment, looking at the arrangement of the dashboard and everything.

"Say, this is pretty keen," he said, running his hand over the smooth wood paneling. "Chloe's got good taste in autos."

"I think it's Harvey's taste, actually. He bought it for her. Just like he bought the Rolls."

Ernie gave his head a quick shake. "Must be nice to have money."

I bit my tongue.

"Glad the top's up," he said next.

Ah, good. A safe topic. "Yes. I figured it would be better to have it up just in case it gets windy."

"Good thinking. All right, here's the first thing you need to do when you want to start your car."

Thus began my very first driving lesson. My goodness, but there were a lot of things to do in order to operate an automobile properly. You had to turn a key, press a button on the floor with your foot, make sure another foot was pressed down on the clutch—which wasn't at all what it sounded like, but rather a pedal on the floor in between the brake pedal and the gas pedal.

"And you'd better never get them confused, either," said

Ernie, "or you're liable to end up driving yourself off of a mountain or something."

Although I felt like slapping him, I only said, "I'll do my very best to keep the arrangement of the pedals in mind."

"Good girl."

Ernie backed the machine out of the driveway and we began our journey to Chavez Ravine, which was about thirty minutes from Bunker Hill. There wasn't a lot of traffic, which seemed a good thing to me. Ernie said it was because we were driving the wrong way. "If you want traffic, you have to head *toward* Los Angeles, not away from it."

"I don't want traffic," I told him.

"No," he said. "You don't."

You'd think he had absolutely no confidence in me at all. I was very nearly depressed by the time we got to Chavez Ravine.

But I cheered up considerably when Ernie turned out to be a considerate and complimentary teacher. I'd expected him to rag me during the entire lesson, but he didn't. He gave me quite a few "That's the ways," and "Good girls." I wasn't awfully fond of being called a girl by him, but I appreciated the thoughtfulness behind the expression.

We spent about an hour in Chavez Ravine, and I was fairly confident I wouldn't stall the Roadster every time I started it by the time Ernie said we should be getting home. "I'll pick you up tomorrow, and we can do this again," he said.

"What time?"

"Hell, I don't know. Does it matter?"

"I don't suppose so. Caroline was going to discuss my book with me, is all. I think she likes to go to church in the morning."

"Good God," said he, a remark that was almost appropriate. "Do you go to church? Don't tell me you and Lulu are still going to the Angelica Gospel Hall?"

"Very well," I said. "I won't tell you that, because we aren't."

"Thank God." Another almost relevant remark, by Jupiter. "So, do you want me to come by in the afternoon?"

"Sure. About one? Or is one o'clock too early for you?"

He gave me an evil look. "Of course, it's not too early for me. What do you think I do with my evenings, anyway?"

"I have no idea." I sounded like a pious choir member. However, it wouldn't have surprised me a whole lot to discover Ernie frequented the many speakeasies sprinkled throughout the Los Angeles area. He was no angel, my Ernie, even though he lived in the City of Angels. When I'd first met him, he'd carried a little flask with him everywhere he went. Still did, in fact. Anyhow, I'd been shocked until I learned the flask carried nothing more dangerous than apple cider. I'm sure Ernie wanted me to think he was concealing liquor in the silly thing.

"One o'clock," he said, sealing the deal.

Then he drove me home, in spite of my pleading with him to allow me to try my hand at driving by myself. "It's my car, after all," I reminded him.

"Wait until you have a little more experience under your belt, and I'll let you drive the car tomorrow. Maybe. It'll be daylight then, and safer."

I suppose I couldn't argue with him about it being safer for a beginner to drive in the daytime.

When he pulled up in front of my house, I stiffened my spine. We'd been getting along quite well during our lesson, but now I had to tell him Miss Peggy Wickstrom's gentleman friend, Johnny Autumn—I still loved his name—had known the murdered Mr. Gossett.

"Thanks, Ernie," I said when he pulled to a stop in my driveway.

"You're welcome."

"Um…Ernie?"

"Yeah?" He turned to look at me, and I noticed his eyebrows had dipped.

"Why are you looking at me like that?" I asked him, annoyed.

"Because when you talk to me in that sweet little voice, I know you're going to tell me something I don't want to hear."

"Fudge."

He was right. Curse the man.

"Spill it, Mercy."

So I spilled it.

EIGHT

"God damn it, Mercy Allcutt! I swear I don't know how you keep doing this!"

"Keep doing what?" I demanded, incensed. "And don't swear at me!"

"Hell, you should be used to me swearing at you by this time. How do you *always* manage to get mixed up with the cases I want you to stay out of? Do you do it on purpose?"

He was serious. I gawped at him. "I certainly don't do it on purpose! I had absolutely no idea Miss Wickstrom's young gentleman friend knew Mr. Gossett until she told us at breakfast."

Ernie's head bowed until it rested on the steering wheel. I think he was only being dramatic, but he muttered, "I can't stand it."

I sniffed.

His head lifted with a snap and he gave me a hideous scowl. "I mean it, Mercy. Don't go poking into this case. There's a lot more involved than you think, and some of the people concerned are folks you don't want to get chummy with."

Folding my arms over my chest and feeling hurt and indignant, I said, "I have no plans to get *chummy* with anyone, Mr. Templeton. And it's not my fault one of my new tenants knows someone who knew Mr. Gossett."

He'd begun drumming his fingers on his former headrest, and he continued to glare at me. "I wonder," he said softly. "I'd swear you do these things on purpose. Did you make her knowing someone who knew Gossett a condition of her tenancy?"

"If that's not the most ridiculous thing I've ever heard in my entire—"

He held up his hand, and I stopped ranting. "I know. It's just some sort of Mercy-type luck, isn't it? You attract these things. You must. I never got mixed up in messes like this until you trotted into my office in your little Boston dress and back-east accent and applied for a job."

I sniffed again. "You hired me."

Expelling a huge sigh as he did so, he said, "Yeah. I know I did. Been sorry about it ever since, too."

"Ernie!" I cried, crushed. "You don't mean it! You *can't* mean it!"

He stared at me, frowning, fully long enough for me to believe he actually did mean it. What a lowering reflection. I felt my chin tremble and firmed my resolve. I would *not* cry in front of this horrid man.

"Take it easy, kid. I know you don't do these things on purpose. Probably. But even you have to admit it's uncanny the way you manage to weasel yourself into all the dirtiest cases I work on."

"It is not uncanny. And I didn't weasel anything. It's not my fault."

"Right."

We sat silent in the Roadster for several more minutes. I contemplated opening my own door and stomping away from my aggravating employer, but he still sat behind the steering wheel, and I didn't quite dare reach for the key in the ignition. He could easily grab my wrist, and then what would I do? Struggle for possession of my own key? Too embarrassing.

At last Ernie gave another weary sigh and said, "I don't suppose I could meet this new tenant of yours, could I? Is she another genteel working girl like Miss Terry and Lulu?"

The notion of Lulu as a genteel anything at all almost made me laugh, which is probably what he'd intended, darn him. However, I wasn't about to give up a good fit of indignation so easily. "Miss Wickstrom," said I in my chilliest voice, "works nights at Clapton's Cafeteria."

"Clapton's, eh? Is she there tonight?"

"I presume she is."

"You don't know?"

I turned upon Ernie like a furious tornado. "I'm not her keeper, curse you, Ernie! I'm her landlady. I have three respectable girls renting rooms from me, and I don't keep tabs on their every movement! I'm neither their mother nor their nanny! For all I know, Miss Wickstrom is enjoying an evening out with her young man, Mr. Autumn."

"Autumn," murmured Ernie meditatively.

"Yes," I said. "His name is Johnny Autumn." I considered telling him I liked the name but knew better.

Ernie sat still for a minute then said, "I'll have to ask Phil if he knows about this Johnny Autumn of yours."

"He's not mine." Boy, was I grumpy. Oh, I'd known Ernie would kick up a dust when he learned about Peggy's boyfriend being acquainted with Mr. Gossett, but I hadn't any idea he'd take it *this* hard. Imagine him accusing me of arranging such a thing! He made me so angry.

"Right. Well, I'll see what I can find out about him. For all you know, he's a second-story man, and this Wickstrom character is only scouting out your place and aims to burgle it one of these days when the rest of you are at work."

"She'd have a difficult time of it," I told him snappishly. "Don't forget Mrs. Buck and Buttercup."

"I haven't forgotten anything," he said.

Suddenly he removed the key from the ignition and opened his door. "I'll see you to your porch," he said.

"Thank you *so* much."

"You're welcome."

I didn't give him a chance to open my door for me. Rather, I opened it myself and hopped out, slamming it behind me. "I don't know what you have to gripe about, Ernie Templeton. At least you have another person to interrogate about the Gossett murder!"

"I'm sure we'd have come across Autumn without your help."

"Oh, I just bet! I'll call Phil myself and ask him if he's ever heard of a person named Johnny Autumn, darn you! He's probably stopped looking for anyone at all since he has Calvin Buck behind bars. I should think you'd thank me for providing you with something of a clue."

"A clue, eh?"

"Well, what else do you have?" I demanded. "Exactly what have *you* done to move forward on the case? How do you expect to spring Calvin Buck from the pokey if you get mad at every single person who brings a little tidbit of information to your attention? I should think you'd thank me, but no. You accuse me of butting in, is what *you* do!"

"A little tidbit of information, eh?" he said. I could hear the sneer in his voice. "Listen, Mercy, if this Autumn character has anything to do with the case, I'm sure we'd have discovered it in due time. Yes, Phil's still investigating. I don't want you involved. At all. Do you understand me?"

I rolled my own eyes, a gesture lost on Ernie because it was dark outside. "You're impossible!"

"So are you."

It was a ghastly end to a rather enjoyable driving lesson, all things considered.

As you can probably imagine, I waited for Ernie to arrive at my home on Sunday afternoon with something less than joyous anticipation. In fact, I wondered if he was so angry with me he might skip the lesson entirely.

But there I wronged him. At one o'clock, as I was quietly reading *The Benson Murder Case,* by S.S. van Dine in the living room (Lulu was reading yet another movie magazine, Caroline was visiting her parents who lived in a town called Alhambra, and I don't know where Peggy was), Buttercup set up her happy "we have a visitor" bark, and the doorbell rang. With a sigh, I put a bookmark in my novel, laid it on the table beside my chair, and slowly walked to the front door.

I knew it was Ernie before I opened the door, because I could see his shadowy form in the leaded glass paneling that took up half the front door. Inhaling a deep breath and praying for no more lectures about my getting involved in criminal cases, I opened the door.

"'Lo, Ernie. Want to come in and say hey to Lulu?"

"Sure." And he stepped into my front entryway as if we hadn't ended our last encounter only hours earlier under most unpleasant circumstances.

As I led the way to the living room and Buttercup ecstatically greeted Ernie, of whom she was inordinately fond for some reason known only to God and poodles, I pondered the problem of Ernie and the lesson to come. Should I mention last night's tiff? Should I pretend it never happened? Or should I leave that part of this day's business up to Ernie himself. By the time we'd reached the living room, I'd decided upon the last course of action. Or inaction.

"Hey, Ernie," said Lulu with a smile for him as he entered the room. She slapped her magazine on her lap. "Gonna take Mercy for another driving lesson, eh?"

"Yup. Pray for me."

I smacked him on the arm, and he recoiled as if I'd used a hammer. "Hey! I'm only saying, is all."

Lulu laughed. "You'd better be nice to her, Ernie. What would you do if she quit being your secretary?"

"Breathe easier," muttered Ernie, sliding me a sideways glance.

Furious, I slammed my fists on my hips. "He's mad at me because Peggy's boyfriend knew Mr. Gossett," I told Lulu, thereby violating my own decision before a minute had passed since I'd made it. Ernie did that to me: made me so angry, I'd lose control of my temper. Nuts. "He's being totally unfair to me!"

"She's right, Ernie. Peggy's boyfriend isn't Mercy's fault," Lulu pointed out, with quiet but brilliant logic. "You can't hold Peggy's guy against her. Mercy, I mean."

"Exactly what I told him." I was ever so glad Lulu and I were friends. We might have come from polar opposite social scales, but we were sisters under the skin.

Ernie'd already removed his hat. Now he slung his long body onto the sofa. "Yeah. She told me about him, all right. What I don't understand is how she manages to get involved with people who know people who kill other people all the time."

"You don't know Johnny Autumn killed Mr. Gossett!" I cried, furious at the injustice of his statement.

Lulu, blast her, laughed. "Yeah, she does have a knack, doesn't she?"

"Not you, too!" I said to Lulu.

"Not your fault," she said.

Before I could defend myself, which would have been a wholly undignified thing to do, Ernie said, "Say, Mercy, it's hot out there. Before we go, I don't suppose you have a glass of lemonade or some water or something for a thirsty gent."

Glaring at him sprawled casually on my own personal sofa, I growled, "I might, if I could find a gent somewhere. The only male present whom I see is *you*."

Both Ernie and Lulu laughed at my riposte, and I felt a tiny bit better.

"Well, can this cad have something to drink? Teaching people to drive is thirsty business."

"I think there's a pitcher of lemonade in the Frigidaire. Mrs. Buck is thoughtful about such things."

"I'll come with you," said Ernie, uncoiling and standing before the sofa.

So he did. I led the way into the kitchen, and I could imagine him glancing around at everything. I guess he was so accustomed to taking in details—being a detective teaches you observational skills, I'd learned—that he did it wherever he went.

The kitchen was big and well-stocked with appliances, thanks to Harvey's largesse and his willingness to furnish his new home with all new appliances and leave his not-very-old ones to me. The stove used gas and had a self-regulating oven, a feature Mrs. Buck said was the latest and greatest in modern cooking inventions, and the Frigidaire was only a year or two old. It kept everything nice and cold, and it even had a freezing compartment where Mrs. Buck kept little trays filled with water for ice. I've already admitted I enjoyed the benefits wealth could supply. Not that I wanted the worker proletariat to go without the things I had, but I was all in favor of manufacturers producing appliances affordable to those of the worker proletariat who actually had to live on their incomes.

"Pretty nice," he said when I opened the Frigidaire and removed the pitcher of lemonade.

"Yes, it is. Harvey bought only the best stuff, you know."

"And he left it in this house for you?"

"Yup."

"Must be nice," said Ernie, not bothering to finish his sentence, the end of which I knew by heart by then.

"Yes, it is. And I'm trying to help others with my own money, so don't start in on me about being a snotty rich girl, Ernie Templeton. It's not my fault I was born to wealthy parents." I sniffed and added, "Would you like some ice cubes?" I got a glass from the cupboard and walked to the Frigidaire.

"I wasn't going to say a word about money, and yes, I'd like some ice cubes. Thank you."

"Hmph."

It was pleasant to discover, when I opened the freezing compartment, that Mrs. Buck had a supply of ice cubes already removed from the ice-cube trays and sitting in a bowl right there, waiting for people to grab. Naturally, I didn't grab. I used the ice tongs.

"No, I mean it," said Ernie. "You have a great place here, and I'm happy for you."

I squinted narrowly at him as I handed him his frosty glass of lemonade. He didn't *look* sarcastic, although it was difficult to tell with Ernie. I opted for a neutral "Thank you."

A big square table sat in the middle of the large kitchen to make it easier to fetch and carry foodstuffs from cupboards to the counters for mixing or to the stove for roasting, sautéing or whatever. I sat in one of the four chairs surrounding the table and gestured for Ernie to take another. I didn't want lemonade, having already drunk three glasses that morning, which, as Ernie had mentioned, was quite warm.

Out of the blue, Ernie asked, "Say, Mercy, can you cook?"

"Cook?" I blinked at him. "Why...I...don't know. I mean, I've never had to cook for myself. And don't say anything about money!" I added before he could mock my background and upbringing.

"I wasn't going to say a single word," he said in a self-righteous tone of voice I didn't believe for an instant. "I was just asking."

"Hmm. Well, I've never tried to cook anything, although I think it might be fun."

"What are you going to do if you ever get married and have a family? Going to marry a rich man so you won't have to learn how to do anything for yourself?"

"Marry? I'm not getting married!"

"Maybe not right away, but you want to marry someday, don't you?"

I eyed my boss, wondering if he'd finally gone 'round the bend. Why was he asking me about getting married?

"I haven't even thought about marriage, to tell the truth," I said, telling the truth. I'd never met a man I wanted to be around for any length of time thus far in my life, and I most assuredly didn't want to marry anyone like my father or my beastly brother George.

"Huh. Well, I just wondered. You might need to learn to cook unless you marry a millionaire. You can probably hook another Harvey Nash if you hang out with your sister and her friends long enough."

"For your information, Ernie Templeton, I have no intention of *hanging out* with my sister and her friends, as you so crudely put it, nor do I aim to *hook* a rich husband. My goal in life at the moment is to gain experience of the world in which we live. As you've so often and so cogently pointed out, I didn't learn a whole lot about the real world in my ivory tower in Boston."

"Hey, don't get mad, kiddo. I just wondered, was all."

"Actually, I think it would be a good idea to learn to cook," I said after pondering for a second or three. "Mrs. Buck can teach me. I'm a good student, darn you."

"Never said you weren't."

"And it might be a pleasant pastime."

"If you say so."

"What about you?" I demanded of my aggravating employer. "Can you cook?"

"Eggs and toast, maybe."

"I hope you add an apple or a piece of celery to your diet every now and then. Man cannot live by eggs and toast alone, you know. At least not for very long."

"So I've heard." Ernie downed the last of his lemonade and rose from his chair. "Well, it's a bright, shiny day out there, so let's get at it, shall we?"

"Gladly," said I.

Before we left the house, I took Ernie's glass to the sink and rinsed it out. Never let it be said that Mercedes Louise Allcutt was a messy housekeeper. Or a woman who made messes and expected her housekeeper to clean them up.

For some reason, all the way to the vacant lot where Ernie aimed to conduct his lesson that day, I thought about learning to cook. Drat Ernie, anyhow!

"We'll have lots of space here," he commented as he pulled the Roadster onto a dirt road off Sunset Boulevard. I'd had an unpleasant experience on one of those unpaved roads once, but I tried not to think about it, because I didn't want to ruin the day. "There's a big place up ahead where they've already bulldozed about six acres for some picture star's new home."

"My goodness. I thought all the picture people were moving to Beverly Hills these days."

With a shrug, Ernie said, "Not all of 'em, evidently."

"Evidently."

Quite soon, I saw what he meant. A good deal of earth-moving equipment lay about, from bulldozers to ladders, piles of wood and so forth, but they surrounded a huge flat space, and as long as we stayed away from the equipment, I wouldn't hit anything. I hoped.

After giving me a brief précis of the basics he'd taught me the night before, Ernie opened his door and said, "Want to give it a go?"

"Absolutely!" I said with glee. I really, really wanted to be a good driver and show my boss I wasn't the dolt he kept treating me like. I think that sentence is grammatically incorrect. Well, it doesn't matter. This is only my journal.

At any rate, I hopped from my side of the car, took the key from Ernie as we passed behind the Roadster's rump, and I got into the front seat.

Only then did I realize my feet didn't reach the various pedals placed on the floor for the driver. Ernie, who stood next to the driver's side of the auto, grinned down at me. I frowned back at him. "What does this mean? Only tall people can drive? Chloe's not any taller than I am, Ernie Templeton, and she drove this car everywhere!"

"Exactly. So I'm going to show you how to move the seat back and forth. Step out for a moment, please."

So I did, and he did, and I resumed the driver's position, feeling slightly humiliated. I mean, I was glad he'd showed me how to move the seat, but I wished he hadn't done it the way he had. I'm sure you understand.

"Thank you." My voice was rather stiffish.

"You're welcome." Ernie's, on the other hand, nearly crackled with laughter.

Trying to keep my temper under control, I started the Roadster. I did it well, too, by golly, and then I gently put my foot on the clutch, put the car into first gear, and even more gently pressed the gas pedal.

We stayed in that flattened lot for at least an hour, during which I only stalled the car once or twice and I never even came close to hitting anything. I saw perspiration bedew Ernie's brow, and he took out his handkerchief to blot it a time or two, but I chalk his perspiration up to the general heat of the day and the fact we were in an open flat field with no shade or anything.

So there, Ernie Templeton.

NINE

"All righty, then, I think it's time to take a rest, Mercy. You've done very well today."

We sat in the Roadster under the baking sun, and I felt like a dripping puddle of moisture. I eyed my boss to see if he was telling the truth about the relative goodness of my driving, and didn't discern anything but exhaustion and perspiration, so I said, "Thank you."

"In fact, you've done so well, I think you deserve an ice-cream soda. Let's go back down to Sunset and find an ice-cream parlor."

"What a heavenly idea!" By that time, I wished I'd thought to bring a jar of Mrs. Buck's lemonade. Maybe a gallon jar. With ice.

As for Ernie, he took a swig from his flask containing apple cider, then held it out to me and lifted his eyebrows.

Did I want hot apple cider from a flask carried around by Ernie Templeton every day of his working life? I decided I wasn't that thirsty. "Thanks. I think I'll wait for ice-cream." I smiled when I said it and hoped he wouldn't be offended or anything.

He only shrugged and stuck the flask back into his pocket. He'd taken off his jacket, which he'd hung on the back of his seat. I was glad I'd chosen to dress for the weather in a light-weight gingham day dress. Even so, it was drenched in parts, and I felt as though I were glued to the Roadster's seat.

"Want to try driving in traffic? It's Sunday, so Sunset shouldn't be too bad. Most of the Sunday drivers are off out of the city somewhere, looking at cows and clogging country lanes."

I'd heard about Sunday drivers: people from the big city who piled into their automobiles and headed out of the crowded towns and drove up and down little unpaved roads in farming communities. I guessed from Ernie's comment they were not universally admired.

"I'd like that," I said, even as my heart hammered. It was, after all, one thing to drive in a flat field where there were no impediments in one's way. It was quite another to drive on a paved street in a big city and have to stay on your own side of the pavement and not hit cars parked at the various curbs.

However, I did quite well. I didn't stall out once on our way down the unpaved dirt road to Sunset, and I took the turn onto Sunset with no trouble at all. Luckily, Ernie was correct about the lack of traffic. Things began to get busier—and, therefore, more sinister as far as I was concerned—as we approached the more populated area of Los Angeles.

"Why don't you take Sunset to Figueroa? I think I know a place where we can get some ice cream."

"Very well." I thought I knew where Sunset and Figueroa met, although I prayed hard the whole way there. I didn't want to have to ask Ernie if I was going the wrong way. But I wasn't! By golly, there was the intersection of Sunset and Figueroa, big as life—with automobiles everywhere, and not a policeman in sight to direct the traffic. Oh, dear.

"Just pull up slowly and watch for your opening," Ernie advised. "And don't forget the arm signals I taught you."

Easy for him to say. He did this sort of thing every day.

But I did it! And only one person honked at me. Mind you, the honk startled me nearly out of my skin, but Ernie leaned his head out of the window and hollered an oath to the honker, so I felt better afterwards.

"Bastard," grumbled Ernie. "You were in the right, Mercy."

"Thank you," I said humbly and sincerely.

My heart nearly gave out before Ernie told me to pull up in front of a seedy-looking place on Figueroa. Then it sort of sank. If I didn't want to take cider out of Ernie's flask, I most certainly didn't want to go into this ugly, run-down building. I didn't say so, being by then a bundle of nerves and painfully close to crying, which would never do.

"If you park here, we can dash across the street," said Ernie, surprising me. "There's a really nice little soda fountain in the drug store on the corner."

After carefully parking the Roadster—the wheel finder things warned me not to get close enough to the curb so as to scrape the running board—I tried to remove my hands from the steering wheel, only to discover they'd frozen into position. Which was patently ridiculous, since the weather that day was in the nineties.

I heard a chuckle from the passenger seat and managed to get my neck unstuck enough to turn my head and look at Ernie. He grinned back at me.

"You're scared to death, aren't you? But you did swell, Mercy. You can stop being nervous now. I'll drive us back to your place after we eat our ice cream."

Then he reached over and removed my fingers, one by one, from the steering wheel. It was terribly embarrassing.

But there you go. At least I'd done it. And Ernie was right about the soda fountain at the drug store. The store itself was pristine and tidy, and the soda fountain was a joy to behold. We sat on our stools, and I ordered a chocolate ice-cream soda. Ernie ordered a root beer float for himself. I was beyond ready when the soda jerk placed our confections before us.

My mouth was so dry, I could hardly stop sipping, but I knew it would be impolite to drink my entire ice-cream soda in one big slurp, so I paced myself. I'd downed about a third of it when I decided I'd better think of a conversational opener to keep my mouth away from the straw.

"Did I tell you I'm giving Chloe and Harvey a puppy for Christmas?" I said, believing dogs to be a safe topic.

"Yeah? That's nice. I had a dog when I was a kid."

"Yes. I think every child needs a dog. Dogs are kind of a… what do you call it? An iconic symbol of childhood. You know, a child and his—or her—dog."

"Iconic, eh?"

When I turned to see his face, Ernie had a grin a mile wide on it, and I sensed he didn't perceive the same romantic notion of children and their dogs as did I. It figured.

"Yes," I said firmly. "Iconic. Heck, artists even paint pictures of boys in ragged trousers playing with their dogs. I've seen them."

"What if the kid's a girl?"

"What if she is? I always wanted a dog when I was a little girl. My mother wouldn't hear of having a dog in the house." I'd always resented her for it, too. Among too many other things to count.

"Why doesn't that surprise me?" Ernie had met my mother, too.

"Exactly. But I think a dog would be a special present for a special little child."

"When's the baby due?"

"Probably in early February. So Chloe can get the dog trained before she has to get used to motherhood."

Ernie chuckled. "If I remember correctly, neither child-rearing nor dog-training are things you 'get used to.' They're both things you have to work like the devil at."

With a sigh, I admitted he was right. "But they do have a whole house full of servants, don't forget."

"How could I forget?"

I sipped again. That was the best ice-cream soda I'd ever tasted in my life, and I honestly think practically dying of thirst played a minimal part in my enjoyment of it.

"What kind of dog are you going to get them?" Ernie asked after another moment or two.

"A toy poodle. Like Buttercup. She's the best."

A huge, empty silence made me glance at Ernie again. He was staring at me as if he'd never seen me before.

"What?" I asked, irked. "Toy poodles are excellent dogs. Buttercup is the best little dog anybody could ever hope to have. I think poodles are marvelous. I read about them at the library, in fact, and dog trainers say they're the smartest dogs on earth."

"But..." Ernie stared some more.

Annoyed, I said, "But what?"

"But what if the kid's a boy?"

"What difference does that make?" I took another huge sip of my soda.

"Mercy, I don't know how to break this to you gently, so I'll just come out and say it. Any red-blooded American boy would rather be shot dead than be seen walking a toy poodle on the street."

I was so startled, I made a slurping sound with my straw and would have been embarrassed if I weren't so astounded. "What do you mean?" I asked, indignant on behalf of poodles the world over.

"Exactly what I said. Think about it, Mercy. You're a little boy in knee britches, and you're taking your dog for a walk or to the park to play. Your dog is a fluffy little poodle with tiny poufy things on its head and tail. With ribbons tied around them, probably. Do you think for a minute the other kids on the block or in the park wouldn't have a field day making fun of you and your dog?"

I opened my mouth to utter a hot retort, in spite of my then-frozen tongue, when the spectacle Ernie had raised suddenly exhibited itself to my mind's eye.

Oh, dear.

"I'm right, aren't I?" Ernie pressed. "You're seeing it, aren't you? A little boy, a boy who aims to impress his pals with his dog, presents his friends with a little ball of fluff. Do you know what his friends are going to think of him?"

"If they're his friends, they won't think anything but that he's got a nice dog," I said defensively, even though I already knew he was right.

"Nuts. They'll either think he's a faggot or a mommy's boy. You've got to get a boy a boy's dog, not a fluff ball."

"But what if the child is a girl?" I said, feeling almost desperate.

"Then a poodle will be okay, although I wouldn't want a daughter of my own to have one. Hell, even girls deserve better than that."

"Better than what, Ernest Templeton? How dare you impugn my wonderful—"

"Dammit, Mercy, I'm not impugning Buttercup or anything else. I just think you need to consider this dog thing a little more thoroughly. When's the baby due again?"

I thought about sulking, knew it would be a stupid thing to do, and said sullenly, "February."

"Well, then, maybe you ought to wait until after the kid's born to decide what kind of dog to get the Nashes."

"But I already told them I'd get them a dog for Christmas!"

He patted my shoulder, a gesture I didn't appreciate. "Don't get all panicky now, Mercy. All you need to do is decide on a dog that won't embarrass a little kid. There are lots of dogs out there. Maybe pick out a spaniel or something."

"Why a spaniel?"

"I don't know! All's I know is that a poodle isn't the right kind of dog to give your sister and her husband for Christmas. Get the kid a fox terrier. They're nice dogs. At least I've been told they are."

My shoulders slumped. "Maybe you're right." Boy, it hurt to say those words.

"You know I'm right," he said.

"No need to sound so smug."

"I'm not smug. I do, however, have a piece of information you might want to think about."

"Relating to dogs?"

"No. This is about something else entirely."

I took one last sip of my soda, wished I had another one waiting for me, and turned to peer at Ernie. "What is it?"

"I went to Clapton's Cafeteria after our driving lesson last night. Nobody named Peggy Wickstrom works there."

Instantly, I saw red. "You checked up on *my* tenant? Darn you, Ernie Templeton! How dare you check up on my tenant! And without even telling me about it beforehand! You're the most—"

It was probably a good thing Ernie lifted a hand to stop my tirade, since people in the store were beginning to look at us. Besides, I couldn't think of any appropriate adjectives that wouldn't have become clogged in my formerly pure Bostonian throat. I might be learning about life, but learning and living are two different things, and I wasn't accustomed to spewing bad words.

"I didn't tell you about it because you were already mad at me, but her story sounded fishy to me, and she definitely knows some shady characters."

"How do you know that?"

"Johnny Autumn."

"I thought you'd never heard of him."

"I hadn't. But after I dropped you off, I went to Phil's, and he said Autumn is a pretty well-known hoodlum in the L.A. area. Either your friend Peggy has lousy taste in men, or she's as bad as he is, and I thought you ought to know it."

"I don't believe it," I said, although I did. Peggy had already begun to give me the jitters.

But this was incredible. Peggy was younger than I, for heaven's sake! And I was only twenty-one. How much trouble could an eighteen-year-old girl get in to? Heck, she was scarcely out of diapers.

"Well, you don't have to believe it, but you might want to ask her about Clapton's, since they don't seem to have heard of her."

Although I wanted to argue with him, I knew it would be a futile thing to do and probably a stupid one as well. "All right. I'll ask her about her employment. Her boyfriend is her own business."

"Not if he's a criminal. Then he might well become your business, too."

I heaved a huge sigh. "All right. I said I'd ask her about it."

"Good girl." He patted me on the back again.

I really wished he wouldn't do that, because the gesture, like him calling me "kiddo," made me feel like a six-year-old. Which was probably how he thought of me, I reflected glumly.

However, we'd both finished our ice-cream treats, and it was time to go home. Ernie drove, thank goodness. Driving down

Sunset to Figueroa and then through the Sunday traffic had almost finished me off. Anyhow, I was too busy contemplating how I aimed to talk to Peggy to pay attention to driving.

When we arrived at my nice home on Bunker Hill, Ernie pulled into the drive, parked the machine, got out on the driver's side, came around to my side of the car and opened my door. I glanced up at him. "Decided to play the gentleman, did you?" I asked tartly.

"Yeah. I know you're disappointed about the Wickstrom girl. I figured acting like a gent is the least I can do, under the circumstances."

"I still think you're wrong about Peggy," I said stoutly, although I thought no such thing.

"I hope I am," was all he said. "May I please have another glass of lemonade?"

"Of course, you may," I said politely, and Ernie followed me into the house, where we were greeted by an ecstatic Buttercup. All of Ernie's reasoning about poodles and little boys rushed back into my head, and I scooped Buttercup up into my arms, hoping she'd forgive me for not giving Chloe and Harvey a toy poodle for Christmas. It then occurred to me I could wait until their child was born to get *it* a dog, but there was no law saying I couldn't give Chloe and Harvey a toy poodle of their own.

The only problem with that was I wasn't sure they really wanted a dog. Nuts. I'd have to have a chat with Chloe.

By the time Ernie and I got to the living room, Caroline had come home from visiting her parents and was relaxing with Lulu. They were playing a spirited game of Old Maid. Lulu looked up as we entered.

"Have a good lesson?" she asked, her eyes sparkling. Have I mentioned Lulu was quite a pretty girl? Well, she was, and that was even without all the paint she usually wore. In fact, I believe she looked better un-made-up, but I'd never tell her so.

"It was a splendid lesson," I said, trying to add a bit of sparkle to my voice, because I was so upset about so many things.

"Yeah," agreed Ernie. "Mercy didn't hit anything, and she even drove through traffic. It's hot as blazes out there, though. I came in for some lemonade."

"There's lots more left," said Lulu. "Caroline and I finished the pitcher Mrs. Buck left, and Caroline made some more. It's really good, too." She beamed at Caroline, who flushed becomingly.

"Nonsense," she said softly. "Lemonade is easy to make."

Which brought to mind Ernie's question about whether or not I could cook. The truth of the matter was that lemonade might well be easy for Caroline Terry to make, but I, Mercedes Louise Allcutt, didn't have a notion in the world how to mix up a batch of it. One more lowering reflection to add to my list of things to feel lousy about.

"Thank you, Caroline," I said. Turning, I told Ernie, "Sit down somewhere, and I'll bring you a glass."

"Thanks, kiddo."

Kiddo again. Before I could dwell on the word, Lulu said, "Why don't you guys join us in a couple of games of Old Maid?"

"I haven't played Old Maid since I was a kid in Chicago," said Ernie. "It might actually be fun."

He sounded eager, and when I turned to look he had a twinkle in his eye, as if he'd really meant what he'd said.

Gloriosky, as one of Chloe's picture friends sometimes said. Perhaps the man (Ernie, not Chloe's friend) really did want to socialize with three young women on a Sunday afternoon. Then I recalled my mother and how horrified she'd be to know I'd entertained a single man in my front parlor on a Sunday afternoon with a card game. In Boston, one doesn't play cards on Sunday. According to my mother, young ladies never played cards at all, not even so innocuous a game as Old Maid. Well, they could play bridge, but only bridge and not another card game.

That settled the matter. Not only did I bring everyone fresh glasses brimming with icy lemonade, but I also decided to give Chloe and Harvey's baby child, whatever its sex, a set of Old Maid cards as a Christmas present. Never mind that the child wouldn't be born until the February following Christmas or that he or she wouldn't be able to play cards for another five years or so. He or she was going to get a pack of Old Maid cards before his or her birth.

Actually, Sunday evening turned out to be one of the most pleasurable I'd spent in a long, long time. Ernie and I not only played Old Maid with Caroline and Lulu, but Ernie ended up the Old Maid three times. I felt almost vindicated. Then, when suppertime came, Caroline and I actually went to the kitchen and made sandwiches together. Well…I cut the bread and watched very carefully as Caroline built the sandwiches.

I considered the experience my very first cooking lesson. So that made two lessons in one day. By the Sunday's end, I'd not only learned how to drive an automobile in traffic, but I could make a ham-and-cheese sandwich like nobody's business. Ham-and-cheese sandwiches, made with mustard, along with sliced apples, made for a satisfying supper.

And I didn't have to confront Peggy Wickstrom, because she hadn't come home by the time Ernie left and Caroline, Lulu and I went up to bed.

Every now and then, things go my way.

TEN

Naturally, that state of affairs didn't last long.

"What do you mean, they told Mr. Templeton I don't work at Clapton's?"

Monday evening. Lulu, Caroline and I were home for the evening and we, along with Peggy Wickstrom, had been served a lovely dinner by Mrs. Buck. I'd asked to speak to Peggy after supper in a little room I called the office, for no better reason than I didn't know what else to call it.

"Mr. Templeton went to Clapton's Cafeteria on Saturday evening, and they told him they'd never heard of you there," I said. I tried to keep the tone of my voice non-accusatory. After all, Ernie might be wrong about Peggy. Besides, I didn't want to make an enemy of this girl unless she proved to be a total rotter. So what if she seemed taciturn and uncommunicative? Perhaps she wasn't awfully bright or preferred to remain on the quiet side.

She sure blushed up a storm at my information. Her cheeks practically blazed with red. "You mean you sent your boss to check up on me?"

I could tell she was torn between fury and fright, and I felt a little sorry for her. "No. I told him you said you worked at Clapton's, and he went there Saturday night to check. He..." I hesitated to impart the next piece of information, then swallowed my qualms and blurted out, "He doesn't trust my judgment."

Peggy bowed her head. "I see."

And then, to my utter horror, she burst into tears.

"Peggy! Please, tell me what's the matter!" I reached for her, and she flinched away from me as if she expected me to strike her. I sat back, folded my hands in my lap and waited for the storm to abate.

When she finally lifted her head, her face was streaked with tears. I felt like a brute. Nevertheless, I didn't speak, deciding it was better she be the first to do so. Perhaps I hadn't learned much during my time in Los Angeles, but Ernie had taught me the value of silence when you wanted somebody to tell you something. He'd more than once accused me of putting the words I wanted to hear into other people's mouths, and I didn't intend to do so on this occasion. Ergo, I waited.

Peggy managed to wrestle a crumpled handkerchief from her frock's pocket. She wore a sober-hued blue dress that evening. I thought to myself she didn't *look* like a lying cheat who hung out with hoodlums. On the other hand, I've been wrong about people many times, as I've mentioned before.

She sniffled pathetically and mopped her face. Then she looked at me, her demeanor pitiable and wringing my heart. I told it to be still because it had led me astray too many times recently.

"I...I'm sorry. I was afraid if I told you the truth, you wouldn't let me live here, and then I didn't know what I'd do."

I said a cautious, "Oh?" I longed to fill in her story for her, but didn't and was proud of myself. Rather, I sat in stony silence. Well, I had a sympathetic expression on my face, because I couldn't help it.

After another sniffle, Peggy began a somewhat watery narrative. "You see, when I moved here from Michigan, my folks didn't want me to come. They were really mad and cut me off completely."

I bit my tongue, which wanted to spew forth my opinion of families who cut their children off without a penny or parental support. My own family wasn't what I considered tip-top in the uplifting-of-one's-morale department, but at least my parents still spoke to me, even though they disapproved of nearly everything I did. I didn't even give her another "Oh," figuring it was better she spill her own beans her own way.

"So I was down on my luck, and I couldn't seem to find work anywhere," she continued after another several sniffles and a sob or two. "I applied everywhere, but everyone told me I was too young. I did apply at Clapton's," she said earnestly. "But they wouldn't hire a girl my age. So...so I finally got a job at a dance studio on Flower."

"You teach dancing?" Teaching people to dance didn't sound so terrible an occupation to me. Heck, it sounded quite respectable. Even my mother didn't object to a foxtrot, as long as the couple dancing it stayed far enough apart for propriety.

"Teach?" Peggy stared at me for a second, as if she weren't quite sure what to say.

"You don't teach at the studio? Er...what do you do there?" Maybe she kept books for the place. That sounded even more respectable, if considerably duller, than teaching people to dance.

She licked her lips. "Um, it's not that kind of dance studio."

"Well, then, what kind is it?" I asked, perhaps a bit too sharply, because Peggy winced.

Then she blurted out, "Men pay to dance with me."

I blinked, astonished. "You mean you work at a dance hall?" I'd heard about dance halls, frequented by men who weren't gentlemen who danced with young women who weren't ladies for a dime a dance.

She nodded, looking as if she wanted to sink through the flooring, although she'd only have hit dirt if she'd done so, since the house didn't have a paved cellar. In fact, they called cellars basements in California. I only kept junk in mine. Not that it matters.

"I-I was afraid if I told you I danced with men for a dime in a dance hall, you wouldn't allow me to move in here, and I didn't have anywhere else to go."

After a significant pause, during which I tried to think of something cogent to say and Peggy stared at me with eyes as round and imploring as any dog's, I said, "I see. What's the name of the, uh, dance studio where you work?" Was that cogent? Well, never mind.

"Anthony's Palaise de Danse. That's Danse with an S instead of a C," she answered promptly, making me think she wasn't making up the name. Anyhow, I could look up Anthony's Palaise de Danse in the telephone directory at work. Then I'd at least know if it existed. In fact, I could darned well ask the person who answered the telephone there if a Miss Peggy Wickstrom worked there. Why leave it to Ernie?

"I see," I said again. "Is that where you met Mr. Autumn?"

"Johnny?" She seemed to perk up a trifle. "Yeah. I met Johnny there. He's a nice young man."

"Is he?" I made my voice stern. "According to Mr. Templeton, your Mr. Autumn has some rather unsavory chums."

"Johnny's not like that!" she said in hot defense of her beloved. "He's not a thug! He may know some people, but he's not like they are."

Right. "Well," I said judicially, "I don't like the fact that you lied to me, Peggy—"

"I'm sorry," she interrupted, sounding miserable. "I'm really sorry. I didn't know what else to do."

"Yes, so you've told me. However, I do believe this breach of confidence deserves my consideration. I won't make you move out or anything, but if any other such misrepresentations come to light, I'm afraid I won't be so forgiving the next time."

"They won't," she said instantly. "Honest. I only lied because I was afraid—"

"You wouldn't be allowed to live here," I finished for her. "Yes, so you've said." After hesitating for a minute, I went on, "You know, Peggy, I'm not a wicked witch. I understand young women have a hard time when they're on their own in the big city."

"You?" she asked incredulously, which peeved me.

"Yes. Me. I come from a well-to-do family, but that doesn't mean I'm blind to the travails of the rest of the women in the world. Why do you think I'm letting out apartments in my home, anyhow? I wanted to give working girls like you a chance to have a decent place to stay. I do *not* expect to be lied to."

Boy, if I could have sounded more like my mother, I don't know how. I guess not all of my early childhood training was for naught. I could scold like a master of the art.

Seeming cowed, Peggy shrank back into her chair. "I'm sorry. You've been very kind to me, and I understand. I…well, I guess I underestimated your…well, your heart. If you know what I mean."

Aw. I appreciated her words. Feeling fairly noble, I rose from my chair. "Yes, well, let's not discuss this any longer. You're on notice as far as your future behavior goes. You may stay here, but any future trespasses on my good nature will not be tolerated. I trust we understand each other?"

"Yes. Yes, I understand." She stood, too, and gave me a tremulous smile. "Thank you, Mercy."

"You're welcome."

"Your name suits you."

Boy, I'd never thought of it before, but her comment made me happy. I smiled back at her. "Thank you, Peggy. I think we'll get along quite well now."

Feeling satisfied with myself and the world, I departed the office behind Peggy, who raced up the staircase. She had to get ready to go to work at the dance hall. What a tawdry way to make a living! I felt sorry for the girl. I also felt an absolute fascination to see what went on in a dance hall and wondered if Lulu would like to go with me one night after I felt more accomplished at driving the Roadster.

The rest of the week passed peacefully enough. Ernie gave me two driving lessons, although they were short because we had to conduct them in the dark due to work eating up most of the daylight hours. But my confidence was growing, and this was in spite of Ernie constantly telling me to be careful because most auto accidents occurred when people became over-confident, which didn't help my meager store of assurance at all.

Also, I kept annoying Ernie by asking him how he was proceeding on Calvin Buck's case, and he kept telling me it was none of my business. I resented those words.

"How can it not be my business when Calvin's parents live in my home?" I asked him on a steamy day late in September when we were both in his office. Did the weather *ever* cool off in Southern California? "And a woman to whom I'm renting a room knows a man who used to do odd jobs for Mr. Gossett!"

He eyed me narrowly. "Yeah. I know both of those things. What's with the Wickstrom wench? Did you ever find out where she really works?"

Drat! I was hoping to avoid this conversation and was sorry I'd brought the matter up, since Ernie the irritating habit of not overlooking things people wanted overlooked. Nevertheless, I answered with the truth.

"Yes. She works at Anthony's Palaise de Danse. I called and checked with the ownership, and they told me she's worked there for six months."

Ernie's eyebrows had shot up at the name of the joint—for there was truly no better word for it—and he sneered. "Anthony's Palaise de Dance? She's a dance-hall cutie? A dime a dance? Like the song?"

I sighed. "Yes."

"Tough job for a young girl like her."

"Yes. I think so, too." After mulling for a moment, I said, "She told me that's where she met Johnny Autumn. I presume his sort frequent such establishments."

"Hoodlums? Yeah, I'd say so."

Feeling slightly depressed at the thought, I sat in one of the chairs in front of Ernie's desk. "Do you think she might get into trouble with him? I mean, do you think *he's* trouble? Have you looked into him? Well, of course you have. I wish you'd tell me something. This is important to me."

"I don't want you involved in the investigation, Mercy. You always get yourself into trouble when you get mixed up in these cases."

"Darn you, Ernie Templeton! I'm involved in this one whether I want to be or not. Better you simply tell me what you find out than I discover things by accident when Johnny Autumn tries to kill me!"

Ernie's gaze paid a visit to the ceiling. "He's not going to try to kill you. But he's no good. He's been involved in shady dealings for a long time. He's twenty-six years old, which is way too old for your precious Miss Wickstrom, too."

"She'd not my precious Miss Wickstrom," said I through gritted teeth. "But I do think it my duty to care about what happens to my tenants. Not to mention the fact that my own interests might well be involved."

Pushing his chair back and flinging his feet onto his desk, Ernie heaved a gigantic sigh and said, "All right, all right. I'll tell you what I know so far, which is pretty darned little."

"Thank you." I felt better about Ernie, the world and life all of a sudden.

"Mr. Gossett was heavily in debt to a gambling organization. Johnny Autumn is one of the goons working for the gambling outfit."

"But would the gambling folks kill him? If they did, they'd never get their money back. I know we talked about this before, but—"

Ernie fixed me with a steely stare, which effectively shut me up. "I'm not finished yet."

Whoops. I waved a hand to let him know he could continue talking, so he did.

"Besides being involved with the gambling syndicate, it seems Autumn's been branching out into…other ventures, as well."

After a moment of silence, I decided it was safe to speak. "What kinds of ventures?"

A hint of color tinted Ernie's cheeks, and I stared, astounded. If I didn't know better, I'd swear the man was blushing!

"Booze and…well, ladies of the night, I guess you might call them. He works for Jimmy the Stinker Pastorale—"

"Jimmy the Stinker?" I nearly burst out laughing. "What kind of name is that?"

Scowling hideously, Ernie said, "It's a nickname he earned the hard way, by working for some goons out of Chicago. Believe me, you don't want to know most of the stuff he's been involved in. He's moved to the west coast, but Phil doesn't know if he's still part of the Chicago mob."

"Good heavens," I said faintly, thinking of the dim but pretty

Peggy in the company of murdering thugs. "You mean Johnny is a...what do you call them? A soldier for the mob?"

With a shrug, Ernie said, "Nobody knows yet, but I guess Autumn's the adventurous sort. According to Phil, it looks as though he's trying to organize his own stable of young women. With or without Pastorale's permission, Phil couldn't say. I presume Pastorale gave his blessing. Otherwise, I suspect Johnny Autumn wouldn't be alive now to sweet-talk your precious tenant."

I was horrified. "Golly! You don't think Peggy is...?"

"No, I'm not saying anything about her. However, this Johnny Autumn guy of hers is bad news. It would be good if you could steer her away from him, but you probably won't be able to."

My back suddenly went stiff. "Why not?" I demanded, feeling what might have been a reformer's zeal invade my soul.

"Gals who hang out with the Johnny Autumns of this world don't usually want to be saved."

I think I blinked at him. "Why ever not?"

He threw his arms out wide. "Hell, don't ask me! I'm only saying what I know to be true. I've seen it before. A girl gets involved with a thug, and it's like scraping barnacles off the hull of a ship to get her to leave off hanging out with the guy. It's one of those...what do you call 'em? It's a mystery of life."

"I wonder why."

"Who the hell knows?" he asked grumpily. "For that matter, who the hell cares, except maybe somebody from the Salvation Army?"

"I care," I told him sharply. "Miss Wickstrom seems like a perfectly nice person, and she's living in my house. I'd hate to see her get hurt by a boyfriend who's not all he should be."

"Oh, Johnny Autumn is definitely not what he should be," Ernie said. "He's a crook. He's served time for petty stuff, but it looks to Phil and me as though he's doing his best to work his way up the ladder of the gambling—and other—rackets."

"He's done *time*?" I cried, appalled. But, really! Peggy Wickstrom was eighteen years old! And she was seeing a certified bad man with a criminal record who was almost ten years older than she!

"Take it easy," said Ernie. "He might be nice to the girl." He didn't sound as if he believed his own words.

I didn't believe them either. I resolved to have a heart-to-heart chat with Peggy Wickstrom as soon as I got home from work. I was certain she'd resent my interference, but I only had her welfare at heart. I got up to leave Ernie's office, my innards in turmoil.

"Hey, Mercy, don't take this too hard. She'll probably come to her senses one of these days. Anyhow, I aim to give you another driving lesson on Sunday."

Frowning and upset, I turned toward my boss. "Thank you. What time?"

"How about one?"

"One is fine with me," said I, and I went to sit at my desk and wish for something to occupy my mind so I could stop thinking about what kind of life Johnny Autumn might be persuading Peggy Wickstrom in to. Before I got to the door leading from Ernie's office to mine, I remembered my manners and turned again. "Thanks, Ernie. I appreciate the information and you teaching me to drive."

"No problem." Ever casual, my boss.

I hadn't been brooding for long before Detective Phil Bigelow opened the outer office door. Looking up from staring at my empty desk, I said, "H'lo, Phil."

"Good afternoon, Mercy. Ernie in?"

"Yes. He's in."

As Phil headed toward Ernie's office, I said, "Do you think Johnny Autumn will turn Peggy Wickstrom into a…you know."

I could tell from the way his back stiffened Phil wished I hadn't asked him that question. Nevertheless, he turned to face me. "I don't know, Mercy. You can never tell what people will do. I haven't been able to dig up any background information on Miss Wickstrom." I saw the instant an idea strike him, because he tilted his head and his expression brightened. "Say, maybe you can help. Find out where she comes from, if her parents are still alive. That sort of thing."

With a sigh, I told him what Peggy had revealed to me: her parents had disowned her when she moved from Michigan to California. His shoulders sagged a bit.

"I'm sorry to hear it. But you never know. Maybe she's hiding something. Wouldn't be the first girl to come to L.A. dreaming of stardom only to fall into the wrong hands. Maybe she'll be glad for a lift up from the Johnny Autumn type."

"Maybe." I considered the light in Peggy's eyes whenever she spoke of her beloved and had my doubts. Why couldn't Peggy be like Lulu: content to paint her nails in the lobby of some office building and await being discovered by some famous producer or director magically strolling in one day? Why'd she have to find such a sleazy job and end up with a slimy creature like Johnny Autumn?

No answer occurred to me.

Phil went into Ernie's office and closed the door, and I resumed brooding. Fortunately, the phone rang shortly thereafter, and to my great joy it was someone wanting to make an appointment with Ernie about business matters. Then, by golly, the phone rang twice more before the working day ended. By then, three (count 'em) potential clients had made appointments with my boss. Business seemed to be picking up, which made me happy, although

I didn't want it to pick up so much that Ernie would turn his attention away from the Gossett case. I knew, if the police didn't, that no son of Emerald and Lottie Buck could have killed a man.

Which, if I'd told Ernie, would have prompted him to point out my own blissful ignorance of the world. But never mind. After work Lulu and I took Angels Flight up to Olive, and walked the few blocks to my—No. Our—home.

As luck would have it, I spotted Peggy Wickstrom at the foot of the stairs, and before she could make a mad dash upward—she seemed to be attempting to steer clear of me, probably because she was embarrassed I'd found out about her lie and her job—I said, "Peggy, may I speak to you for a minute? Come into the office with me, please."

Her shoulders slumped, and Lulu looked at me oddly, but I only marched firmly to the office with Peggy straggling behind me.

I sat behind the desk residing there and waved Peggy to a chair. Folding my hands on the desk, I spoke to her gently. "You know, I think, Peggy, my employer is looking into the murder of Mr. Milton Halsey Gossett."

"Yes. What does that have to do with me?"

I detected a note of defiance in her voice, but didn't allow it to deter me from my course of action, which was to save this young woman from her baser instincts and Johnny Autumn. "I hope and pray it has nothing whatsoever to do with you, Peggy, but I fear that, during the course of his investigation, Mr. Templeton has discovered some rather unsavory facts about your intended." I presume he was her intended. For all I knew at this point, he aimed to ruin her and abandon her to her fate. Wicked man!

She sat upright at my words. "Johnny is a good man!" cried she with vigor—and untruth, if what Ernie had told me was correct, and I'd bet it was.

"Not according to his police record."

"Oh, that." She shrugged off Johnny Autumn's criminal past as if it was nothing.

"Yes, that," I said, doing my best to sound stern. I drew upon memories of my mother's many lectures to guide me, only I attempted to imbue the process with warmth. My mother didn't believe in warmth. "What's worse is that he's apparently involved in a gambling syndicate, run by a fellow from Chicago. Worse even than gambling is that the police believe him to be involved in…" I sucked in a big breath, loath to say the word aloud. "…prostitution."

"What?" Peggy jumped up from her chair. "It's not true! It can't be true!"

"Sit down, Peggy." My mother came to my aid again. Perhaps I would thank her one day. Not any day soon, but one day.

Peggy sat, and I saw tears well in her eyes. The girl was a watering pot. "It is true Mr. Autumn has served a jail term, although I must say I don't know what for."

"Petty theft," Peggy said promptly. "And he deeply regrets it."

It sounded to me as if she believed what she was saying, and I was hard pressed not to sigh in resignation. What's the old saw? There are none so blind as those who will not see? I think that's it. It's probably from the Bible. Or maybe Shakespeare. Or Oscar Wilde. All of our best epigrams come from those three sources, in my experience.

"Hmm. I wonder if he's not bamboozling you, Peggy." She wanted to leap to her feet and speak in Autumn's defense again, but I held up my hand. "Please hear me out."

She slumped and said, "Very well." But she wasn't happy about it; I could tell.

"I'm not in any position to pass judgment on you or Mr. Autumn, Peggy, but I do believe you might want to reconsider your employment and your choice of friends. Most of us go through our entire lives without meeting people who have served jail sentences, you know. There are many more non-criminals in the world than there are criminals. I'm sure you could find a nice fellow who isn't as shady as Mr. Autumn if you could only get out of that dance hall and secure another position somewhere else."

"But I *tried*!"

"Yes, I know, but perhaps I can help you. There must be something you can do that doesn't require you to dance with strangers for a living."

"Maid work," she said in a voice clearly indicating what she thought of maid work. "Or maybe I could wash dishes for a living."

"Either one of which modes of employment would be more satisfactory than dancing with strangers for a dime a dance," I said icily. "What's wrong with being a waitress? Or working at a department store? Or being a receptionist. Or a telephone operator? Why do you choose to work in a disreputable establishment catering to disreputable men?"

"I didn't choose it!" she all but screeched at me. "It was the only job I could find!" She passed a hand over her eyes to catch her tears, which were now falling fast. "Anyhow, Johnny is a good man. It's not his fault he got in trouble when he was a kid."

"He's not a kid any longer," I pointed out dryly. "He's ever so much older than you are. You ought to be seeing a young man closer to your age, Peggy. Don't you have *any* family willing to help you?"

"Oh! You don't understand! I could go back home and work on the farm, but I don't *want* to be a farmer! Johnny is exciting! Besides, I *love* him!"

Well, there you go. Even I, who was young and inexperienced at life, knew you couldn't argue with a young woman who thought she was in love. Oh, for the good old days when parents selected suitable husbands for their children.

Wait! What was I thinking? I didn't mean that! For heaven's sake, I'd moved to Los Angeles to get away from precisely that sort of supervision.

Why, then, did I get the unpleasant sensation Peggy was somehow doomed? It all beat me. Feeling discouraged, I said, "I wish you'd think about what we've discussed here, Peggy. God knows I don't want to interfere in your life, but I hate to see a girl as young as you making what I see as a terrible mistake only leading her to tragedy."

"You don't know that!"

I gave up. "You're right. Perhaps your young man will all of a sudden decide to live a good and virtuous life, marry you, and you'll have many bright and lovely children together."

Her nose wrinkled. Evidently she didn't care for the described scenario for herself any more than I cared for it for myself. Unfortunately, I got a strong impression I possessed a more stalwart character and probably one or two more cranial convolutions, than Miss Peggy Wickstrom. I decided not to despair of her. Yet. I gave her one last option.

"Please keep in mind that if you ever do want to change your circumstances for the better, I'll be more than happy to help in any way I can, Peggy. I don't want you to think I'm a self-righteous prig, only I can't help but worry about your involvement with a man who is definitely on the wrong side of the law."

"Maybe he was," she said stubbornly. "He isn't any longer."

"According to the police, he is involved in an illegal gambling syndicate and probably bootlegging and prostitution, as well," I reminded her.

"Then why don't the police arrest him? Answer me that! I tell you, he's not involved in any such thing."

That's when I gave up.

ELEVEN

Yet it seemed my little lecture had some effect on Peggy after all. I'd considered her all but a lost child, but the Sunday following our meeting in the office—Lulu asked me about it, but I didn't believe I should tell her another tenant's business—she seemed brighter and more chipper than I'd ever seen her.

The Bucks had spent the morning at church as they always did on Sundays, and now I presumed they were visiting their son in jail. What a disheartening way to spend your day off. But Peggy helped brighten the day when she offered to make lemonade for Lulu, Caroline and me as we waited for Ernie to come over and give me another driving lesson.

"My Aunt Margaret used to make this lemonade. It's her recipe," she said, acting for once like the adolescent she was. "She's the one I was named after, you know. My real name is Margaret, but everyone's always called me Peggy."

"Thank you," I said, pleased to see her on her way to reformation. "That would be very nice of you."

"Yeah," said Lulu, who had been engrossed in the latest issue of *Screenplay*. "I could use some lemonade. It's hot again today."

I sighed. It certainly was warm again. And the calendar was creeping perilously close to October. Shoot. In New England, we'd all be getting out our woollies.

"I'd like some lemonade," Caroline said. Shyly, I need not say. Well, I just did, but I'm sure I didn't need to.

"I'll be right back."

Peggy all but skipped to the kitchen. I called after her, "Need any help?"

"No, thanks," she called back cheerily. "I'm fine."

I stroked Buttercup, who had curled up on my lap, and resumed reading *The Mystery of Angelina Frood*, by R. Austin Freeman. It was one of his Dr. Thorndyke mysteries, and I loved all of them. I wanted to be like R. Austin Freeman when I got published. Well...not exactly like him, but...you know, successful. I don't mean the kind of success that brought in wads and wads of money (I already had enough money), but the kind of success that meant people loved reading my books. Everyone loved Dr. Thorndyke. Creating my own character, one whom people would want to read about over and over again, was my idea of success. Like Agatha Christie had done with Hercule Poirot. Or, on the other hand, perhaps I'd like to be another Mary Roberts Rinehart. Mrs. Rinehart didn't write about the same person all the time, yet her books were wonderful, too.

But enough daydreaming. Lulu, Caroline, Buttercup and I waited for Ernie, and Peggy went to the kitchen to make her Aunt Margaret's lemonade. Gee, from the way she spoke about the folks back home in Michigan, I was surprised she'd bothered to bring any recipes with her to Los Angeles. But mine was not to reason why, as they say. I was only glad she seemed to be coming out of her shell.

Shortly after she went into the kitchen, she came out again, carrying a tray with a pitcher of lemonade and four ice-filled glasses. She set the tray on a coffee table—she didn't even rattle the glasses, which convinced me she could be a waitress if she really wanted to be one—and poured out lemonade for all of us.

"Here you go," she said, smiling as she handed around the glasses.

"Thank you," we said one at a time as we accepted our lemonade.

I sipped mine tentatively, wondering how Aunt Margaret's lemonade could be so different from anyone else's. Except for an odd bite to it, it tasted just like lemonade to me. "Very nice," I said in order to be polite. In truth, I'd drunk tastier lemonade, but I didn't want to discourage the girl now that she seemed to want to socialize with the rest of us.

"Mmm," said Lulu, licking her lips. I got the impression she liked her lemonade better than I did mine.

"Tasty," said Caroline. I don't know if she was merely being polite or if she really liked it.

"Thank you," said Peggy, and I think she blushed a little. I thought her blush was sweet.

We resumed our former occupations, Lulu reading *Screenplay*, Caroline knitting, and me reading Dr. Thorndyke, when Lulu giggled. I looked up and noticed her lemonade glass was empty and Peggy was refilling it. I considered this gesture nice of her.

"What is it?" I asked.

"It says here that Theda Bara is still carrying a torch for Rudolph Valentino," said Lulu, and she giggled again.

"And you think it's funny?" I asked, surprised, never having pegged Lulu as a callous young woman.

"Well, no. But that…what do you call it? Phrase? 'Carrying a torch.' I think it's funny. I got a mental image of Theda Bara carrying a torch all over Hollywood."

"Ah," I said since no more appropriate word leapt to my mind.

Then Caroline giggled, too. I glanced up from my book to peer at her.

"Drink your lemonade, Mercy," urged Peggy. "It's really good. My Aunt Margaret swore by it during the hot summer months."

And how many hot summer months did one get in Michigan? I wondered. Wasn't Michigan one of those states that froze over for nine months out of a usual year? Well, I didn't want the girl to think I didn't appreciate her efforts, so I took another swallow of lemonade.

"It really is funny, the things people say," said Caroline after a moment. "Carrying a torch, indeed."

"Yeah," said Lulu. "It's like when people say applesauce when they mean something's nonsense."

"Or when they say they're beating their gums when they're gossiping," said Caroline, grinning.

I realized some of our slang expressions truly were pretty funny, so I decided to join in. "Or the big cheese. My father's the big cheese at his bank." The notion of my father as a cheese actually tickled me a good deal. Especially when I visualized a big square of Swiss cheese, holes and all, wearing one of Father's prosperous "banker" suits.

"And Ernie's the big cheese at his office," said Lulu, laughing harder.

"And what about calling a pretty woman a tomato," said Caroline, beginning to laugh in her turn.

Now that was funny. I began to laugh too.

Peggy said, "One of the gentlemen who came to the dance club had been drinking. He said he was spifflicated."

"He doesn't sound like a gentleman to me," observed Caroline.

We all roared at her words. Even Buttercup gave a happy little yap.

"And why do they call coffee Joe? Or java?" asked Lulu. "And what does Jake mean? Like 'Everything's Jake.' I never did understand that expression."

"Me, neither," I said, believing she'd made a valid point. What did Jake mean, for heaven's sake?

"Some of the men who come to the club call me a hoofer," said Peggy, referring to her job again. "But it reminds me of heifer, which is a female cow, and I don't like it."

Lulu whooped. I regret to say I did, too.

We were, as luck would have it, in hysterics by the time Ernie rang the bell to pick me up for my driving lesson. Buttercup and I, still laughing—I was, I mean. Buttercup wasn't—went to the front door to let him in. Wiping tears from my eyes, I said, "Come on in, Ernie. Have some lemonade. Peggy made it for us."

Ernie frowned at me, an expression I didn't appreciate. "What?" I asked. "There's nothing wrong with drinking lemonade on a warm afternoon."

"Right," said Ernie. He stalked past me and on into the living room, where he surveyed the ladies gathered there, fists on hips and with a withering glower.

"'Lo, Ernie," said Lulu. And she giggled.

"How do you do?" said Caroline, pronouncing each of her words carefully.

"I'm Jake," said Ernie.

We all but exploded in laughter.

Then Ernie grabbed me by the elbow, tucked Buttercup under his arm, and aimed me out the door and into his Studebaker.

"Wait!" I cried. "I need to get my key and my handbag."

"You don't need your key today. Or your handbag." He sounded grim.

"But I thought you were going to give me a driving lesson!"

"I was, but things have changed."

"What things have changed?"

He didn't answer until he'd started his Studebaker, backed out of the drive, and we were heading down the street. I noticed his lips had pressed into a thin line, and I couldn't imagine what the matter was. Therefore, I asked him. "What's troubling you, Ernie? Why are you in such a foul mood?"

He pulled to a stop at an intersection and gave me such a ferocious frown, I actually shrank back in my seat, glad I had Buttercup to hold on to. "Who made that so-called lemonade of yours?" he asked.

I shook my head, confused. "Why are you changing the subject?"

"I'm not changing the damned subject. Who made the lemonade?"

"Stop swearing at me!"

"Damn it, Mercy Allcutt, tell me who made the damned lemonade!"

He'd roared the question, totally intimidating both Buttercup and me. She cowered in my lap, and I said in a small voice, "Peggy."

Slamming his fist on the steering wheel, he said, "I knew it."

Greatly daring—I didn't trust this mood of his one little bit—I said, "What's the matter with Peggy making lemonade?"

We'd made it to Sunset, and Ernie was driving along at a pretty fast clip, his motorcar shaking like an autumn leaf in a high gale—his was an elderly car—before he answered my question, which I was too afraid to repeat.

Finally, he turned onto one of those dirt roads leading off Sunset and drove into the lot where he'd given me one of my first driving lessons. He stamped on the brake and the clutch and slammed the gear lever into neutral. Then he turned and glared at me.

I tried to glare back, but not awfully successfully.

"You have no idea, do you?" he said through gritted teeth.

Totally befuddled, I stammered, "Um…I guess not. An idea about what?"

"You and your pals are looped, Mercy!"

Looped? What did that mean?

He must have guessed I had no idea what he'd just said, because he said, "You're ossified."

"Ossified? You mean we're turning into rocks?"

He allowed his head to fall forward until it rested on the steering wheel. "Damn it, Mercy, you're all buzzed! That Peggy woman put something in the lemonade."

My brain finally began to function, sort of. When Ernie had come to the house, we'd been laughing about modern slang expressions, and I now recalled some of the ones we'd tossed about. I was horrified. "You mean she put liquor in the lemonade and we all got *spifflicated*?"

Without lifting his head, he turned a gazed at me. "Spifflicated? Good God. And you didn't know what ossified meant?"

"How do you know what she did?"

"I can tell when people have been boozing it up, Mercy. Believe me. I've seen plenty of them before this. I've never seen three nice young ladies in your condition before today, however. The fine, upstanding Miss Wickstrom of yours is a bad egg, Mercy."

Unfortunately, I remembered the big cheeses we girls had been discussing and giggled.

Lifting his head so fast I'm surprised his neck didn't snap, Ernie slapped the steering wheel and roared, "What the hell is so damned funny? You think it's *funny* that the woman deliberately put booze in your lemonade to get you all drunk? I'll be surprised if you don't find your whole house ransacked by the time you get home and Peggy and her boyfriend gone after clearing out your place."

I felt my eyes widen. "No! She wouldn't do such a thing. She was...she was being cheerful for once."

"I just bet she was."

"Oh, dear."

"Right. Oh, dear."

"You must be wrong about her, Ernie. She said it was her Aunt Margaret's recipe. Her aunt wouldn't have put liquor into her lemonade, would she? An old lady like her?"

"Her aunt Margaret, my aunt Fanny," said Ernie, letting me know exactly what he thought about my reasoning.

I felt tears well in my eyes and lowered my head so Ernie wouldn't see them. Poor Buttercup got used as a handkerchief; however, you must remember Ernie hadn't allowed me to take my handbag with me.

"Have you ever drunk alcohol before, Mercy?"

I sniffled, feeling stupid. "No."

"I didn't think so. So you wouldn't know. Did the stuff taste like regular lemonade?"

"Um...not really. It had an odd bite to it."

I heard him say, "Damn," under his breath but didn't bother to scold him for it.

"I'm sorry, Ernie." I sounded pitiful. I felt pitiful.

"Sorry ain't going to cut it, Mercy. You're going to have to get rid of the Wickstrom girl, and the sooner the better. I'll kick her out for you if you don't want to do it yourself." He swore again. "I *knew* it was a mistake to let you interview the woman by yourself."

"But she's only eighteen years old!" I cried.

"Eighteen's plenty old enough."

"But..."

He held up a hand, and I shut my mouth. "Listen, Mercy,

I'm not trying to be hard on you. I know you're a nice girl and trust people. But this is the big, bad city, and you're not living in your parents' house, all protected, like you were in Boston."

"I know it."

"So you really kind of have to depend on people like me, who know what's what and how life goes on in L.A."

"I know it." I sniffled again. "Thank you."

"You're welcome."

I scooted a little closer to him on the seat, suddenly feeling awfully lucky to have such a nice, upstanding, handsome man as a boss, even if his suit jackets were generally a little rumpled. I'd rather be around Ernie than any of my father's friends or, God forbid, my awful brother George's pals.

Putting my hand on his arm, I whispered, "You're very good to me, Ernie."

He eyed me doubtfully. "Yeah?"

"Yeah." I smiled up at him. "In fact, I really appreciate the way you try to protect me and take care of me." I couldn't help adding, "Even thought I don't really need your help all that much."

Naturally, he rolled his eyes.

I tried not to take offense. "Really, Ernie, I do appreciate you."

"How nice."

"In fact, I've been thinking lately it might be fun if we were to get better acquainted."

Don't ask me where this bold statement came from, because I honestly don't know. Ernie, however, did.

"That's the booze talking, Mercy. You're not going to take advantage of me in your present condition."

I blinked at him. "Take advantage of you?"

"Dammit, Mercy, move over to your side of the car! You're

drunk, and I may not be a fine Boston gent, but I know better than to ravish an innocent young woman in your condition."

Crushed, I scooted over to my side of the car, tears sliding down my cheeks, feeling like a total fool. Buttercup crawled back onto my lap as if her feelings, too, were hurt.

In a softer voice, Ernie said, "Here," and handed me a clean handkerchief. God alone knows where he got it. "Don't cry, Mercy. I didn't mean to make you cry."

"You think I'm a hussy," I whispered, mopping tears.

"Ah, God." Ernie's head hit the steering wheel again.

"You do, don't you?"

Without looking up, he said, "Mercedes Louise Allcutt, you couldn't be a hussy if you tried. In fact, I think you just did try, and it didn't work."

How depressing.

We sat in the machine for about ten minutes or so, Ernie with his head on the steering wheel and me trying to control my emotions. Buttercup just sat on my lap and looked from one to the other of us in turn, as if she didn't understand human beings, never had and, what's more, didn't want to. I couldn't say as I blamed her.

After I'd calmed down, Ernie turned to peer at me once more. "You all right?"

I nodded.

"You look okay."

"Do I look as though I've been crying?"

He squinted at me. "Naw."

"Good."

"You ready to go home now?"

"I guess." My spirits were by that time hovering somewhere under the automobile, clinging to any pipes that might be there.

"Do you want to stop for coffee or anything on the way home?" he asked politely.

"No, thank you." I, on the other hand, was much too formal, probably to make up for having behaved like an idiot earlier.

"Right. I'll drive you home then."

"Thank you."

"But I'm going to walk you to the door and take a look inside. Just to make sure everything's Jake in there."

I didn't feel the least inclination to laugh at his use of the word Jake this time.

TWELVE

Unfortunately for me, not to mention Lulu and Caroline, Ernie had been correct in predicting I'd find my home looted when I returned to it.

Not only had the place been ransacked, but I discovered Lulu and Caroline sound asleep, Lulu in an armchair and Caroline on the sofa. Gentle snores permeated the air, along with a not-altogether pleasant fragrance.

Peggy, naturally, was long gone.

Glancing around with grim satisfaction, Ernie said, "Looks like I got you out of here just in time. The ever-noble Miss Wickstrom probably put a Mickey Finn in the lemonade right after we left."

Gazing at my friends with regret and a good deal of guilt, I didn't react to Ernie's sarcasm, but only said, "What's a Mickey Finn?"

"Probably chloral hydrate. The Wickstrom dame could have put a few drops in a glass of lemonade, and it would be nighty-night for Lulu and Caroline."

I put Buttercup down, sank onto another chair and covered

my face with my hands. "Oh, Ernie, what a fool I was! I had no idea."

"Don't take it so hard, kiddo. You're not the first young woman who's been duped by a doxie."

I looked at him through my fingers. "Do you honestly think she's a doxie?" Could I be *so* mistaken in my judgment of the girl?

Ernie waved his hand at the sleeping women in my living room, giving me my answer without having to use words. Yes. I had been so mistaken in my judgment. Again. I didn't want to think about it.

"So what should I do now? Call the police?"

Ernie flopped himself on the stool in front of my armchair. "I guess you might as well call the coppers. I doubt they'll find the Wickstrom dame."

"Why not?"

He shrugged. "L.A.'s a big place, and Miss Wickstrom clearly knows plenty of folks in the underworld who can assist her. In fact, it wouldn't surprise me if her *Mr. Autumn* had a hand in this day's work."

Covering my face again, I murmured, "Oh, my God."

Ernie patted me on the shoulder and stood. "But before we go off half-cocked, we'd better look around and see if she actually took anything or if she just played a trick on you and your friends."

"Some trick," I muttered, feeling bitter and abused.

"Right."

However, Ernie was correct again. Conquering self-pity and guilt, I rose from my chair and made a cursory glance around the living room. I noticed Peggy hadn't bothered to clean up after her so-called trick. I reached for the lemonade pitcher, but Ernie caught my arm and stopped me.

"Hold on there, Mercy. Don't touch anything. The coppers might not be good for much, but they can check for fingerprints."

Holy cow, I'd forgotten all about fingerprints. Perhaps the ardent Prohibitionists were right in their stance against alcohol if it had fuzzed my brain to this extent. I know I'm innocent of the world and too naïve for my own good and all that, but even *I* knew about fingerprints.

"Right," I said. "Sorry."

"Don't be sorry. Just take a look around."

So I did, with Ernie accompanying me. Things were missing, all right, although Peggy and her Mr. Autumn evidently knew nothing about expensive rugs, because the Caucasian rug in my room was still on the floor. My handbag had been rifled and all my money was gone. There hadn't been much in it in the first place, since I kept most of my cash in a safe behind a picture in the office. All my jewelry was gone, including Great Aunt Agatha's opal ring. I never wore the ring, because wearing opals is supposed to be bad luck for anyone not born in the month of October—which is silly superstition, but I couldn't help myself. Anyhow, the ring was gone, and so were a couple of other bits of jewelry. Fortunately for me, I didn't have much of the stuff, and what little I did own that was worth anything was in a safe-deposit box at the bank. I might be rich and ignorant, but I wasn't totally stupid.

I suppose it need not be said that Peggy's room was as empty as if she'd never lived in it.

"I expect she took it on the lam with her Autumn beau. Which is probably why they didn't take more of your things. They had to stuff his machine full of her property."

"She didn't have much," I told him. "I thought I was being kind to her."

"You were being kind to her."

"I think you told me once that no good deed goes unpunished," I said in a voice droopier than any I'd ever heard issue from my own personal mouth.

"Yeah, I probably did. But I didn't mean this."

What worried me more than my own losses were those of Lulu and Caroline. I prayed hard as I went through their rooms, feeling wretched as I did so, since I didn't like intruding on my tenants' privacy. Not that it mattered. I couldn't tell if anything was missing or not.

"I guess we'll have to wait until they wake up, and then they'll have to tell me if any of their property has been taken."

Ernie, who had been noting missing items in his little pocket notebook, nodded. "Yeah. In fact, we'd probably better see what we can do to get them conscious again. Chloral hydrate can be tricky stuff."

I stopped in my tracks and stared at him, appalled. "Oh, my goodness! Do you mean to tell me they might be *dead*?" I raced toward the staircase, but again Ernie caught me up.

"Stop panicking, Mercy. They aren't dead. I already checked."

Shutting my eyes and breathing a heavy sigh of relief, I said, "Thank God. Thank God." Then, thinking he deserved at least this, I said, "Thank you, too, Ernie."

"No problem, kiddo."

So far it looked as though Peggy had taken easily portable things: a jade Chinese goddess, my aunt's ring and my other jewelry, a porcelain shepherdess that used to reside on a table in the upstairs hallway because I didn't know what else to do with it and thought it was sappy, the living-room radio, a couple of other ornamental pieces that weren't worth much, and some other items of the like. By the time Ernie and I had made our way back to the living room, he'd filled two pages in his notebook.

"She must have used a big sack," I muttered, disgusted with Peggy Wickstrom and, mainly, myself.

"Looks like it. Or she had help."

"Johnny Autumn," I said bitterly.

"Probably."

We stood together, gazing at the two sleeping beauties decorating my front room for a minute or two until Ernie asked, "Do you know how to make coffee?"

"Coffee?" I gazed up at him. "No. Why?" Suddenly it seemed pathetic to be so helpless that I didn't even know how to make coffee.

"We'll need coffee. So I'll make the coffee while you call the cops. That okay by you?"

I didn't want to call the cops. I felt like an utter fool, and confessing this mess to anyone other than Ernie nearly gave me hives. Yet I knew I had to face the music. This was my fault; I had to rectify it. And the police needed to be informed that Peggy Wickstrom looked very much as though, young as she was, she was a low-down, dirty crook.

"I'll call." My voice was small. "Thank you for making the coffee."

"You're welcome. Don't be scared, Mercy. The cops are used to this sort of thing."

Maybe they were, but I wasn't.

Nevertheless, I made the call. The officer who answered the telephone at the police station didn't sound sarcastic or nasty when I told him I'd been burgled while I was out of the house, which I appreciated. When I told him two of my tenants appeared to have been drugged with chloral hydrate, he made a disgusted noise in his throat and asked if I knew who'd done the drugging.

With my heart in my throat, hating for some reason to name the obvious suspect, I said, "Another tenant of mine. A young woman named Peggy—Margaret is her real first name—Wickstrom." Because I couldn't help myself, I then blurted out, "But she's only eighteen years old!"

The fellow on the other end of the wire said, "Don't matter how old they are. If they're rotten, they're rotten."

"I guess so. I do know she associates with a fellow named Johnny Autumn, and I understand he's a bad apple."

The policeman snorted. "You can say that again."

I didn't bother.

"I'll send a car right out."

"Thank you."

"Ma'am?" he said before I'd put the receiver back on the candlestick.

"Yes?"

"You might want to check references before you rent out rooms to tenants in the future."

"Yes. Thank you."

By the time I got off the 'phone, the aroma of coffee had begun filling the air of my formerly wonderful new home on Bunker Hill. Well, the home was still wonderful. I was an arrant nincompoop, but my failures as a human being weren't the house's fault.

Feeling pretty dejected, I walked into the kitchen, where Ernie was busily gathering cups and saucers onto a tray. He glanced at me. "Don't look so downhearted, kiddo. We all make mistakes."

It was nice of him to say so, although his words didn't hearten me much. "Maybe. But this mistake hurt my friends, and I'm responsible for it."

To my utter surprise, Ernie set down a cup, came over to me, and wrapped me in a warm embrace. "It's all right, kiddo. Everything will turn out okay. At least you don't have to evict the girl. She's already evicted herself."

"I suppose so," I said into his shirt front—he'd hung his suit coat on the rack in the entryway. "Thanks for helping me, Ernie. You're a nice man."

"In spite of myself." I could feel him chuckle.

"No. You're a nice man. Period."

"Don't tell anyone. It'd ruin my reputation."

I was disappointed when he let me go.

"Well, we'd better try to wake up your sleeping tenants. Maybe they'll be able to help the police when they arrive."

"Good idea." What I wanted was for Ernie to hold me some more. I needed comfort. It looked like I'd have to use Buttercup for comfort, however.

Ernie carried the tray into the living room and set it on a chair-side table, since the table in front of the sofa still contained the lemonade tray, pitcher, etc. Every time I glanced at that blasted pitcher, I wanted to break it. Guess I'd have to wait until the police checked it for fingerprints; "dusting" is, I believe, the term used for lifting fingerprints from objects. The notion made me feel marginally more cheerful: I'd get to watch a procedure I'd only read about before this. Too bad I'd be seeing it in my own house and for such an onerous reason.

As Ernie and I shook Lulu and Caroline and tried to awaken them, Buttercup announced the arrival of the police. I left Ernie to continue the awakening task and went to the door. Two uniformed policemen I hadn't met before stood on the front porch. One of them was gazing around the neighborhood as if he approved—well, it was a lovely neighborhood—while the other one, looking dour, stared at the door, which I opened.

"Good afternoon," I said, although it was anything but.

"Are you Miss Allcutt?" asked the serious copper, holding out his shield, which said he was Sergeant Vincent Croft.

"Yes. Please, come in. My friends are in the living room, and another friend is trying to revive them."

"The desk sergeant said you suspect they were given chloral. Is that so?" asked Sergeant Croft.

"Yes."

"And you say this Wickstrom woman is an associate of Johnny Autumn's?"

"She called him her boyfriend."

"Huh. And you think she and Autumn did this together?"

"That's what Ernie thinks."

"Ernie?" said the other copper, whose name was Officer Lawrence T. Williamson. His name barely fit on his shield. "Ernie who?"

"Mr. Ernest Templeton. He's my employer."

"Ernie's here?" said Sgt. Croft. He didn't sound particularly pleased. "Why's he here if he's your boss? You two have something going on or something?"

As odd as it sounds, it needed only that tone in Sergeant Croft's voice to bring my Bostonian upbringing back to me with a vengeance. I straightened my shoulders, gave Sergeant Croft my frostiest glare, and said, "Mr. Templeton and I are friends, Sergeant, which should be of no concern to you. He's also my employer, and he's teaching me how to drive my Roadster. That's the reason he came to my home today. After the lesson, we drove back here to find two of my tenants drugged and the third one gone. It looks to me as if she stole quite a few things on her way out. *That's* the reason you're here. You're *not* here to ask personal questions. Do we have this matter clear, or will I need to telephone Detective Philip Bigelow?"

Both men stepped back a pace. I can do Boston extremely well when I get angry enough, and Sergeant Croft's snide question had done the trick.

"I didn't mean anything, Miss Allcutt," said Sergeant Croft hastily. "I just wondered, was all."

"Well, you can jolly well wonder about the job you're

supposed to be doing and forget the personal questions." Then I snapped out an order. "Follow me. I trust you have the materials necessary to obtain fingerprints from the pitcher and the glasses."

"Yes, ma'am," said Williamson in a placating sort of voice.

I led them into the living room. Ernie had succeeded in getting Caroline to sit upright on the sofa. She pressed a hand to her forehead and appeared dazed as Ernie held a cup of coffee to her lips. He glanced at us as we entered the room and frowned.

"Were you two the only cops on duty?" he growled at Croft.

"Yeah. We were," said Croft in a snotty voice.

I bridled. "If you can't be courteous to my guests, Sergeant Croft, you may leave my home this instant. You aren't here to quarrel with Mr. Templeton. You're here to solve a crime. If you don't have your priorities straight about the work you're expected to do, you might as well go away, and I shall procure help from someone else."

"Bigelow," whispered Williamson. He looked nervous.

"Detective Bigelow is a good friend," I said, fibbing only a little. "I'm sure he'd like to know some of his officers are impudent rascals."

"We aren't under Bigelow," said Croft in an irritated voice. "Let's get down to business. Exactly what happened here?"

So I related the story to him, although I left out the part about me partaking of the doctored lemonade. Ernie didn't tell on me, for which I was grateful.

"So you think as soon as you left for your driving lesson, the Wickstrom girl drugged the lemonade?"

"That's my hypothesis," I said coldly, although it was Ernie's hypothesis, really.

"Huh," grunted Croft. He turned to his partner. "Got your kit, Will?"

"Yes, sir. I'll dust for prints." Glancing at me shyly—I guess Boston had made quite an impression on the young man—he said, "You say the Wickstrom girl is the one who handled the pitcher?"

"Yes. I suggest you try the pitcher first. I'm not sure which glasses are whose." That sentence didn't come out exactly the way I'd wanted it to, but evidently Williamson understood it, because he withdrew a little kit from his belt—they both wore leather belts full of all sorts of things, including nasty-looking guns—opened it up, squatted down in front of the table, and began delicately dusting the pitcher with some grayish powder.

But I wasn't allowed to finish witnessing how fingerprints were taken because Sergeant Croft said he needed to speak to me. I didn't like the man, but it was my duty as a citizen, not to mention the victim of a crime, to aid him. I graciously asked him to be seated in one of a pair of matching Louis XIV chairs across the room, so he sat and pulled out a notebook and pencil. I sat across from him. Harvey's taste in furniture was quite elegant. If I'd furnished the place, I'd have done it up in a more modern fashion. But furniture is irrelevant to the problem at hand.

"Can you tell me anything more about Peggy Wickstrom?"

"She works—or worked—at a place called Anthony's Palaise de Danse. It's on Flower and—"

"I know where it's at," said Croft, not only interrupting me, but doing so in a shockingly ungrammatical manner. He squinted at me. "You always get your tenants from dives like the Palais?"

I sucked in about a gallon of air, with which I aimed to blast him, but Ernie cut in before I had the chance.

"Miss Allcutt has only begun letting out rooms in her home recently, Croft. She's trying to give young women who have to work for a living a break. It's not her fault she got a cuckoo in her nest right off the bat."

Scowling at Ernie, Croft said, "I'll ask the questions here, Templeton. You're not on the force any longer, remember?"

"How could I forget?" said Ernie in a scathing voice.

"That's enough!" I barked at Croft. "Mr. Templeton has brought up a valid point. When I allowed Miss Wickstrom to live here, I believed she worked at Clapton's Cafeteria. It was only when Mr. Templeton checked on her references I learned she worked at the dance hall."

"Why didn't you kick her out then?" asked Croft.

"My reasoning has nothing to do with the matter at hand," I told him with some heat. "The only thing you have to worry about is how to find her and get our belongings back."

"That's not going to be as easy as it sounds."

"Yes. So Mr. Templeton told me. I suppose it would help if you actually were to *look* for Miss Wickstrom and Mr. Autumn."

"We'll look for them," said Croft irritably.

I sniffed.

By this time, Caroline was barely *compos mentis*, and Lulu had begun groaning softly.

"What happened?" asked Lulu, always more talkative than Caroline.

"Peggy drugged you," I said baldly. "And I'm afraid she may have stolen some of your possessions. I know she took my jewelry."

Caroline gave a little cry of dismay.

Lulu stared at me, aghast. Then she said, "So *that's* why she was so friendly all of a sudden. I knew there had to be a reason."

"You got it," said Ernie.

It was really disheartening to know Lulu and Ernie both had pegged (so to speak) Peggy for what she was while I was still trying to save her from herself and her precious boyfriend. Would I *ever* learn to pay attention to those who knew more than I? My mother would answer my question with a firm negative, but I vowed to learn from this ghastly circumstance.

"I'm so sorry, Lulu and Caroline. I should never have allowed her into my home."

"It wasn't your fault," said Caroline. "How could anyone know she'd do anything like this?"

I thought about suggesting she ask Ernie to explain it to her, but restrained myself.

Both Lulu and Caroline had drunk some coffee at this point. Neither girl looked particularly perky, but Sergeant Croft asked if they could visit their rooms and check for missing items. With Ernie helping Lulu and me helping Caroline, we climbed the stairs. Croft, who clearly disliked Ernie and whose dislike was returned in full measure, stayed with Caroline and me while Williamson went with Ernie and Lulu.

"I don't have much for anyone to take," said Caroline, sinking onto her tidily made bed. "Give me a minute. My head's all muzzy."

"Take your time," I told her. "You've been through an ordeal."

"We don't have all day," growled Croft.

I gave him the Boston eye and was pleased when he flinched. "You have all the time it takes for Miss Terry to recover herself enough to look through her belongings. That's your *job*, if you'll kindly remember it. If you don't care for it, perhaps you might try another line of work."

Croft huffed, but he didn't say anything else of a spiteful nature.

Eventually Caroline pulled herself together and looked through her things. "My charm bracelet is gone. My grandmother gave me a new charm to put on it every year on my birthday." Her eyes filled with tears, and I put my arm around her. She sniffled. "I don't suppose it's valuable. My family isn't rich. But it meant a lot to me."

"Of course, it did," I said soothingly. "We'll try to recover it for you." I shot Croft a good scowl to let him know he wasn't supposed to interject a negative into the room. Poor Caroline was unhappy enough without a policeman telling her there was no way she'd ever see her grandmother's charm bracelet again.

After a half-hour or so, Caroline determined the only personal items of hers that had been snatched by Peggy, besides the charm bracelet, were a nice leather handbag she used for church and a couple of brooches. Naturally, her handbag, too, had been rifled.

"I don't get paid until next Friday, so there wasn't much money to take, and I put most of my paycheck in my bank account. The other things weren't expensive," she said.

"The worth of the items doesn't matter," I said firmly. "They were yours, and Peggy was vile to have stolen them."

"Do you know how much money was taken, Miss Terry?" asked Croft in a civilized tone of voice.

Caroline shook her head slowly. "I'm not sure. I think I had maybe seventy-five cents."

Thank God she hadn't just been paid.

About then Ernie, Lulu and Officer Williamson entered Caroline's room. Naturally, Peggy had stolen all the cash in Lulu's handbag, although Lulu said she only had about sixty-five cents at her disposal at the time. I got the feeling she spent most of her money on makeup and fingernail polish and clothes.

When the others entered her room, Caroline's look of shock told me she wasn't accustomed to strange men interfering with her privacy, so I said, "Let's gather in the living room, everyone. We can write up what's been taken and perhaps, if we put our heads together, we can discover if one of us knows something pertinent about Peggy Wickstrom that might help us find our missing property."

Croft and Williamson exchanged a speaking glance, but I ignored it. Darn it, they were cops! If they wouldn't do their duty on their own, I'd make darned good and sure they did it at my insistence.

THIRTEEN

The policemen left about an hour later. Ernie had been going to give them the list he'd made up of my own missing property, but I insisted upon copying his list and adding to it the items stolen from Lulu and Caroline.

"We don't want our list to get lost by accident, do we?" I asked in an astringent voice and directing the question to Sergeant Croft.

"We won't lose the list," grumbled Croft.

"Good idea, Mercy," said Ernie. He gave me a cheeky grin. "You can never be too careful, especially when it comes to L.A. coppers."

"So I've heard," I said dryly.

The policemen left, and Ernie and I returned to the living room where two pale and shaky tenants of mine sat looking unhappy.

"Is there anything I can do for you, Lulu and Caroline? I feel just awful about this. I'm so sorry I allowed Miss Wickstrom to live here even after I learned she had lied to me about her employment."

"It's not your fault," said Caroline faintly but staunchly. "How could you know what she was like? She's so young. One never expects so young a girl to behave so badly."

My sentiments exactly, but Ernie and Lulu snorted in chorus.

"A rotten apple's a rotten apple," said Lulu, "no matter how young it is. I learned that when I was a kid. There was another kid in school with Rupert and me, and he was a terrible bully. He was only eight years old when he beat another kid almost to death."

I stared at Lulu in horror.

She licked her finger, drew a cross in the air and said, "True story. They kicked him out of school, but the last thing I heard was that he'd got drunk on bathtub gin and shot up the town. He's in prison now, and I hope he says there. There's no doing anything with people like him except locking them up."

"But…but do you really think Peggy is as bad as that dreadful person?" My voice seemed awfully small.

Lulu shrugged.

Ernie said, "Yes. She's what we call a black widow. Pretty on the outside and poison on the inside. Give her time, and she'll be up to her neck in vice and corruption."

"What a…terrible thought," I said, feeling sick. Which reminded me of something. "Say, girls, would you like some powders? Do you have headaches or anything?"

"I could use a powder," Lulu said. "My head's pounding like a drummer in a speakeasy band."

"My head aches, too," said Caroline, again pressing a hand to her forehead.

"I'm sorry. I should have thought to give you something earlier." Guilt piled on guilt as I rose to go to the kitchen cabinet and fetch clean glasses—the policemen had taken the pitcher and the other glasses away as evidence, so I wouldn't have the pleasure of smashing the pitcher any time soon—and fixed up two glasses of water with aspirin powders stirred in. Aspirin came in pill form in this modern age, but Harvey swore by the powdered variety, claiming it began working more quickly than the pills, and I was still using his stock.

The kitchen was clean out of trays by then, so I carried the glasses back to my friends and tenants in my two hands, thinking how crass my mother would consider this behavior on my part. Thank God she'd never know.

Ernie was talking to Lulu and Caroline when I set a glass down in front of each girl. "Come on. It'll make you feel better. Get a little food in you, take some of those powders and a little more coffee, and you'll both be right as rain."

"I dunno, Ernie," said Lulu. "I don't feel much like eating anything."

"Trust me. You will. I know about these things."

I was about to ask him where he aimed to find food for the two girls when I recalled he'd mentioned he could fix eggs and toast. Well, I supposed eggs and toast would be better than nothing. I felt stupid, ignorant and worthless because I couldn't even do *that* much in the kitchen. I could, however, make a ham and cheese sandwich, which made me feel minimally brighter.

"I'll fix some sandwiches," I offered.

"Don't bother. I know where to get some good roast beef sandwiches. I'll have 'em wrapped and bring them back here. This calls for something substantial. These girls need meat. You know. Protein."

They did? Well, who was I to argue with Ernie Templeton, who probably had lots of experience dealing with the aftereffects of overindulgence in spirituous liquors. The thought made me sad for some reason. "Where will you go for sandwiches?" I asked, curious.

"Place called Philippe's on Alameda. It won't take long to get there, and they have the best roast beef sandwiches in town. They call 'em French dip sandwiches."

"Oh." I gaped at him.

"Don't worry. I'll get you one, too." He winked at me.

"Oh, but you shouldn't have to pay for them," I said, hurrying after him as he headed toward the door. Buttercup followed at my heels, always happy to give a departing guest a polite send-off. "This is my fault, after all. Here. Wait and I'll get some money."

"Keep your damned money, Mercy. I can afford a few sandwiches."

"But…"

But nothing, I guess. He was gone. I sighed and meandered back to the living room, plopped myself on a chair and picked up Buttercup. Comfort time.

Lulu, Caroline and I sat in the living room, chatting in a desultory manner. Neither of them felt awfully chipper, and both still suffered the after-effects of the chloral hydrate they'd been given. Mind you, we were only speculating about the chloral. Officer Williamson said the forensics people at the police laboratory would test the lemonade remaining in the pitcher and the glasses to ascertain exactly which substance had been used to drug my friends.

I still felt guilty, and I told both Lulu and Caroline so over and over as we waited for Ernie to return with sandwiches.

"Stop it, Mercy," Lulu said at last. "Your problem is your heart is too big for you. You're always trying to help people, and some people aren't worth helping."

"Ernie told me the same thing," I admitted glumly.

"Oh, my, but do you honestly believe that?" asked Caroline, who appeared shocked at this callous assessment of Peggy Wickstrom.

"You bet I do," said Lulu firmly. "Remember the kid I told

you about? His name was Gerald O'Flannagan, and my daddy said somebody should have drowned him at birth and done the world a favor."

I saw Caroline gulp.

"But really, Lulu, you can't tell if a baby's going to grow up to be a bully or a thief, like Peggy," I said, putting in my own two cents' worth, although my words probably weren't worth even that much. I felt lower than a snake.

"You can if you look at their parents," she declared.

"Oh, but Lulu, that's not always true. One of the girls I went to school with came from a terrible family, but she turned out very well. Why, the last I heard, she was actually attending college," said Caroline in her soft voice.

Lulu sniffed. "Well, let me tell you, it doesn't work out that way very often."

I sighed, feeling out of my depth. I'd grown up in the upper echelons of Boston society and, while I knew there were some bad apples among my parents' acquaintances' children, all the juicy details had been scrupulously kept from Chloe and me. It seemed a pity now, because I had no entertaining stories to add to the conversation.

Eventually Ernie returned with our sandwiches. I set the table in the kitchen—it seemed silly to eat sandwiches in the dining room—and Ernie laid everything out quite artistically, which surprised me. He'd even brought a jar of potato salad, which he said Philippe's made better than anyone else and which would go well with the sandwiches.

Eyeing the table dubiously, Lulu said, "I dunno, Ernie. My tummy feels a little queer."

"Mine doesn't," said Caroline, surprising me. I'd have pegged her for the wilting lily of the two girls. On the other hand, I don't believe she'd drunk as much of the alcohol-laced lemonade as Lulu had.

"Well, I'm starving," said Ernie in the hearty voice he sometimes used to get people to do his bidding. "Have a seat."

So we sat. I was hungry, too, although I didn't think I deserved to be. I felt bad that Ernie hadn't allowed me to pay for the fare we aimed to eat.

Blushing faintly, Caroline said, "May I say a prayer? I was brought up always to thank God for the food I eat."

"This time you ought to thank Ernie," said Lulu, although she said it softly.

"I think it's a splendid idea," I said, coming to Caroline's rescue. "After all, we lost some material things today, and our faith in a person was shattered—which is my own fault—but at least we weren't hurt." I swallowed, feeling guiltier than ever. "Well, you two were. Oh, nuts." I had to wipe my eyes.

"Calm down, Mercy," said Ernie. "You're taking too much of the blame for this on yourself. Peggy Wickstrom is a bad egg, and you were too nice to notice until it was too late."

The others at the table nodded solemnly, and I felt worse than ever. After sniffling to maintain my composure, I said, "Shall we take hands?" We always held hands in Boston.

We took hands, and Caroline recited a brief blessing over the food. To tell the truth, although it does me no credit, I agreed with Lulu and thought Ernie was the one she should be thanking, although perhaps it was God who'd made him think of Philippe's. The sandwiches and potato salad were *very* good.

The girls and I cleaned up after our delicious meal. I wouldn't allow Ernie to help. "You were the founder of the feast, after all," I said, thinking he wasn't at all like Ebenezer Scrooge. Of course, I wasn't at all like Bob Cratchit, either.

Probably in order to make us laugh, Ernie said, "Bah," and followed it up with a "Humbug."

It worked. The three of us giggled. Lulu washed, Caroline

dried, and I put away, since I knew where everything went. Well, so did they by then, but that's the way it worked out.

When the last dish was put in its place, the table wiped down and the dishtowel hung on the rack, we all retired to the living room, where we sat and looked at each other.

"Golly," said Lulu. "Too bad they took the radio. A little music might be nice."

"Yes," said Caroline with a sigh. "I can't imagine what possessed Peggy to behave in such a way."

Ernie said, "Johnny Autumn would be my guess, although she had to be well on her way to ruin in order to pull a stunt like this on people she lived with and presumably had nothing against."

"She was probably mad at me for lecturing her," I said, culpability once more assaulting me. Buttercup, bless her heart, licked my chin.

"Nuts," said Lulu. "If she only had a grudge against you, she wouldn't have stolen our stuff, too. No, Mercy. You'll just have to face it. Peggy Wickstrom is a bad person."

"How sad for her," whispered Caroline.

Lulu looked at her as if she'd gone crazy. "Sad for *her*? What about us?"

"But, Lulu, we only lost a few material items. Peggy seems to have sold her very soul to the devil."

Oh, my goodness, what a bleak thought.

So as not to dwell on it, I turned to Ernie, who sat sprawled in a chair drinking some warmed-up coffee. "Do you think the police will actually look for Peggy, Ernie? Please tell me the truth. Is there any hope at all that our missing possessions will be recovered?"

He eyed me narrowly for a considerable space of time before he said a concise, "No."

Caroline gasped.

Lulu said, "It figures."

"Honestly? They won't even try?" I asked, hoping he was only being pessimistic to teach me a lesson, although I knew better.

"They've got big stuff to worry about, Mercy," Ernie told me in a kindly voice, as if to humor me. "A petty burglary like this won't even register on their scale of crimes. Heck, another big Hollywood fellow got killed last night, just like Milton Halsey Gossett."

"Good Lord. Another murder?"

I spoke the words, but we all goggled at Ernie.

"Yup. Producer named Gregory Preston."

"Oh, my!" Lulu cried. "Isn't he the one who made *Guardian of the Plain*?"

"That's the one."

"And he was killed the same way Mr. Gossett was?" I asked.

"Exactly the same. Point-blank range. Found him at the foot of the stairs, just like Gossett."

Something almost pleasant occurred to me. "Well, they can't blame Mr. *Preston's* murder on poor Calvin Buck! And don't you think the same person must have committed both crimes?"

"Yes, I do, but don't bet your money on the police letting go of a viable suspect just because he didn't do both murders."

"How discouraging," I muttered, stunned, although Ernie was right. If the police had what they considered a sure thing, they wouldn't look any farther. I'd learned this salient fact after the police accused Ernie or murdering a former client. Idiots. The police. Not Ernie or the client.

"Anyhow, the cops have murders, book-making rings, bootleggers, and all sorts of other, bigger, crimes to worry about. I doubt they'll put out a team to look for your stolen items." After eyeing me for a second, he said, "They might send out a notice to pawn shops in town. Sometimes pawnbrokers will rat someone out if he—or she—attempts to pawn stolen merchandise."

I could almost hear him say, "Fat chance of that happening," although he didn't do so aloud. Feeling worse than ever, I peered at Lulu and Caroline. "I'll make this up to you. I'll pay for your losses. And I'll definitely buy another radio as soon as I can. The police might not care about your stolen property, but I do."

"Mercy," said Lulu, sounding as if she were trying to maintain her patience. "This wasn't your fault. Crumb, I ought to have known the lemonade had booze in it. I've tasted enough of Uncle Junior's corn liquor to know alcohol when I taste it."

I felt my eyes widen, not sure if I was more shocked over her revelation about drinking corn liquor or about her having an uncle named Junior. "Really?"

"Really." Lulu heaved a gigantic sigh. "We lived in a real backwater, Mercy. You've never seen anything like where we lived. L.A. and Boston are centers of the civilized world compared to my little town in Oklahoma. Lots of folks made liquor in their own stills. The revenuers would try to find them and bust them up, but Uncle Junior was smart. He had his still in a cave, and no revenuer to date has been able to find it. Heck, the rest of the family doesn't even know where it is."

Feeling stupid, I asked, "What's a revenuer?"

Ernie laughed. He would. "A G-man sent to quell the manufacture and distribution of illegal liquor, Mercy."

I almost asked him what a G-man was, but then realized the G must stand for Government, so I said merely, "Oh."

"Prohibition's a lost cause anyway," he went on. "People like a glass of beer every now and then, and it sure doesn't hurt them any." He saw me open my mouth to rebut this statement, I guess, because he went on quickly, "I know. There will always be people who abuse both liquor and drugs. And probably lots of other things that aren't in themselves evil. But to quash an entire industry isn't the way to go about anything. I'm from Chicago, and when Prohibition started, it put thousands of people out of work, especially in the German and Polish sections of town, because they were the main brewers. Well, and the Russians, too. They like their vodka."

"Goodness. I'd never even thought about the industry itself. I've only ever thought about men drinking away their families' food money in taverns and stuff."

Ernie nodded. "Carrie Nation has a lot to answer for."

"But I don't approve of drinking, either," said Caroline, her voice even softer than usual.

With a shrug, Ernie said, "Nobody has to approve of drinking. Just don't drink if you don't want to. What one person likes or doesn't like shouldn't mean the rest of the world can't have a little tot if it wants one."

Caroline frowned but said no more. She was definitely not the argumentative sort.

"But Ernie," said I after thinking about it for a minute, "if we carry your scenario to its logical conclusion, you'd condone drug-taking and gambling and all those other sorts of vices, too."

"I don't necessarily *condone* anything at all. But hell, yes! Make the manufacture of all those things legal, give the government oversight, and you'll create a million jobs. You probably won't have any more drunks or addicts than you have now, but you'll at least have full employment rosters and empty jails."

I frowned, recalling some of the things my father had said about the government interfering in the banking industry. On the other hand, my father was a banker. "Do you really think that would work?"

"Lord, I don't know. All I know is Prohibition isn't working for anyone except the bootleggers."

"You might just have a point there," I conceded. I didn't want to, though. Ernie's jaded view of the world troubled me sometimes, although I appreciated his coming to my defense about the Peggy situation.

"I think you're right," said Lulu.

And her comment pretty much put a cap on the conversation. Shortly thereafter, Ernie rose from his chair, stretched, and said, "Well, I'd better beat it. Tomorrow's Monday." He eyed Lulu and Caroline. "You gals going to be all right to go to work in the morning?"

"Yeah," said Lulu. "I feel much better now."

"Indeed," said Caroline, smiling a tiny smile. "Your recipe for recovery worked very well, Mr. Templeton."

I expected him to tell her to call him Ernie, but he didn't. For some reason, I was glad of it.

"Happy to help," he said, and he took off for the front door.

Buttercup and I rose to follow him. He slapped his hat on his head, donned his jacket and said, "Don't take any wooden nickels, Mercy. You've already taken too many of 'em lately."

"You've got that right," I said despondently, wishing he'd give me another hug.

But he didn't. He only winked at me and left my house. I dragged myself back to the living room.

FOURTEEN

Lulu and Caroline still sat where I'd left them. They both appeared slightly less under the weather than they had when Ernie and I had come home and found them unconscious from the drug Peggy had given them.

Although it was only about six-thirty by then, Caroline said, "I think I'd better go to bed. I need to rest up, and I still don't feel too well."

Naturally, as soon as the words left her lips, my feeling of responsibility nearly drowned me again. "I'm so sorry, Caroline. I truly will do everything I can to get your belongings back. And if they can't be found, I'll do my best to replace everything."

She gave me one of her sweet smiles. "I know you will, Mercy, but truly, this wasn't your fault." Shaking her head sadly, she said, "I guess it's true what people say: sometimes the big city can corrupt vulnerable youth."

Lulu and I both stared at her as she went slowly out of the living room and up the staircase. I felt lower than dirt.

"I'm going to get her a new charm bracelet," I told Lulu. "At the very least."

"That would be nice of you, but it wouldn't be her grandma's," said Lulu, telling the truth even though I didn't want to hear it.

"I know."

Silence settled over us. I didn't know how Lulu was feeling, but I was drained. I felt as though I didn't want to move for about ten years or so. I was so pooped, I didn't even stroke Buttercup, who had curled up on my lap. She didn't seem to mind; actually she seemed to be sleeping quite soundly without any stroking on my part.

After what seemed like a century or two, Lulu broke into the quiet. "I wonder if there's any way we could find Peggy on our own. I know darned well the coppers aren't going to try to find her."

"You want to find her?"

With an incredulous glance at me, Lulu said, "Yes, I want to find her! Then I want to get our things back and then beat the stuffing out of her! What she did is just plain wrong. Don't you want to find her?"

Goodness. I hadn't known Lulu to harbor violent thoughts about anyone or anything until then, although now that she'd brought them to the surface, I discovered within myself a certain desire to do something hurtful to Peggy Wickstrom. While I didn't believe I could ever beat the stuffing out of anyone, I could darned well stamp on her feet or kick her in the shins or something. What's more, I'd feel good doing it.

Therefore, after thinking for a moment or two, I said, "Yes. I'd like to find her. I'd like to know why she stole from us. We never did anything mean to her. If she didn't like me for lecturing her—and I know I lectured her, and I know she didn't like it—why didn't she just move out? Why did she do this to us?"

Lulu rolled her eyes in an Ernie-like gesture. "Mercy Allcutt, you still haven't learned there are evil people in the world, have you?"

Frowning, I said, "Well...yes, I know there are evil people in the world. For heaven's sake, I've met enough of them since I moved to Los Angeles. I...oh, nuts. I feel stupid saying it, but I still have a hard time believing Peggy is all bad. She's only *eighteen*, Lulu! When I was eighteen, I was attending tea parties and dances and trying to avoid the boys my mother wanted me to marry."

This revelation about my privileged background made Lulu laugh. "Mercy, you slay me! Shoot, when I was eighteen, I was on the bus to Los Angeles, determined to become a movie star. I found myself a job at the Figueroa Building, and I've been there ever since, supporting myself. Nobody's ever invited me to a tea party in my whole life."

"I suppose not," I said, chastened and feeling every iota of my sheltered youth. "But I invited you to the Ambassador Hotel for dinner with John Gilbert."

"Yes, you did, and I love you for it," said Lulu, suddenly serious. "You're a good person, Mercy. You can't help it that you always think the best of people. You didn't grow up living in a town with the likes of Gerald O'Flannagan."

With a sigh, I said, "There were probably lots of people like him in Boston, but I didn't have to deal with them."

"Exactly."

Silence descended upon us again until I said, "I wish I could think of a way to find Peggy. If we can't get her to give us our belongings back, maybe we could at least get her arrested. That would be satisfying."

"True. And it might shake her up some, too. She *is* young. You're right about that. Maybe a stint in jail would cure her of her bad tendencies. I know Rupert swore he'd never even jaywalk again once he got out of the clink."

"That was a terrible miscarriage of justice," I said in firm defense of Lulu's hapless brother, who'd been in the wrong place at the wrong time and been arrested for it.

"Well, you got him free again," said Lulu, giving me a warm smile.

She was right. Realizing the truth made me feel marginally less like an ineffectual nitwit. "I wonder..." My voice trailed off, since I truly hadn't a clue how to go about finding someone who didn't want to be found.

Her forehead wrinkled in concentration, Lulu said, "Where'd you say she worked? Some place on Flower?"

"Anthony's Palaise de Danse," I said, my nose wrinkling, much as Lulu's forehead had done. "I think it's near Flower and Seventh."

"Hmm. I wonder if she's going to keep working there. She might not if she thinks the cops are after her."

"Do you think they'll check on her there?"

With a shrug, Lulu said, "They probably will. It's called making a token effort, I think."

Shoot, she sounded more like Ernie than Ernie did. "Well, there's no law that says we can't make our own token effort, is there?"

Lulu smiled again. "By golly, there sure isn't."

"Then let's do it."

"Okay. I'm game. But not tonight. I'm too bushed. And we both have to go to work tomorrow."

"Right. But maybe we can snoop around after work."

"Sounds like a plan to me."

I went to bed Sunday night not happy, but at least pleased Lulu and I aimed to do something constructive about righting the wrong that had been done to us and Caroline.

Ernie arrived at the Figueroa Building early on Monday morning. That is to say, he didn't arrive *early* early, but he arrived earlier than he generally did. I'd only been at my desk, after doing my morning chores of dusting and straightening things, for a half-hour or so before he strolled in. With him strolled Detective Phil Bigelow.

I was interested to see them both. "Hey, Ernie and Phil. Are you here about the burglary, Phil?" My heart lightened to think that the L.A.P.D. might honestly be going to work on my own personal case.

"Yeah, Ernie told me about what happened at your place," said Phil, removing his hat. He was much more gentlemanly than Ernie, who never took off his hat until he went into his office, even though there was a lady—me—in the outer office. "It's too bad, and I'm sorry you lost some things."

Those words didn't sound as if he was champing at the bit to work on my case. "You're not here about my losses, are you?"

"Well…" Phil scuffed his toe on the Chinese rug I'd bought and placed before my desk. This rug wasn't expensive, but it was darned pretty. "To tell the truth, Mercy, that's not my department. I'm a detective in homicide, and I've got another murder on my hands. The burglary boys are handling your case."

I sniffed. "It didn't sound to me as if they aimed to handle it very much."

With a sigh, Phil said, "I know it's hard for a civilian to understand these things, Mercy, but petty crimes like what happened to you happen all the time, and it's virtually impossible to find and prosecute the offenders. By this time, I expect your property has been fenced and your former tenant and her friend are probably drinking up the profits."

My jaw dropped momentarily, but it snapped shut because I needed to know the answers to a couple of questions. "What does *fence* mean in this context, Phil?"

Ernie had stopped to listen to our conversation, and he answered my question for me. "It means your Peggy and her Johnny have likely sold your belongings to a second party, Mercy. Like a pawnbroker. As I said before, the police will probably send a notice to the pawnbrokers, but it's also probably already too late for them to do anything. And Phil's right. I imagine Peggy and Johnny bought booze with the proceeds and had themselves a dandy little party."

Before I could stop myself, I blurted out, "But Peggy's only *eighteen*!"

I saw and resented the look that passed between Ernie and Phil.

"All right. I know I'm naïve," I said hotly. "But, darn it, she's just a child! It makes me sick to think that terrible Johnny Autumn character has warped her so badly."

"He might not have done as much warping as you think," Ernie said wryly. "Some folks are ripe for the picking."

"That's…really discouraging, Ernie."

"Yeah. It is. I agree."

"But you know, Mercy," said Phil as if he were running interference between us, "it's certainly possible we'll nab this Autumn character, and if we do, chances are we'll pick up his cronies, too, and one of them seems to be this Miss Wickstrom of yours."

"She's not—"

"Mercy disavows any ownership of Peggy Wickstrom, Phil," Ernie interrupted. "She only tried to give the girl a break."

Although I didn't appreciate his rudeness, I had to appreciate his sentiment. "Ernie's right," I said, nodding.

"Very commendable," said Phil. He didn't sound as if he meant it.

"But in the meantime, we're working on the Gossett and Preston cases. I know it might not seem like it to you, but for a homicide guy like Phil, a murder is a little more important than the theft of a few bucks and a few trinkets."

"Well, of course it is!" I all but shouted at my boss who, as you have undoubtedly guessed, had said the above.

Phil gave me a commiserating look as he and Ernie walked on into Ernie's office and closed the door. Stupid men. On the other hand, perhaps Phil was right in that the police might arrest Johnny Autumn for something, and his arrest might lead the way to finding Peggy Wickstrom. It appeared as though our stolen property was gone for good, however, and that made me feel pretty awful—not for myself, but for Caroline and Lulu. Especially Caroline, whose grandmother had been giving her charms to put on her charm bracelet for years and years.

I vowed once more to get the girl another charm bracelet. It wouldn't be the same, but it seemed the least I could do. And in the meantime, I'd replace the radio on my lunch hour. Later on Lulu and I would do a little snooping of our own. The least we could do was go to the Palaise de Danse and find out if Peggy was there. I thought about 'phoning the place again to find out, but didn't want anyone to tip Peggy off that we were looking for her. If she was still working there, which I doubted. Peggy might not be the brightest candle in the box, but she wasn't stupid enough to return to her place of employment after perpetrating a burglary.

Monday night after dinner, Caroline excused herself and went upstairs to read her latest acquisition from the public library, *The House Without a Key*, by Earl Derr Biggers. I'd read the book and loved it and, while I felt a little sad Caroline didn't seem inclined to spend time with Lulu and me, it was actually better she didn't remain with us that evening. Lulu and I had plans to discuss. Although I plugged the new radio into a socket in the living room, we didn't turn it on.

We huddled together on the living room sofa and, to the

gentle clanging of Mrs. Buck cleaning up dinner dishes in the kitchen, we discussed how to find Peggy Wickstrom.

"I guess the first thing we should do is go to the Palaise de Danse," I said doubtfully. "They told me a week or so ago she worked there. I guess they can tell us if she still does." I gave her my reasoning as to why we should put in a personal appearance and not telephone the place.

"Good idea. Do you have the address?"

"Um…no. But I can look it up." So I went to the desk in my office, opened the Los Angeles telephone directory and found the address. I wrote it down just to make sure I wouldn't forget it, not that I anticipated doing so.

"Good," said Lulu when I gave her the address of the dance hall. Then she frowned. "How're we going to get there?"

"Why, I thought we could…" Shoot. I hadn't thought about transportation. Then I brightened. "I'll drive us!"

"That's right!" Lulu cried with pleasure. "You know how to drive your Roadster now, don't you?"

Hesitating slightly before telling a blatant lie, I ended up telling the truth. "Well, I'm no expert, but I know how to start it, back it up, turn on the head lamps and not bump into other cars parked at various curbs."

"Sounds good enough to me." Lulu stood up, seemingly energized by our upcoming activity.

I knew how she felt, because I felt the same way. We were actually going to *do* something and not sit around waiting for the police not to discover Peggy's whereabouts. "Of course, if she's not at the Palaise de Danse, I don't know where to look next."

"She must have made an acquaintance or two while she worked there," said Lulu. "We can talk to the other girls."

"Great idea."

"But we can't go like this."

I looked down at my brown suit, the same suit I'd worn to

work. Long gone (for me) were the days I dressed for dinner. Not Mercy Allcutt, the working girl. I put on my clothes in the morning, worked in them, and then went home in them. Sometimes I'd change into a comfortable house dress to wear in the evenings, but that night, both Lulu and I had been too excited about our upcoming mission to bother changing clothes.

"I guess not. I look too respectable, don't I?"

"Yup."

I didn't say so, but Lulu didn't suffer from the same problem as I. She still wore the brilliant crimson frock she'd worn to work during the day. Her lips and fingernails complemented her ensemble amazingly well. What with her blond hair and her red everything else, she looked to me as if she could pass for a lady of the night. Mind you, to my knowledge, I'd never seen a lady of the night, but I supposed they wore bright colors.

"So...what should we wear?" I asked, not having a clue of my own.

"I've got something I think will work. We have to look as though we belong in a joint like that Palais place, and a brown suit just won't do."

"I know it," I said, nettled.

"Don't get mad. Let's just go up and look in our closets."

So we did and, oh, my goodness, if I didn't know who I was, I wouldn't have known who I was by the time Lulu got through with me. Not only was I wearing a perfectly scandalous black evening gown that wouldn't have been at all scandalous if I'd worn the vest supposed to go over it, but Lulu had painted my lips and nails the same bright shade as her own. Then she worked on my hair until I looked like a tart out of an issue of the *Police Gazette*! And then she rummaged in her closet, found a long red boa, and threw it around my shoulders. If I hadn't seen me for myself, I wouldn't have known I had it in me to look so ghastly. I wished my mother could see me; she might ease up on her anti-working theme. In fact, she'd probably believe I'd sold my soul to the devil.

Lulu looked as awful as I did, although on her the change wasn't as astonishing as it was on me, since she was accustomed to dressing more boldly than I. She had put on a vivid purple frock with a zigzag hemline, had rolled her stockings down, rouged her knees, and found a white boa for herself. Naturally, she still wore her crimson lipstick and fingernails. She made quite a sight. Well, so did I, but at least I was all in black and red and not purple and white with red highlights.

At any rate, we looked like two women who weren't ladies when we left the house at about eight o'clock in the evening. I carried a black handbag with a shoulder strap—Lulu had advised me to take the strapped bag, since the neighborhood in which we aimed to do our snooping wasn't the best and I could hold it to my side so it couldn't be snatched—and I took out my key. My heart hammered like a maddened woodpecker as I unlocked Lulu's door and then got behind the steering wheel.

"This is going to be fun!" said Lulu, giving every evidence of believing her own words.

"I hope so." My own voice sounded a trifle less hearty.

"Let's go get 'em!" cried Lulu.

"Very well, but please don't talk for a minute, Lulu. I have to remember all of Ernie's instructions."

I'd only had five or six lessons. And I *had* driven in traffic. Rather heavy traffic, too. But I'd done so on a bright, sunny day, not a dark, dark night. Also—and this was no little thing—before when I'd driven my Roadster, Ernie had been with me. That night I realized what a comfort his presence had been. Now I only had Lulu, and she didn't know how to drive any more than I'd known two months prior.

But nothing ventured, nothing gained, as they say. Whoever "they" are. I stuck the key into the ignition, turned it, pushed the starter button, pressed one foot on the clutch and the other on the brake—I didn't want the machine to get away from me—and put the shift lever into reverse. Very, very slowly, I inched out of the drive. I hadn't practiced my backing-up skills much at all, but at a snail's pace and with Lulu and me both watching, I managed to get the Roadster out onto the street without scraping against anything. I felt better then.

"Good job," said Lulu, making me feel even better.

"I hate to admit it, but I'm scared to be driving at night."

"You'll do fine. You know how to drive this thing. You only need a little practice. Think of this as practice."

Not a bad idea. I tried to keep Lulu's suggestion in mind as I slowly maneuvered the Roadster down the street and around the corner. Flower wasn't too far away from where we lived, so it didn't take long to get to it. The farther we traveled down Flower, the busier the traffic became and the less savory the neighborhood seemed to be.

"Jeepers," said Lulu as we neared Fifth. "I expected her to work in a dump, but I didn't realize it would be like this."

Oh, happy day! Even Lulu was worried. I tried to remain calm. "Well, let me see if I can find a good place to park the Roadster, and we can walk to the Palaise de Danse."

"Better park it on a side street," advised Lulu. "If you leave it around here, somebody's likely to steal it."

Better and better. Nevertheless, bravely daring, I did as Lulu suggested and decided to park the Roadster near the Los Angeles Public Library. Heck, nothing of a criminal nature ever happened at a library, right?

"It's going to be a hike," said Lulu.

"But you said—"

"I'm not complaining. I'm just saying we're in for a walk."

So we exited the automobile, and I locked all of its doors.

Even though we were near the library, there was no sense in taking chances.

By the time we got to Anthony's Palaise de Dance, I'd come to the conclusion Lulu had worked her magic a little too well on both of us. No fewer than three men who were *not* gentlemen had made unsavory suggestions to us.

"I can't believe these people think I'm what they think I am," I whispered after the third man left us, grumpily telling us we were no better than we should be.

"It's all in how you dress," said Lulu. Well, she should know.

I was ever so grateful when we finally saw Anthony's Palaise de Danse on the other side of Flower from where we walked. At the corner, we crossed the street, wolf whistles following us. I knew I was blushing but doubted anyone could tell since Lulu had slathered rouge on me and the night was dark except under the electric street lamps, which were placed too far apart for my peace of mind.

But we got there at last. I was shocked when a man at the door asked us who the hell we were and what the hell we were doing there. I'm not accustomed to being sworn at by strangers—or anyone else, for that matter. Ernie doesn't count, because he doesn't actually swear *at* me; he just swears.

"We're looking for a friend," said Lulu, sounding harder than I'd ever heard her sound. "What's it to you?"

"It's a dime apiece is what it's worth to me," said the man with a sneer. What an ugly customer *he* was.

"Oh, yeah? We don't want to buy any dances, for the love of Pete. We only want to see if our friend is in there."

"Sez you. Who's your friend?"

"Peggy Wickstrom."

I have to admit to a cowardly gratitude to Lulu for taking over the speaking role in this little play of ours. I wouldn't have known how to talk to a creature like the man confronting us.

"Peggy? Hell, she ain't been here for days. She and that guy she hangs out with stole money from the till and lammed it out of here a week or so ago. The cops are looking for 'em. You got bum friends, missy."

"Don't you missy me," growled Lulu. "Is that guy friend of hers named Autumn, by any chance?"

"What's it to you?"

Deciding it was past time to do my part in our drama, I held out a quarter to the man. "It's worth this." I tried to sound as hard and world-weary as Lulu, but don't think I succeeded very well.

He snatched the money out of my hand and sneered some more. "It's worth more than two bits."

"The hell it is," said Lulu, shocking me.

I know. How foolish can one person be? Lulu was acting. She was, what's more, good at it. I'm surprised a director or producer hadn't snatched her up yet, although I still believed her staunch refusal to go anywhere but the Figueroa Building had a lot to do with her failure to hit it big in the pictures.

"One more quarter, and you tell us the name of the guy Peggy's with," I said, doing a little growling of my own. Only this time, I held the quarter between my thumb and finger. Never let it be said Mercy Allcutt doesn't learn from her mistakes.

With another sneer—or maybe it was the same one. I wasn't keeping track—the man said, "Yeah. The guy's name is Autumn." He snatched at the coin, which I deftly put behind my back before he made contact. "Hey, gimme that."

"What else can you tell us about Peggy and the Autumn guy?"

"Not a damned thing. Now gimme that quarter."

"Did Peggy have any friends here? Any of the other dance girls?" Lulu asked.

"She didn't have no friends at all. She was standoffish, that one. Nobody liked her."

Hmm. Interesting.

Lulu and I exchanged a questioning glance, and I saw Lulu shrug. So I gave the man his two bits. Two bits, indeed.

As we turned to walk away, he spoke again. "I'll tell you one thing for free."

He had our attention. We turned around again. Lulu snarled, "Yeah?" as if she'd been speaking to people like this terrible man forever.

"Autumn's a bad character. If Peggy is a friend of yours, you'd oughta try to get her away from him."

Lulu said, "Huh."

And that's when a uniformed policeman confronted us.

FIFTEEN

"All right, ladies, what do you think you're doing?"

Shocked, I said, "Nothing, Officer. We were just walking the streets."

Lulu said, "Mercy!" and I realized what I'd said might be taken the wrong way.

"I mean, we were trying to find a friend who used to work at this place." I pointed at the Palaise de Danse.

"Yeah. I think I heard that one before."

"But it's the truth!" I said, shocked that this man might not believe me.

"I think you were right the first time," growled the policeman. "Come along with me. We try to keep riffraff like you off the streets. It ain't easy, especially around these blasted dance halls, but we do our best."

"But, Officer! We were truly only trying to find a friend!"

By then, the policeman had Lulu and me each by an arm and had begun dragging us along the street. Talk about a humiliating experience! Fortunately, if anyone I knew was watching, whoever it was wouldn't recognize me. Small comfort when one is about to be clapped in the slammer.

"She's telling the truth," said Lulu, sounding a trifle panicky.

Truth to tell, I was glad she was taking this matter seriously and hadn't continued her role as gangster's moll, which she'd been doing very well.

"She isn't even a friend, really," I said, my anxiety clear to hear in my voice. "Her name is Peggy Wickstrom, and she stole money and personal effects from us. She lived in my home, you see, renting a room, and she drugged my friends and stole things from us!"

"Tell me another one," said the copper as we approached a parked automobile.

Another uniformed man who'd been leaning against the police car and whom I presumed to be our captor's partner, threw down the cigarette he'd been smoking and asked mildly, "Whattaya got there, Pete?"

"Coupla hookers. They was struttin' their stuff at the Palaise de Danse."

The man who wasn't Pete shook his head sadly. "Ain't it a shame? Two broads who should ought to be married and home cooking for their families. And here they are, walking the street."

I *wished* I hadn't used that expression when Officer Pete first confronted us.

"They're young ones, too. Don't know if it's the booze or the drugs, but it makes me sick," said Pete.

"It's not liquor or drugs!" I cried in growing desperation. "We were honestly trying to find Peggy Wickstrom! Or her boyfriend Johnny Autumn! He's led Peggy astray!"

"Cripes, you know Johnny Autumn?" The man who wasn't Pete shook his head again. "You should ought to keep better company, lady."

"But I *don't* know Johnny Autumn!" I said. "All I know is he led Peggy astray, and she drugged my other tenants and stole from us. We were trying to find her!"

"Yeah?" The other officer opened the back door of the police sedan and Pete shoved Lulu and me inside. It smelled putrid in there. "You were trying to find your friend at the Palaise de Danse? Funny friend you have there, girly."

"Oh, Lord," I whispered, looking despairingly at Lulu, who looked despairingly back at me.

"You can say that again," said Lulu.

So I did.

The ride to the police station didn't take long. In one sense, that was good, since the back seat of the police vehicle stank abominably. Later Lulu told me the police had probably picked up drunken people, stuffed them in the back seat, and they'd lost their excesses all over the upholstery. I almost wished she hadn't explained the stench to me.

In another sense, I wished that stupid ride would last forever, because I didn't know what would happen to us once the policemen took us inside the station. Mind you, I'd been inside a police station before, but it was for legitimate business, and it wasn't the one toward which we were headed. I knew that because the other one was in the opposite direction. But I'd never been inside a police station as a—good Lord, I don't even want to say the word—suspected criminal. A lady of the night. A scarlet woman. A prostitute. A streetwalker. And what a time to remember *that* euphemism. Stupid Mercy.

Along the way, Lulu said, "I think we'll each get to make a telephone call, but I don't know who to call."

"Oh, my." My brain awhirl, I tried and failed to think of whom I should call. Chloe? Good Lord, no. Not in her delicate condition and certainly not under these circumstances. No matter how much Chloe wouldn't want to rat me out to our parents, she'd probably be unable to avoid doing so. Our mutual mother had a stare that would induce a stone monument to confess, even if it hadn't done anything wrong.

Then inspiration struck.

It evidently struck Lulu at the same time it did me, because we looked at each other and said in unison, "Ernie!"

Boy, was I ever grateful I'd put my little address book into my bag. I'd almost left it out because the bag was small but had decided to take it with me because I'd thought we might need paper and pencil. And, while I hadn't been correct about the paper and pencil, I was definitely in need of the addresses and telephone numbers contained therein.

"What if he isn't home?" Lulu asked, beginning to sound worried again.

Darn, I wished she hadn't asked that question. But it didn't take too long for me to think of a good answer. "If Ernie isn't at his apartment, I guess I can always call Phil Bigelow. He probably won't be at work at this hour, but I can explain what happened and somebody at his police station will probably call him for us."

"Bigelow," Lulu spat out. She hadn't cared for Phil ever since he'd arrested her brother.

Personally, although I agreed with Lulu that the police had been precipitate in arresting Rupert in the other case, I thought Phil was a pretty good man. At least he could help get us out of jail. I hoped.

"What do they do after they take us to the station?" I asked.

"How should I know?" asked Lulu. "You're the one who's always reading mystery novels."

She was right. So I cast my mind back to the various novels I'd read over the years, thought through the bits and pieces of information I'd picked up on the job, and came up with a possible scenario. "Well, first I think they'll book us."

"What does 'book us' mean?"

She had me there. "I think it means they'll get our names and addresses and...and maybe fingerprint us?"

"What for? They think we're loose women, not thieves or murderers."

"Well, maybe they won't fingerprint us. But I'm sure they'll ask for our names and addresses. Maybe take our pictures?"

"Do you have a lawyer?"

"A lawyer? No. Why?"

"I don't think you have to tell them anything if you ask for a lawyer."

This was the most promising thing either of us had said yet. "Will they still let us make a telephone call?"

"I don't *know*," Lulu said. "Like I said, you're the one who's always reading mystery books."

"Oh, dear. I wish I'd asked Ernie or Phil about what happens when someone is arrested."

"Weren't you at the station when that guy who tried to kidnap you was taken in?"

I sat up, revived. Slightly. "You're right! I was right there bleeding, because I'd scraped my knees when Ernie knocked me down."

"He knocked you down?"

"Only because people were shooting at us."

Lulu buried her head in her hands. "Good golly, Mercy, for a fine lady from Boston, you sure get yourself in a lot of pickles, don't you?"

Frowning, I said, "None of that matters. Let me think."

Lulu let me think.

I didn't have to think very long, because the police car drew up in front of the station on Sixth Street. Phil's station was on First Street. Rats. Even if Phil and Lulu didn't get along, he'd understand why we'd done what we'd one, while the officers who'd nabbed us never would. Not that Phil would have approved of our behavior any more than Ernie would. But his approval didn't matter. If neither Phil nor Ernie could be found on that dismal night, Lulu and I'd probably have to stand in front of a judge and tell our story to him. I don't recall anyone ever saying judges were easy to get along with if you were already considered a criminal by the coppers. I sighed heavily.

"All right, ladies," said Officer Pete. "Let's go and get you booked."

Lulu nudged me. "You were right about the booking part."

How encouraging. I piped up, "Aren't we allowed to make a telephone call? Or call a lawyer?"

"Sure. You can call anyone you like after we take your mug shots, print you, and search you."

"*Search* us! You certainly can't mean you're going to...*search* us!"

"Nobody's laying a hand on me," said Lulu with more grit than I'd ever heard from her before.

"We got ladies to search ladies," said Pete's partner. "Although why you two should care, I don't know. After what you were going to do." He shook his head yet once more. I got the feeling he didn't have a whole lot of gestures at his disposal and found head-shaking an undemanding way of getting his point across.

"We weren't going to do any such thing!" I all but bellowed. "I wish you'd believe me! We were looking for Peggy Wickstrom! Do we look like streetwalkers?"

This, clearly, was the wrong thing to say. Both officers only stared at us, and I recalled Lulu's artful work with the makeup, powder, eyebrow pencil, mascara and rouge pot.

"Listen, lady," said Pete, who didn't have his partner's compassionate nature. Or maybe he just didn't shake his head as much. "Nobody who's ever been brought through them doors was guilty. To hear all the pimps and grifters and bootleggers tell it, they're all as innocent as the Mother Mary."

"There's no need to blaspheme," I muttered, knowing I'd get no understanding from this quarter. Or two bits.

Never mind.

The next forty-five minutes were among the most humiliating of my life. Not only were pictures taken of Lulu and me—and I must admit we looked like the types of women the officers thought we were—but we also had our fingerprints taken and we were searched. Fortunately, a woman did the searching, but still, the whole thing was ghastly and embarrassing, and I swear, if anyone ever tells my mother about it, I'll personally strangle whoever does it.

After the search and through gritted teeth, I asked the female police person, "May we make our telephone calls now?"

The woman glanced at Pete, who was doggedly filling out forms. It looked to me as though he was having a difficult time of it. Neanderthal. Buttercup had more brains in her head than three Petes put together.

Can you tell I was quite ruffled?

"Pete? These here girls want to make their calls."

Pete peered up, squinting. "Find anything on 'em?"

"Naw. They're clean."

"Huh."

"I think they're who they say they are," offered the woman.

Pete merely grunted again. *Not* a man of large understanding, or one who liked to have his assumptions overset. The lady police officer shrugged. "Go ahead. You can use the 'phone on my desk. It's over here." She led the way.

Lulu and I both thanked her. By then, even though she'd been the one to do the searching, I'd come to think of this female police person as our only port in this particular storm. Then I said, "May I please have my handbag? I need to get my address book out."

"I'll get it for you," said she.

I felt my eyes open wider. "Don't you trust me? You already know there's nothing in there that can do anyone any harm!"

The woman shrugged. "Rules are rules. I don't make 'em. I only have to follow them."

I think I growled. However, the woman dug in my handbag—not a difficult task, since it was so small—and withdrew the address book. It was a pretty one with a Chinese fabric cover I'd bought in Chinatown on a luncheon break once. I took it from her gently, not snatching it away as I wanted to do. The woman was right, whether I liked it or not: she was only following rules.

"When you pick up the receiver, the operator will ask for the number you want," said the woman. "Give her the number, and she'll place the call."

"What if the person I'm calling isn't at home?"

The woman glanced at a clock on the wall, which told us the hour was growing on toward midnight. Good heavens. "If your party ain't home, let your friend call someone."

"You mean I only get one call, and if the person I'm calling isn't there, I don't get to try another person? That's not fair!"

"Honey," said the woman, "life ain't fair."

I felt another growl rise in my throat, but Lulu touched me gently on the arm and said, "Ernie's probably home, Mercy. He's not one to carry on much during the week."

Although I wanted to, I didn't ask her how she'd come by this interesting tidbit of information. Rather, I picked up the telephone receiver and, through gritted teeth, asked the operator to connect me with Ernie's telephone number.

The phone rang and rang and rang. I was about to give up in despair when I heard a click, and a groggy voice said, "Templeton."

"Oh, thank God! Ernie, it's Mercy. Listen, Lulu and I were trying to find Peggy Wickstrom tonight, and a policeman arrested us! He thought we were...well, never mind. We're at the police station. The one on Sixth Street. Can you come and pick us up?"

Silence greeted this spate of information.

"Ernie?" Panic made my heart thunder in my chest.

After fully long enough for me to have several heart attacks, the voice on the other end of the wire said, "Is this some kind of joke? Because if it is—"

"No!" I all but shrieked. "It's Mercy, Ernie, and I'm telling the truth. Would I joke about something like this? You have to help us! I only have this one telephone call. You have to come and get us out of here!"

"Shit."

Goodness. While Ernie used words like damn and hell a lot, I'd never heard that one come from him. I stepped back, startled. Then I said in a small voice, "Ernie? I'm sorry."

"Yeah, yeah. I know. You're always sorry when you get yourself entangled with things that are none of your business."

"Peggy Wickstrom is—" I began indignantly, but Ernie interrupted.

"Shut up. I'll be there as soon as I wake up and get dressed. How much is your bail?"

Bail? I glanced with abstraction at Lulu, who didn't have a notion what Ernie and I were discussing. Returning my attention to the receiver, I said, "Um...bail?"

Again Ernie said, "Shit."

"I have money," I told him hastily. "I can pay...whatever it costs to get us out of here." Oh, Lord, bail! I'd never in a million years have believed I, Mercedes Louise Allcutt, would one day have to be bailed out of a Los Angeles City jail.

"I know you have money," he spat at me. "I'll be there as soon as I can be. You say you're at the Central Station on Sixth?"

"Is it the Central Station? I thought Phil's was—"

"Mercy! Answer my damned question!"

After jumping three or four inches, I said, "Yes. Central Station on Sixth."

Ernie said "Shit" once more, and then the line went dead.

Lulu put a hand on my arm. "I heard his voice," she said softly. "He's real mad, huh?"

"And how," I answered.

"But he's coming?"

"He's coming."

After asking, we were told we could sit on a couple of the cold, hard folding chairs lined up against the wall near the lady policeman's desk. I was glad she didn't lock us in a cell or make us sit nearer Pete or his partner. Pete still seemed to be struggling with his paperwork.

I looked at the name plate on the lady policeman's desk, and discovered her to be named Officer Mary Johnson. Since we had nothing to do but wait and Officer Johnson didn't appear awfully busy, I decided to talk to her.

"Um, do you know how much bail my employer will need to have to get us out of here?" I didn't have much money in my handbag, but I could certainly get my hands on any amount I needed.

"No bail's been set yet. That's for the judge to decide."

"The judge! But...Are we going to have to stand before a judge?"

The woman shrugged. "I doubt it. I think you two were just in the wrong place at the wrong time. Pete gets carried away sometimes. Anybody but a halfwit could see you're not used to the streets."

I gulped hard. "Thank you for believing our story. It's the truth."

"Uh-huh."

Not awfully promising, but I persisted. Ernie had once—perhaps more than once—said I had more persistence than brains, a comment I didn't take kindly. "We really were looking for a girl named Peggy Wickstrom. She used to work at the Palaise de Danse, and we figured maybe someone there would be able to steer us in the right direction."

Officer Johnson lifted an eyebrow.

"You see, I rented her rooms in my home, and she drugged my tenants and ran off with some of our personal property."

"Yeah? Well, it's probably long gone by this time."

"That's what Ernie and Phil told me," I said, feeling dispirited.

"Who're Ernie and Phil?"

"Ernie Templeton. He's my boss. I'm his secretary. Phil Bigelow is a detective with the Los Angeles Police Department."

Officer Johnson's other eyebrow lifted to meet her first one. "You know Detective Bigelow? He's kind of a hotshot." She glanced at Officer Pete, and I think she smirked. Perhaps she was hoping, as I was, that Officer Pete would be reprimanded for jumping to illegal conclusions. Well, inappropriate conclusions, at any rate.

"Yes. He's a friend of mine," I said, stretching the truth only a tiny bit. Phil and I were on friendly terms with each other, but we weren't what I'd call true friends. Officer Johnson didn't need to know that.

"Yeah? You know the mayor, too? Or the district attorney? We don't get too many folks in here with highfalutin friends."

Perhaps Officer Johnson thought I was boasting. Or perhaps she didn't think it appropriate to throw names at her. I always hated it when people bragged about all the movie stars they knew, probably because I'd met many so-called stars myself and wouldn't give you two cents for most of them, with a few exceptions.

"I wasn't trying to imply Detective Bigelow would come

storming down here to spring Miss LaBelle or me," I told her, striving for a humble tone. "I only—"

"LaBelle? Who's Miss LaBelle? This here paperwork says your friend's name is Mullins."

"Cripes, Mercy," muttered Lulu at my elbow.

I wished I'd kept my fat mouth shut. "LaBelle is her…um, stage name," I said lamely.

"Stage name, eh?"

"Yes."

"She an actress, is she?"

"She's only chosen a name for the future, when she makes it big in the pictures."

A hard elbow poked in my side let me know Lulu didn't appreciate me relating her history to this person. I cleared my throat. "Anyhow, it's my boss, Mr. Templeton, who'll be coming down here to get us. Um…he mentioned bail. You don't know how much bail will be unless we see a judge first?"

She heaved a huge sigh. "It'll probably twenty-five dollars. We haven't found any priors on either of you. We don't have night court here, so you'll have to come back to see the judge. I expect you'll get the money back once the judge realizes Pete and Mac jumped to the wrong conclusion. Although," she added severely, "you two sure look like a couple of hookers at first glance. A second glance would have shown them two idiots they were wrong about you."

Relief flooded me. "Oh, *thank* you! Do you really think so?"

She nodded. "Yeah. I've seen enough of the real thing to know you ain't it."

Oddly comforting, I thought, feeling better about our predicament. Not that sitting in a stark police station, even though an honest-to-goodness police officer believed you to be innocent, was much fun.

And then Ernie arrived.

SIXTEEN

You'd have thought General Custer, the Seventh Cavalry and the entire Sioux Nation had stormed the doors of the Central Police Station when the door banged open and Ernie stomped inside.

"Where's Mercy Allcutt!" he bellowed to one and all without bothering to look around first. I got the clear impression he was annoyed at having been awakened in the middle of the night, especially by me, and especially for the reason I'd called.

With my heart in my throat and dreading the tongue-lashing Lulu and I—especially I—were about to receive from the source, I waved. "We're over here, Ernie!"

Officer Pete got up and went to Ernie, a scowl on his face. Well, both men wore scowls. There were a few minutes of heated discussion between them. I didn't hear much of it; only the occasional swear word and Ernie scoffing at Officer Pete's depiction of us as—I absolutely *hate* using this word, but it's the one he used—whores.

"*Whores?*" hollered Ernie. "They're no more whores than you are, dammit. They thought they were being smart and going out to find the girl who burgled Miss Allcutt's home. Idiots. I'll grant you they're both idiots, but idiocy's not a criminal offense or half the L.A.P.D. would be locked up instead of going around locking up innocent, if stupid, people."

"Now see here, you—"

And so it went. I don't know how long Ernie and Pete fussed at each other, but eventually Officer Johnson got up from her desk and joined them. The argument didn't last long after her appearance. Spotting Lulu and me scrunched back against the wall and doing our best to disappear into the dirty plaster, Ernie barged toward us, not bothering to allow Officer Johnson to lead the way.

"Get the hell up, and let's get out of here," he commanded.

I noticed he looked only slightly more rumpled than usual. He'd combed his hair, at least. He assuredly didn't look sleepy. He looked as though he aimed to take us up to the top of the highest Hollywood Hill and throw us over it.

Lulu and I got up. Lulu said, "Thanks, Ern."

"Yes. Thank you, Ernie." My own voice sounded much feebler than I wanted it to. However, this experience had shocked me. Badly.

"Yeah, yeah. Get a move on."

"Don't we have to post bail?"

"No. After a little friendly discussion, your captor decided he'd made a mistake. I don't think he wanted to face the day you and Lulu showed up in court and presented yourselves to the judge looking normal. Anyhow, after I pointed out that you could sue the police for false arrest—and win—he decided to let you go." He spoke the last sentence very loudly. I didn't look to see how Officer Pete took it.

Ernie hurried us to the front door of the police station, opened it and shoved us both out into the dark night. Taking each of us by a shoulder, presumably so we couldn't escape, he aimed us toward where I suspected he'd parked his Studebaker. As we walked, he eyed us with patent disfavor. "What the hell did you think you were doing, dressing up like streetwalkers and parading around in that lousy neighborhood?"

Lulu, I noticed, had her lips pressed tightly together, and I got the impression she was going to let me do the talking. Fair enough. Ernie was my boss, after all, and I was the one who'd called him.

"You already know what we were doing. You shouted it to the whole of Central Station."

"Yeah, I know. You were looking for Peggy Wickstrom. But why were you looking for her like *that*?" He shot us both a disparaging glance. "I don't blame the policeman for thinking you were wh——"

"Don't say that word!" I said.

"Why not? Whores are what you look like. What's more, it's what you *wanted* to look like. Cripes, Mercy, I don't know how the hell you get into the scrapes you get in to. If I didn't know better, I'd think you *wanted* to get arrested."

"Darn you, Ernie——"

Lulu finally unzipped her lips, probably in order to prevent an all-out war. "It's my fault, Ernie. I thought we should look as though we belonged in that neighborhood."

Ernie stared at Lulu for so long, he nearly stumbled over a curb. "*You?*"

Lulu nodded. When I glanced at her, I saw her eyes glittering strangely, and I hoped she wasn't going to start crying. I knew from experience Ernie didn't care for women weeping at him.

"She's not to blame," I said in staunch defense of my friend. "She just thought we'd stick out like sore thumbs if we went to Anthony's Palaise de Danse dressed in our regular daytime clothes."

"I see. That's why you painted yourselves to look like red Indians instead, is it?"

"We didn't—"

"Yes," said Lulu, interrupting another hot rejoinder on my part. "I figured we'd fit in better there if we both wore lots of makeup. Shoot, Ernie, you know what dance halls are like."

"Yeah, I do. I didn't know *you* did."

"I read the papers," Lulu said.

Curious, I said, "I thought you only read movie magazines."

"Well, those too. But the papers have some pretty juicy tidbits in them if you look for them. I knew we wouldn't get any information from anybody at that dance joint unless we looked the part."

"God save me," muttered Ernie. It sounded more like a profanity than a prayer to me, but who am I to judge?

Speaking of judges…"Does this mean we won't have to appear in court before a judge?"

"No. I mean yes, it means you won't have to appear before a judge. Christ Almighty, it would serve you right if you did have to spend a day in court. Or a night in jail."

"We were only trying to find Peggy, Ernie! It's not our fault Officer Pete is stupid!"

"It's not his fault you look like a couple of—"

"All right! You've already said as much. I'm sorry we had to get you out of bed at this hour." I looked around. The street was totally deserted. Ernie's Studebaker was the only one parked there, and it reminded me I'd left my Roadster at the public library. "Um, can you take us to the library?"

Ernie stopped dead in his tracks and stared at me. "The library? Why in the name of holy hell do you—"

"Stop swearing at me! My Roadster is parked there! That's why we need to go there."

"You parked your car at the library? Why, for God's sake?"

"So no one would steal it. Lulu and I thought the Palaise de Danse wasn't in a very good neighborhood, so we parked it at the library and walked."

I couldn't see his face, but I knew Ernie was rolling his eyes.

"First of all, you're not driving you and Lulu home. I'm taking you home after we stop for a bite at the Pantry. I'm hungry. Second of all, I'll take you to the library tomorrow, in the daylight, and you can pick up your Roadster then."

"But—"

"God damn it, Mercy Allcutt, don't argue with me! You woke me up out of a sound sleep, it's damned near three o'clock in the morning, and I'm hungry. The Pantry is the only place I know of that's open all night long and has decent food. So just shut your trap, will you?"

He sounded so angry and determined, I decided I'd better do as he said. However, I did say, "I'll buy your breakfast."

"To hell with that."

We'd reached his Studebaker, and he opened the door. Lulu and I couldn't both sit in the front seat, so I stepped back and let Lulu get in first. Ernie gave me an evil smile when he opened the back door for me. I could see his smile because he'd parked under one of the sparsely spaced street lamps. I didn't respond, but only climbed into the back seat of Ernie's automobile feeling meek and sad and sorry. Which, all things considered, was no more than I deserved, even though Lulu's and my motives had been pure. Well, if not pure, at least well-intended.

It didn't take long for Ernie to drive us to the restaurant called the Pantry on Ninth and Figueroa. It was a brightly lighted place, and I was surprised to see so many people seated at its counter. I said so.

"People gotta eat," said Ernie. "Not everyone has a cook at home."

"I know it," I grumbled. "I'm only surprised to see so many people dining at this hour."

"People work all hours, Mercy. It's not a nine-to-five world anymore."

I hadn't known it ever was, although I sensed it would be better not to say so.

Ernie opened the Pantry's front door, and Lulu and I trooped in, Ernie scowling at us. When I scowled back at him, he said, "I should have made you wipe that junk off your faces. You look like a couple of circus clowns who fell off the train."

Better a clown than a whore, I thought bitterly.

Ernie found three seats together at the counter. The waiter who came to take our orders looked at Lulu and me rather oddly, however, and I decided to take steps. Smiling at the waiter, I said, "May I please have a glass of water and a napkin?"

"You'll get a napkin with your silverware," muttered Ernie.

"I'd like a second napkin, please," I said.

"Yes, ma'am," said the waiter, who looked as if he'd seen worse than me walk through the doors of the Pantry, although not very often. Hmph. I thought he should expect anything at all, if the place stayed open all day and all night. It was a small restaurant. In fact, it was hardly a restaurant at all, but really only a hole in the wall with the counter and some stools. It looked to me as if they made do with a grill and a hot plate to assuage their diners' appetites.

After we sat in the last three seats available, I was surprised when I saw people begin lining up at the door. I pointed this out to Ernie and Lulu.

"Good grub," said Ernie, explaining the line outside in his own pithy way. "They'll probably expand one of these days. I want breakfast. How about you two?"

Lulu and I glanced at each other. My stomach took that

moment to growl. It would. "Breakfast sounds good, although I won't be able to eat Mrs. Buck's breakfast if we dine here."

"We're going to *eat* here, Mercy, not dine," said Ernie.

"Well, if you're going to be picky—"

Lulu interrupted what might have turned out to be another row, which was probably a good move on her part. "Anyhow, tomorrow's Tuesday, and Caroline will still have to eat something."

This was a good point and not one I'd considered before.

I was about to say so when Ernie spoke again. "Besides, I have to talk to you about Mr. and Mrs. Buck's son."

"You do?" My heart started thumping again. I wasn't sure it was going to survive until morning. Well, later in the morning, it being technically morning already.

The waiter set a napkin and a glass of water in front of me, and I dipped the napkin in the water and began scrubbing at my face.

"Jeez, Mercy, all that face paint will ruin the napkin!" said Lulu. "I don't think the management will be happy with you."

"I'll pay for the stupid napkin," I said. I wasn't accustomed to wearing so much makeup, and I didn't like the feel of it, especially the rouge, which, when I caught sight of myself in the shiny surface of a toaster, stood out starkly against my pallid face. Lord, Lord, what had I allowed Lulu to do to me? Well, it was too late to worry about it.

As I scrubbed, I asked, "What about Calvin Buck?"

"The housekeeper at Gossett's is sticking to her story. Only now she's claiming she saw Calvin Buck at the Gossett place on the day of the murder."

"She didn't mention him being there before," I said. "Besides, he was studying at my house at the time of the murder. And he was in jail at the time of the Preston murder."

"His parents say he was there. You didn't see him, and

neither did anyone else. The police don't give a rat's ass about his being in jail when Preston was murdered. They've got him for Gossett, and they aren't going to let him go."

"That's disgusting."

"It's the truth."

Sometimes I hated the truth. "Maybe. But somebody must have seen *someone* else at the Gossett place! Calvin can't have been the only person besides the cook to visit Mr. Gossett's house that day."

"According to the cook, she thinks, but isn't sure, another man and a woman visited him."

"Who was the man?"

Ernie shrugged.

Therefore, I pursued the point. "And a woman? What woman?"

"Who the hell knows? Gossett sure can't tell us."

"Hmm," I said, scrubbing. "A gentleman and a lady."

"Not a gentleman and a lady," said Ernie, correcting me wryly. "The housekeeper said a *man* and a *woman*. Believe me, servants know the difference between ladies and women."

"Oh."

Lulu asked, "Didn't somebody tell me Johnny Autumn was involved in a bootleg operation and maybe a—" She stopped speaking suddenly and shot me a look.

Ernie stepped in. "A prostitution ring. Right. Gossett might have been visited by a prostitute, and Johnny Autumn might have delivered her, but the cook didn't get a good look at either of them."

I was so shocked, I stopped scouring my face for a moment. "A prostitute? On a Sunday? Good heavens."

Ernie and Lulu both rolled their eyes then, and I felt foolish. But honestly. Hiring a prostitute on the Lord's day? Doing such a thing at any time was reprehensible, but…Well, I got the distinct impression neither Lulu nor Ernie shared my sentiments, so I went back to removing makeup and said not another word about it.

"So," Ernie continued, "yes. Johnny Autumn is known to run with bootleggers, and he's suspected of having a string of girls, one of whom may well be Peggy Wickstrom."

My mouth dropped open and rougey water trickled into it. I snapped it shut instantly and wiped my lips with the dry end of the ruined napkin. "Peggy? *Peggy*? Do you really think she's a... one of those? But she's only—"

"Eighteen," Ernie said wearily. "Yeah, I know. And I don't know if she's one of those, but it's a thought."

"Good Lord," I murmured, stunned.

"So it's probably a good thing you didn't find her," said Ernie. "Or God alone knows what she or her precious Johnny might have done to you."

"But..." I couldn't think of anything to say.

Fortunately, the waiter returned and took our orders. By that time I was famished. I guess being arrested, booked, fingerprinted, searched, photographed and left to languish in a police station's squad room does that to a person. Speaking of fingerprints, I surveyed the tips of my fingers. "I wonder if this ink will ever come off."

"It will. Might take a day or two, but it will." Naturally, it was Ernie who supplied this information, I presume because he knew.

I sighed. "If my mother ever finds out about this night's work, she'll kill me."

"She might have to line up for the privilege," said Ernie before downing a gulp of the coffee the waiter had brought us.

I decided not to respond to his sally.

The Pantry served a delicious, very filling breakfast, and by the time Ernie finally dropped Lulu and me off at my house, I was nearly asleep on my feet. Ernie walked us to the door.

"Sleep in tomorrow morning, both of you. Don't bother coming to work. I'll come over sometime during the day and drive you to the library to get your Roadster, Mercy."

"Thank you, Ernie," I said, feeling quite humble by that time.

Lulu and I mumbled our good-nights. After I jotted a little note to Mrs. Buck to spare her making us breakfast that morning, we separated at the head of the staircase, I to go straight ahead into my own suite of rooms, and Lulu to turn right and go to the west wing to her suite of rooms. I presume Caroline Terry was slumbering peacefully, not having done anything insane to interfere with a good night's sleep.

Buttercup woke me up before I was ready to arise, but since it wasn't her fault I'd gone out the previous evening looking like a lady of the night, I didn't scold her. Rather, I rose, yawned, noticed Buttercup fairly crossing her legs with discomfort, threw on a robe, and staggered downstairs, where I allowed my sweet doggie to go out into the yard and do her duty as a well-trained poodle. Because I was so exhausted, I sank onto the cement stairs leading from the back porch to the yard and waited for her to finish.

I'd neglected to look at the clock as I'd passed through the kitchen with my pooch, although my eyes were so gummy I might not have seen it had I remembered. Squinting at the sunlight and thinking perhaps Los Angeles might actually receive some cooler weather as autumn progressed—mainly because I'd begun to shiver—I heard an automobile in the drive. I figured it was Mrs. Buck or a delivery wagon or something. Mr. Buck had undoubtedly gone to work already, but I didn't know what Mrs. Buck did during the day when I was supposed to be at my own job. The house always looked immaculate, so I presumed she was somewhere inside cleaning something. Or perhaps she'd gone to the Grand Central Market, which was just down the street after you got off Angels Flight. Even though I knew very little about running households, I knew groceries didn't appear by magic.

My state of exhaustion didn't allow for enough curiosity to investigate the source of the noise. Whoever was in the automobile could jolly well go to the front door and ring. Either Mrs. Buck would answer the door or nobody would, and then whoever it was could go away again.

Can you tell I wasn't in a rosy mood that morning? At least I thought it was still morning.

My scheme for the person in the automobile didn't come to fruition. All of a sudden Buttercup began to make ecstatic happy, yappy noises and danced to the gate separating the drive from the back yard. Oh, no. It must be someone I knew. And, of all the people I knew, my own personal bad luck assured me it was Ernie Templeton. And here I was: gummy-eyed, hair askew, and in my bathrobe. Shoot, I hadn't even put my slippers on!

Burying my head in my hands, I hoped against hope he'd just go away when no one but Buttercup greeted him.

Naturally, he didn't. I heard the gate open mere seconds after I heard him greet Buttercup. I sent up a prayer for help, but figured God had better things to do than save me from my own stupidity yet again. So, rather than slink back into the house and pray Ernie wouldn't see me, I lifted my head from my hands and glared at him.

"My, my, aren't you bright and chipper this lovely Tuesday morning?" he said. With evil intent, I'm sure I need not add.

"Go away," I said.

"Not on your life." He plunked himself down on the steps next to me and petted Buttercup. "I've always wanted to see what your mistress looks like on an average morning, Buttercup," he said to the dog. "I'm surprised you haven't moved to another home."

I said, "Huh."

He passed a slitty-eyed glance at me. "Your face is all red where you scrubbed it at the Pantry last night. Did you know that?"

Wonderful. Exactly what I wanted to hear. "You don't have to look at me," I snarled.

Naturally, he laughed. "Aw, buck up, kiddo. You don't look so bad. I thought you'd be up and at 'em this morning. Being that your Roadster is stuck at the library and all."

"What time is it?" My voice was as froggy as my face was red, I guess, and all I wanted to do was go back to bed.

"It's time for you to go upstairs, wash up, don some clothes, and come out with me. We might as well get in another driving lesson while we're at it."

"I don't want a driving lesson. I want to go back to sleep."

"Tsk, tsk. The intrepid private investigator never sleeps when he—or she—is on the job."

"Nuts. You were asleep until I woke you up last night."

"Indeed I was, which is exactly why I'm here at ten o'clock on this particular Tuesday morning. Never let it be said that Ernie Templeton doesn't pay his debts."

I tilted my head and squinted at him. "You mean you came here early on purpose? To pay me back for waking you up and asking you to bail out Lulu and me?"

"You got it in one," said Ernie, grinning like the fiend he was.

Burying my head in my hands once more, I said, "Uuuuh-hhh. But I really don't want a driving lesson today, Ernie."

Ernie slapped me on the back in a gesture that might have been considered comradely except he nearly sent me sliding off the porch steps. "All right. You don't have to have a driving lesson. But get a move on, kid. I don't have all day."

But I did. I knew it would be senseless to say so. Ernie was here, he was determined upon a course of action, and I was too darned tired to oppose him in any meaningful way.

Therefore, I rose creakily to my feet, turned around and trudged back up the steps to the kitchen door. Buttercup, who was delighted to have company on a bright Tuesday morning, dashed ahead of us into the house and danced around her food and water dishes. I said, "All right, all right. I'll feed you."

"Why, thank you!" said Ernie.

I turned upon him a scowl that had him clutching his chest in mock horror. "You mean you weren't talking to me?"

"Uh."

"It's all right. I'll martyr myself. I'll make coffee. Then, after you feed the dog, go upstairs and get presentable. Then we'll go fetch your Roadster."

I gave him another "Uh."

He only laughed at me.

SEVENTEEN

By the time I'd bathed—taking exactly as long as I wanted to take, darn it—washed my hair, brushed it into a neat little cap on my head (I'd recently had my marcelled waves bobbed into a sleeker cut), and put on a plain brown skirt and white shirtwaist, I was almost awake.

As an aside, I wasn't as pleased with my new haircut as I'd hoped to be. For one thing, I don't have the coloring to carry off the look properly. You really need to have dark hair and pasty-white skin. I have light brown hair, fair skin, and too many curves to be fashionable. I didn't present nearly as dramatic an image as did some of the women you saw on the silver screen. On the other hand, I was a secretary, not an actress, so I guess it was all right.

What wasn't all right was that Ernie had assessed the redness of my cheeks absolutely correctly, drat the man. I'd rubbed my face nearly raw the night before, and even powder didn't cover the bright pink cheeks bespeaking more a healthy farm lass than a sophisticated woman from the City of Angels. Bah.

Buttercup had remained in the kitchen with Ernie, hoping,

no doubt, for him to slip her a tidbit. I doubted Ernie was doing anything but making coffee, but when I stepped into the kitchen, he offered up one more surprise for me. Not that I was eager for surprises that morning, but this one wasn't too bad.

Lulu had come downstairs, too, and sat at the breakfast table, looking as groggy as I'd felt half an hour earlier. I said, "'Lo, Lulu."

She said, "'Lo, Mercy."

"Here," said Ernie in a too-hearty voice. "I fixed some scrambled eggs and toast for you and Lulu. Sit down and eat."

Except that his words sounded like an order, I appreciated his industry. "How come you're so peppy today?" I asked in a growly voice.

"I got lots of sleep last night. The fact that it was interrupted doesn't mean I didn't get a full night's rest."

"Huh."

That "huh" came from Lulu. My own "huh" joined hers a mere second or two later.

But the eggs and toast were just what the doctor would have ordered if Ernie hadn't got there before him.

"Where's your housekeeper today?" asked Ernie as Lulu and I shoveled food into our mouths.

Lulu shrugged.

I said, "I dunno. I left her a note telling her Lulu and I wouldn't be down for breakfast."

"You did?" Lulu. "Shoot, I was so tired, I never even thought about Mrs. Buck."

Although it was silly of me, I was rather proud of myself for remembering my housekeeper under trying circumstances. Naturally, I didn't say so. "Least I could do," I muttered, savoring the revivifying effects of coffee on a too-tired body.

We discovered where Mrs. Buck had been when she walked into the kitchen just then, laden with a basket full of goods from the Grand Central Market. She clearly wasn't expecting anyone to be in her kitchen, because she gasped and nearly dropped her burden. Ernie, much more chipper than Lulu and I, leaped to his feet to help her out.

"Here. Let me take that for you, Mrs. Buck."

"Lord save me, Mr. Ernie. I didn't expect to find you here this morning."

"I'm sorry, Mrs. Buck," said I, feeling contrite. The woman had enough to worry about without having people invade her space unexpectedly on a Tuesday morning.

"I didn't even know you was home, Miss Mercy. Your note said you and Miss Lulu wouldn't be here for breakfast, but that's all I knew."

"We had a late evening," I told her, shooting Ernie a keep-you-mouth-shut glare.

"Mercy and Lulu were out investigating the Gossett murder," he said, which goes to show how much my glares meant to him. "They got themselves into a little bit of trouble."

Mrs. Buck gaped at Lulu and me and pressed a hand to her heart. "Lord a'mercy, child! You don't want to do nothing like that! You leave the investigating to the police and Mr. Ernie here. Mr. Buck and I would never forgive ourselves if anything was to happen to you on our account."

"We weren't really investigating the Gossett murder," I said to her, giving Ernie another hot scowl, which did about as much good as my first one had. "We were looking for Peggy Wickstrom."

"Miss Peggy? She didn't come down for breakfast either," said Mrs. Buck.

I sighed. "I know." Then I told her what had happened while she and her husband were spending a blameless day at church and visiting their poor son in the county jail.

At one point during my narrative, she clutched the sink, and I told her to sit at the table and have some coffee with us. She appeared slightly shocked at the suggestion, but did as I'd recommended. Ernie poured her coffee for her. By the time I'd come to the end of the story, Mrs. Buck's head was shaking slowly back and forth.

"I knew that girl was trouble the minute I saw her," she said somberly.

"You did?" I shot yet another glance at Ernie, who carefully peered at the ceiling so as not to garner unto himself any more of my fury.

"Yup. Sure did. She has the *trouble* look about her, you know?"

Clearly, I didn't know. I admitted as much to Mrs. Buck and prayed Ernie would keep his mouth shut. "No. I thought she was just another girl who had to work for a living, like Lulu and me."

Mrs. Buck shook her head. "Naw. She's not like you two or Miss Caroline, who's sweet as can be. She's bad, that other one."

So there you go. My ability to judge a person's worth was right there in the gutter with my sleuthing skills. The knowledge was downright demoralizing.

Ernie smacked me on the back again, jogging my coffee cup, which was empty at the time, thank heaven. "Cheer up, kiddo. You can't win 'em all."

"It seems I can't win any of them," I grumbled under my breath.

Ernie laughed.

Mrs. Buck said, "Get along with you now. I'll put up them groceries and wash up the dishes."

"Thank you, Mrs. Buck," I said politely.

Lulu said, "I think I'll go back upstairs. I need a bath. And a nap."

"Sounds like a good plan to me," said I. "But Ernie's going to take me to get the Roadster first."

And then it was I had what I thought was a bright idea. I

trailed after Lulu when she climbed the stairs while Ernie sat chatting with Mrs. Buck in the kitchen. When we reached the head of the stairs, I whispered to Lulu, "Say, Lulu, would you like to do a little detective work with me when I get back with the Roadster?"

Lulu eyed me askance. "Like what we did last night? We won't get arrested again, will we?"

"No! I only thought…" I peeked over the banister to make sure Ernie wasn't eavesdropping. But I heard him in amiable converse with Mrs. Buck in the kitchen, so I continued. "I thought maybe we could pay a visit to the Gossett house and talk to the cook. You know. The one who fingered Calvin Buck for the crime. I want to find out first-hand what she has to say for herself. She says she saw him there, but he was here. Doing his homework."

Although earlier Lulu had looked approximately as hale as I had when Buttercup first woke me up that morning, she revived a trifle at my suggestion. "You mean it? I was thinking we should probably go to work, even though we're late."

"Ernie told us to take the day off," I reminded her.

"Yeah. Taking the day off is fine for you, but I don't work for Ernie."

"Ernie can give you a note for an excused absence," I told her, wondering where that idea had come from. Grade school, I guess.

Lulu blinked at me. "He can?"

"Sure. If he tells your boss—who is your boss, by the way?"

She shrugged again. "I don't even know. The building is owned by some corporation. When I'm not there, they send over some girl from another building they own."

"Hmm. How curious." I gave myself a mental shake because we were straying from the subject. "Anyhow, if Ernie vouches for you,

you can't get into trouble for taking one stupid day off. You can say you were sick." I attempted to be as persuasive as I could be, since I didn't really fancy tackling the house of the murdered man all by my lonesome. Yet I truly did want to speak to the woman who had accused Calvin Buck of having been there on the day of the murder. Besides, I wanted to find out if she remembered anything else about the man and woman she'd seen at the residence the same day.

"Well...I don't know, Mercy. You know how last night turned out."

Did I ever! "I promise you we won't get into trouble."

"How can you promise that?"

She asked the question with curiosity and not animosity, for which I was grateful. Still, I didn't know how to answer her. "Oh, heck, Lulu, for all we know the housekeeper doesn't even live there any longer. Maybe she figured her job ended when her employer was killed. I only want to try it, is all."

After hesitating for another second or two, Lulu came through for me. Bless her heart!

"Oh, what the heck, why not?" she said. "Go get your machine. Then you can drive us to the Gossett place."

"Thank you!"

It was only when Ernie pulled up beside the Roadster I realized I still had another obstacle to overcome in order to pursue my day's planned activity.

"You coming to work now?" he asked casually.

Work? He'd told us to take the day off! Still..."Um...is it okay if Lulu and I come in after lunch?" That ought to give us time to question Mr. Gossett's cook, if she was still at his house.

Frowning, Ernie said, "What are you planning, Mercy? I can see the wheels turning in that twisted brain of yours."

"I don't have a twisted brain, and I'm not planning anything!" I retorted with as much heat as I could muster. It wasn't a whole lot, since I was still tired. Which gave me a brilliant notion. "I really need another hour or two of sleep."

"Is sleeping all you're planning to do?"

"Why do you always suspect me of ulterior motives?"

"Because you usually have 'em."

"Nuts. I'm tired, Ernie. You *said* Lulu and I could have today off." Which reminded me of Lulu's plight. "Say, Ernie, can you write Lulu a note to excuse her absence today? She's worried about losing her job if she takes today off, but she's as tired as I am and only wants to sleep some more."

"A note?" Ernie threw his head back and laughed. "This isn't the second grade, Mercy. I already called the corporate office and told 'em Miss LaBelle had been taken ill but will make every effort to return to work tomorrow."

He had? How *nice* he could be sometimes. When he wasn't being horrid. "Thank you, Ernie," I said, meaning it. "I'll tell Lulu. It'll ease her worries." I added a quick, "When she wakes up again," for good measure and to throw Ernie off the trail of our true intentions. Golly, being devious was hard work! I don't know why some people—like, for instance, Peggy Wickstrom—didn't find evil-doing exhausting.

He eyed me keenly for a second or two, but he either believed my innocent expression or didn't feel like arguing with me. With an airy wave and a, "Stay out of trouble if you can. See you tomorrow," he was off, back to the Figueroa Building. Or perhaps he aimed to do some sleuthing of his own.

I climbed into the Roadster, started the engine, and very carefully headed for home. Although I'd had several lessons and it was broad daylight, I still felt a little nervous about driving on busy Los Angeles streets.

Lulu was fully prepared to go investigating by the time I drove up to the house. I parked the motor in front of the house, mainly so I wouldn't have to try backing it out of the driveway again. Driving the machine forward was difficult enough.

"Let's take Buttercup," I said on impulse. "She'd probably love to go for a ride."

"We can't take her into the Gossett place with us," Lulu pointed out. "It would look queer."

"I'm sure she wouldn't mind staying in the machine for a bit while we talk to the cook/housekeeper."

"Okay, but you'd better bring her leash in case we have to tie her to the steering wheel."

A sudden, insane mental picture of Buttercup in driving goggles at the wheel of my Roadster flitted through my brain. I knocked the image out again with a vigorous shake of my head. "Right," I said. We'll take her collar and leash. We might stop at a park and give her a walk on our way home.

"I dunno," said Lulu. "All I want to do is go talk to that lady and come home and nap some more."

"Napping does sound a good deal more appealing than going for a walk," I admitted, feeling guilty about my darling doggie not getting a nice walk in the park that day. Well, maybe I'd take her for a walk after I awoke from my afternoon nap. I felt better after making that semi-decision.

When we entered the house, we were greeted by an overjoyed Buttercup, as usual. Mrs. Buck also met us, dust mop in hand. She'd been buffing the foyer tiles, I suppose. I greeted her warmly.

"I'll fix sandwiches for when you want lunch," she told us. Then she said, "Mr. Ernie told me as to how I wasn't to let you out of the house again today, Miss Mercy. He wasn't joking, either. He says as to how you always get yourself into trouble by trying to pretend you're a detective."

My mouth fell open in shock for an instant before it snapped shut. "What utter rot!" I said with as much indignation as I could summon. It wasn't, after all, Mrs. Buck's fault Ernie had saddled her with an impossible task. Not let me out of my own home, indeed!

"It's what he told me, ma'am," Mrs. Buck said. "I told him I couldn't do nothing to stop you leaving your own house, but he told me to tie you to a chair." She grinned at me.

"He would," I muttered.

"He's a card, that Ernie," said Lulu. She didn't sound awfully convincing.

"Lulu and I are only going to take Buttercup for a spin in the Roadster, Mrs. Buck. We won't get into any trouble. Honest," I added when a look of worry crossed her face. "I'm not going to *pretend* I'm a detective." Boy, it galled me that Ernie had expressed his concern in those words.

"I told him I couldn't do nothing to stop you leaving," repeated Mrs. Buck. "So he told me to telephone him if you left the house."

"He didn't!" I already knew Ernie had a managing disposition, but I hadn't realized how far he might go in achieving his aim of total control over my humble person.

"Yeah. He did."

"Well, if that isn't the most—"

"Calm down, Mercy," Lulu advised. Then she spoke to Mrs. Buck. "Ernie's only a little worried that Mercy might get arrested again, is all, but—"

"She might get *what!*" Mrs. Buck all but screeched.

Oh, brother. That tore it. I gave Mrs. Buck a brief précis of Lulu's and my overnight adventures, leaving out the lurid parts, then said, "But it's broad daylight today, and we're only going to take Buttercup for a ride. Then we're coming back home to take naps. We were out very late last night. Or this morning."

Throughout my narrative, Mrs. Buck clutched the dust mop. If it had been a person, she'd have strangled it. She also persisted in shaking her head, as if I were telling her a tale so shocking, she couldn't quite believe it. I hoped to heck she wouldn't quit her job once she learned her mistress was a jailbird.

But when I finally got through my edited version of our adventures, she only said, "I thought Mr. Ernie was funnin' with me about tying you to a chair, but I reckon he wasn't. You stay out of trouble, young lady, you hear me?"

There wasn't a hint of Boston in Mrs. Buck's voice, but she had me standing up straight and squaring my shoulders as if I were being confronted by Mother in one of her lecturing moods.

"Oh, we will," I assured her meekly.

"We sure will," said Lulu, adding her assurance to mine.

"You better, or Mr. Ernie will hear about it from me."

I figured it was probably better to allow Mrs. Buck to have the last word, so I only gave her a reassuring smile and hightailed it to the kitchen, where I grabbed Buttercup's collar and leash. I didn't keep the collar on her all the time, since she was mainly a house dog, but when she saw the leash in my hand, she became almost hysterical. She loved going for walks, and another pang of guilt struck me.

I *would* take her for a walk. Just as soon as I woke up from my nap. Maybe even before I took it.

EIGHTEEN

Mr. Milton Halsey Gossett's Carroll Street home was not very far from Mr. Gregory Preston's residence on Alvarado. It occurred to me this area of Los Angeles wasn't an awfully lucky place for motion-picture folks to live, what with the murders of William Desmond Taylor and Gregory Preston on Alvarado and Milton Halsey Gossett on nearby Carroll. I almost hoped my friend, Mr. Francis Easthope, would move to a more savory location before someone decided to shoot him, too.

You'd never have known murders took place on that street when I finally, very carefully, maneuvered the Roadster around the corner and drove toward the Gossett residence. Manicured lawns and stately homes lined the road. I didn't see any elegant bungalow courts on Carroll Street, as there were on Alvarado, only big houses and pretty lawns and gardens, ablaze now with chrysanthemums. The entire street bloomed with color.

"What was the address again?" I asked Lulu, who was acting as navigator. Buttercup, on her lap, was helping with the job, which accounted for Lulu having to juggle a couple of pieces of paper from underneath my dog's feet, since Buttercup had her head hanging out the window and was enjoying the wind as it flapped her ears around.

Lulu told me the address, and I squinted at numbers. Nothing so squalid as a mailbox marred the beauty of the street here. The numbers were painted discreetly on curbstones. This made the street lovely to look at, but the numbers were cursedly difficult to read sometimes. Lulu squinted, too, and we eventually drew up in front of the Gossett place.

Mr. Gossett had either bought or rented himself an imposing two-story dwelling set back from the street and hidden behind tall hedges and trees. Hmm. I didn't like the looks of all those hedges and trees. Nor did like it when the word *hidden* crossed my mind.

I told myself to stop being stupid. It was broad daylight, and I had Lulu and Buttercup with me. I then told myself to heck with Buttercup staying in the car while Lulu and I tackled the cook/housekeeper. The dog could jolly well accompany us on our intrepid journey.

"Let's take Buttercup with us."

The statement didn't come from me. Rather, it had been spoken by Lulu, who was clearly as unsettled by the concealed nature of Mr. Gossett's former home as I.

"Good idea."

Buttercup thought it was a grand idea, too. She nearly tore the leash from my hand in her eagerness to dash up the walkway past all those hedges and trees. I took this enthusiasm on her part as a good sign, figuring if danger lurked ahead, surely she'd detect it sooner than we mere humans would. Weren't dogs supposed to be good at sniffing out trouble?

Lulu and I followed my poodle up the path, which curved a few yards along, revealing the front of the house, which had a big porch.

"It looks empty," said Lulu.

"How can you tell?"

"I don't know. Maybe I'm just hoping it's empty."

"You can't back out now," I told her bracingly.

"I'm not backing out. But I sure don't much like the looks of this place."

Neither did I, but I thought I'd better not say so. "Well, there's no harm in knocking on the door," I said, still trying to be bracing. In truth, the place was giving me the creeps.

However, Buttercup remained keen on her journey up the path, and I took her attitude as assurance there was nothing to fear by continuing on our way.

I still felt creepy as I climbed the porch steps and pushed an electric ringer button. My own home still had one of the old-fashioned twist varieties of doorbells, but Mr. Gossett must have tried to be up to date with the times. He'd had a relatively visible position in Hollywood to uphold, after all.

"Nope. Nobody's home," Lulu said with great relief approximately six seconds after we heard the bell toll in the house.

"Nonsense. Nobody's had time to get to the door yet," I told her, even though I, too, had the urge to turn around and run back to the car. But I kept my faith in Buttercup, whose tail still wagged.

"Nuts, Mercy. I'm scared."

"Buck up," I told her, not letting on that I was scared too. "I'll just ring the bell one more time and then—"

I didn't get to finish my sentence, because the door opened in our faces. I know I jumped, and I suspect Lulu did, too. Buttercup just kept wagging.

"C'n I help you?" asked the woman who stood in the doorway politely. "What a sweet doggie!"

Very well, this comment sealed the deal for me. I decided anyone who appreciated Buttercup couldn't be all bad. I smiled ingratiatingly at the woman. "My name is Miss Allcutt, and this is Miss LaBelle. My dog is named Buttercup. We came here today because we have a few questions about the late Mr. Gossett's untimely demise. I," I continued, as I saw the woman's eyes widen, "work for Mr. Ernest Templeton, who is assisting the police with their investigation."

The woman glanced from Lulu and me to Buttercup and back again. "You always go investigating with your dog?" She gave me a squinty-eyed look.

I laughed unconvincingly. "Oh, no. But Buttercup loves to go for rides, and I didn't think her coming along would do any harm."

"You got any identification? You with the cops, you said?" The woman appeared quite doubtful.

Looking back on the situation, I can't say I fault her much for being dubious. We must have presented an odd picture as investigators.

"No," I said, and tried to explain the inexplicable. "I work for Mr. Ernest Templeton. Mr. Templeton is an investigator who's working on the case. I'm just here to ask you a couple of questions."

"What questions? The cops already asked me every question they could think of."

So I decided to dive right in. She might slam the door in our faces, but she might not. "Well, for instance, I understand you told the police you saw Calvin Buck, the fellow who's been arrested for the crime, in Mr. Gossett's home on the day of the murder."

"Yeah? So what?"

"But the first time the police spoke with you, you didn't mention Mr. Buck being inside the house. I just wondered why that was. Did you recall later that you saw him? Did you speak to him or anything?"

"Speak to him? No. I just seen him, is all."

"Where did you see him?"

"What do you mean, where did I see him?"

Oh, brother. The woman wasn't the sharpest tack in the box. "I mean, did you see him inside the house? Did you see him on the grounds?"

"Oh. Naw, I just seen him on the sidewalk when I was going to church on the other side of the street."

"I see." In other words, she hadn't seen Calvin Buck at all, but only a Negro fellow walking on the sidewalk. Racial prejudice was a terrible thing. "You also mentioned a man and a woman who came to the house the same day."

"Yeah? What about 'em?"

"Can you give me a description of the two?"

The woman cocked her head to one side and thought. I hoped she wouldn't burn any of her little gray cells by doing anything so unusual for her. "Well, I didn't see the girl too good. The guy was a slick customer."

"A slick customer? How so?"

"Oh, you know." She flipped her hand in the air, as if to describe what she meant, although the gesture meant nothing to me.

I waited for a second, but she didn't seem inclined to continue, so I said, "Um, no, I don't know. What does a slick customer look like?"

She chuffed out an aggrieved breath. "Oh, you know. Had his hair slicked back with grease and wore one of them, what do you call 'em? One of them slick suits like the gangsters wear and one of them whattayou call 'em. Fedoras."

I hadn't known gangsters wore any particular types of suits, and I didn't know what was sinister about a fedora hat, but I'd be sure to ask Ernie about these items of men's fashion the next day when I went back to work. "And you didn't see the woman who was with him?"

"Wasn't no woman. She was a girl."

"A little girl? You mean she was a child?"

"No. More of a young woman, like. Seventeen. Eighteen. Somewheres around there. She looked a lot younger than the slick customer, I can tell you that." She sniffed. "Looked like a flapper to me in her short skirt." She chuffed again.

Instantly I thought about Peggy Wickstrom. Then I reminded myself Los Angeles was full of young women who'd come to the City of Angels with the hope of becoming movie stars, most of them tried to look all the rage, and the rage was focused on the flapper at the moment. It was unlikely that Peggy Wickstrom had visited Milton Halsey Gossett on the day of his demise.

The man with the woman might well have been Johnny Autumn, however, bringing Mr. Gossett one of the fallen women from his flock. Darn it! Now I wished I'd got a description of Autumn from Ernie. Or, since he probably wouldn't have obliged me, from Peggy herself.

"Do you know why the man and the young woman called on Mr. Gossett?"

She gave yet another sniff and appeared undecided for a moment or two. However, her pent-up emotions managed to get the better of her at last, and she blurted out, "No, but I can guess! If I'd'a known what kind of a man Mr. Gossett was, I'd never of took up keeping house for him, I can tell you that much. Why, the man was a gambler! And he visited—"

Her mouth clamped shut, as if she couldn't say the words aloud. I tried to help her along. "Loose women?" I suggested, trying to show her I shared her opinion of men who frequented gambling establishments and other dens of iniquity.

"Yes," she snapped. "What's worse is that he had loose women visit him. Right here. In this house! I didn't know it, or

I'd've quit months ago. His chauffeur told me all about the evil things the man did after he died." She shook her head. "I've never been so took in by a fellow."

"Learning he was of low moral character must have come as quite a blow," I said, my voice oozing sympathy.

"You can say that again."

I didn't get the chance, because she continued, "Say, I was just about to make me a cup of tea. I haven't had the chance to talk to anyone in days and days, trying to get this place cleaned up and ready to let, except the chauffeur, and he's a chump. You gals want to take a cup of tea with me? I have some fruitcake, too."

"Thank you very much! That's awfully kind of you."

"Nuts. There's no reason I can think of why I shouldn't use up Gossett's supplies so long as I gotta stay out the rest of the month here. But I've got me another job lined up, and this time I know the place is respectable, because I'll be working for a family. Goes to show you should never work for a bachelor, I guess."

Ernie was a bachelor, and to the best of my knowledge, he was a man of good character. Of course, I couldn't vouch for his non-working hours, but still...

"Thanks," said Lulu. "Mind if we bring in the dog?"

The woman waved her arm to beckon us into the house. "Why not? Nobody's here to complain, and that there doggie's better company than most of the *people* who've been through those doors."

"It's so good to meet you and for you to speak with us like this, Mrs.... um..." I murmured as we followed her.

"Name's Wallace. Mrs. Wallace."

"This is very kind of you, Mrs. Wallace."

She grumbled some more about if she'd known about Mr. Gossett's immoral habits before she'd been hired for the job, she'd never have taken it as she led us through to the kitchen. In order to get there, we had to walk through the living room, and I interrupted her monologue for a moment.

"Is this where you found Mr. Gossett's body on Monday morning?" I stopped and, I regret to say, pointed. My mother would have a fit if she ever saw me pointing. Phooey on my mother, say I.

"Lord a'mercy, what a jolt *that* was," cried the woman, fanning her face with one hand and pressing her other one to her bosom. "No. He was more over there, near the staircase."

I looked at the staircase. "Was his head toward the staircase, or were his feet pointed at the stairs?" I asked. God knows why. I certainly couldn't come to a conclusion about who'd shot the man by knowing the position in which he'd died.

The woman surprised me, though. "Here," she said. "I'll show you." In an aside, she said, "The coppers took out the rug, or I wouldn't do this, but there's no harm in helping you with the investigation, I figure. Might help. I think they ought to hire more women in the police department. Females got more sense than men, most of 'em."

I agreed wholeheartedly with this pronouncement and decided not to remind her we weren't with the police. I knew the police sometimes used dogs in their investigations, but to the best of my knowledge, the dogs they used weren't toy poodles.

"My first name's Aggie, by the way. Aggie's short for Agatha, just like that lady who writes them books."

"I see. Thank you, Mrs. Wallace. Is there a Mr. Wallace?" Don't ask me why I asked the question, because it was surely none of my business and nothing to the purpose.

"Not any longer. He died. That's why I had to take up working as a cook/housekeeper. Mr. Wallace, he kept me pretty well when he was alive, but he didn't have no savings." She heaved a huge sigh as she got to her knees a few feet from the foot of the staircase. To my surprise, she lay on her stomach. "This is how I found him."

"My goodness," I said. "For some reason, I thought he'd been lying on his back when he was found."

"Nope. Whoever done it shot him in the back of the head, like a dirty coward."

I considered shooting people cowardly no matter how they did it—well, unless one were defending oneself, of course. And then I understood Mrs. Wallace's point. If a person was heading away from one, shooting him in the back of the head did seem a cowardly act. However, it looked to me now as though whoever had shot Mr. Gossett had done so as he'd been walking away from the staircase. Could the shooter have been on the stairs? Did it matter? Crumb, I didn't know.

Lulu and I each took one of Mrs. Wallace's arms and helped her to her feet. "And you have no idea who did the ghastly deed?"

"It was that boy they arrested, of course. There was no reason for him to come by the house on a Sunday."

"Were you working on that Sunday?" I asked, my curiosity piqued.

"Well, no, but I go to church on the corner. That's when I seen him. What else could he have been doing in this neighborhood, a colored man and all?"

I could think of any number of reasons for a colored man to be walking on Carroll Street on a Sunday morning, ranging from leaving or going to a home in which he worked to walking to church just as Mrs. Wallace had been doing, but I didn't offer them to Mrs. Wallace, who seemed determined to see things her way.

"And you're sure the man was Calvin Buck?"

"Listen, I know it was him, 'cause he was the only blackie I ever seen in the neighborhood."

"I see. No one else on the street has a colored maid or a colored man working in his or her employ?"

"Well...as to that, I can't say as I know for sure," she admitted.

By this time we'd made it to the kitchen, and she gestured Lulu and me to take a couple of chairs arranged around a small table. The kitchen in Mr. Gossett's house reminded of my own, which made me think kitchens must all be pretty much alike in the overall scheme of things: a table and chairs, a stove, an ice box or a refrigerator, knives, a cutting board, a pie safe. I suppose there's some variation in decoration schemes, but kitchens were kitchens.

"You knew Calvin Buck pretty well by the time of the murder, didn't you?" I asked as Mrs. Wallace lit the gas burner under the tea kettle.

"Not to say I knew him well. But I knew him. He served meals here and tidied up for Mr. Gossett."

"Had he ever seemed to be a boy who was drawn to trouble?"

"How should I know?" she demanded. "He's colored. What can you expect?"

Oh, boy. I could see what Ernie was up against in attempting to help the Bucks. I'd venture to guess most of the Los Angeles police department believed as firmly as did this woman that colored people were naturally drawn to criminal activities.

"But he was always polite to Mr. Gossett and his guests? And to you?" I tacked the last part on at the end just to make sure she didn't feel left out.

She shrugged. "I reckon."

To my surprise, Lulu took up the conversational gauntlet. "Just because a boy's colored doesn't mean he's a criminal," she said, sounding a shade defensive of Calvin Buck, probably because she knew and liked his parents.

"Oh, Lord, I don't know. Who else could of done it?" asked Mrs. Wallace, a distinct whine in her voice.

"My money's on the man and woman who visited him that Sunday," said Lulu. Then she asked, and astutely, I must admit, "Say, you said you weren't working here that day. How'd you manage to see those two, anyhow?"

Mrs. Wallace had turned away from the stove and was reaching for a canister of tea. I could tell it was tea because the canister said so. She also blushed a bit. "I seen them, too, getting out of a machine when I walked past Mr. Gossett's place." She measured some tea into a tea infuser and laid it aside.

"I see," I said, thinking there surely ought to be a follow-up question to that one.

Fortunately for me, Lulu thought of it. "What kind of machine was it?"

"Mercy sakes, child, I don't know automobiles! It was big and black. That's all I know."

Big and black. Big help. Half the cars on the road were big and black.

"Did it look sporty?" asked Lulu.

"Sporty? I don't think so," said Mrs. Wallace, although her voice carried doubt.

"Was it low-slung?" Lulu again.

"Low-slung? Naw. It was big and boxy. You know, like one of them big Buicks or something."

"Did it have any kind of hood ornament?" asked Lulu.

Hood ornament? What in the world was a hood ornament?

Mrs. Wallace apparently knew, because she thought about Lulu's question for quite a while. Then the kettle began to whistle, so she returned to the stove and poured hot water into the teapot, rinsed it out, put the tea infuser in the pot and then added more hot water. I determined to ask Mrs. Buck if this pouring-hot-water-into-the-teapot thing and pouring it out again was something one was supposed to do before making tea. Maybe it was some sort of cooking rule. I really wanted to learn more about cooking!

"You know," she said as she set the teapot on the table and returned to a cupboard for some teacups, "now that you mention it, I think I did notice a hood ornament. It looked kind of like a red Indian chief. In one of them...what do you call 'ems? Head dresses? You know, with the feathers and stuff?"

Lulu's hand slapped the table, making me jump and Buttercup bark. "It's a Pontiac! The nineteen twenty-five Pontiac has a hood ornament just like that!"

"Oh, yeah? I never much noticed 'em before. Hood ornaments, I mean."

Boy, and here I didn't even know what a hood ornament was. I could learn a lot from these two women, which just went to show you never could tell about people. These two might not have a whole lot of book-learning, but they had practical knowledge that could be much more important in investigative work than literary knowledge.

"A Pontiac," I mused, wondering how I could find out what kind of automobile Johnny Autumn drove.

"I guess it was, if Miss LaBelle says it was," said Mrs. Wallace.

We drank tea, ate fruitcake and chatted a while longer. It seemed to me Mrs. Wallace had managed to give us all the information she had to bestow when we took our leave around three in the afternoon.

As soon as we got home, Buttercup and I ran up the stairs, and I jotted down a list of things to tell and/or ask Ernie when I went to work the next morning. I was rather proud of Lulu's and my excursion onto Carroll Street that day.

We'd learned the brand name of the automobile used by the couple who had visited Mr. Gossett, we'd learned Mr. Gossett had been shot in the back of his head, perhaps by someone standing on the stairs, and we'd learned Mrs. Wallace didn't have a notion in her head about why she'd fingered Calvin Buck as the killer except that he was colored. And that, as I knew full well, was no kind of reason at all.

And yes, I took Buttercup for a walk around the block when I awoke from my nap.

NINETEEN

"You did *what?*" Ernie, who'd arrived at the office earlier than usual on Wednesday morning, stared at me as if I'd just told him I'd jumped out a fourth-story window.

"We went to visit Mr. Gossett's house on Carroll Street. And we learned quite a number of pertinent things."

"God damn it, Mercy! I told you to stay out of the investigation! You already got yourselves arrested! I don't suppose you and Lulu will be happy until you're laid out on slabs in the damned morgue!"

"Don't exaggerate," I told him, peeved. "We learned some relevant things, and I think you ought to know about them. So stop scolding me and listen!"

Ernie's gaze paid a visit to the ceiling of his office, and he heaved one of his more enormous sighs. "I'll bet you ten dollars you didn't discover anything the police and I don't already know," he grumbled.

"We'll see," I said primly. Without being invited to do so, I sat on a chair before his desk. "For instance, did you know the person who shot Mr. Gossett did so from behind?"

"Yeah, I knew that."

Crumb. "Well, did you know that whoever did it was probably standing on the staircase when the deed was done?"

I could tell he hadn't anticipated this information, because he squinted at me. "How'd you figure that?"

"Mrs. Wallace showed us exactly where she found the body. In fact, she acted Mr. Gossett's part."

His eyebrows arched. "She what?"

"She laid herself down on the floor in exactly the position in which she discovered Mr. Gossett's body."

"How'd you get her to do that?"

"I didn't *get* her to do anything. She offered of her own free will, because she was trying to assist two young investigative females with a darling toy poodle who'd come asking questions. I'll bet she didn't act out the scene for your stupid *police*."

"I won't take that bet. Criminy." Ernie passed a hand across his brow. "I can't believe what you can get away with."

"I didn't get away with anything!" I cried. "I only asked politely! From what I've seen of your precious police department, that's more than *they* ever do!"

"You're probably right." In a resigned voice, he said, "So what else did you discover?"

"We learned she didn't even see the face of the colored person she noticed the Sunday of Mr. Gossett's death. She only glimpsed a man in passing from across the street as she was walking to church."

"Figures."

"And, what's more, she didn't see the man and the woman who visited Mr. Gossett that day, but she *did* recollect the hood ornament on the big black car they drove. The hood ornament was in the form of an Indian chief, and Lulu says that means the automobile is a nineteen twenty-five Pontiac." I spoke with perhaps a tiny trace of triumph in my voice, but I'm sure you can't fault me for it.

Ernie's reaction was all I could have hoped for. He stared at me for probably thirty whole seconds, and then he said, "How'd you find *that* out?"

I gave credit where it was due. "Lulu asked Mrs. Wallace if she recalled the car having any kind of a hood ornament."

"I'll be damned."

"I'm sure you will be," I said drily.

"I wonder if Phil knows about the hood ornament."

"I have no idea." I sniffed.

"I'm going to call and tell him."

"Tell him who discovered the information," I said caustically. "We wouldn't want him to think we women are totally worthless, now, would we?"

"Don't worry. I'll let him know how I found out." He eyed me for a moment, but I wasn't about to remove myself from his office until I'd listened to his conversation with Detective Phil Bigelow. I still had questions of my own I wanted Ernie to answer. Ernie scowled at me. I crossed my arms over my chest and remained seated. He finally gave up, heaved another sigh, and dialed the telephone.

After he'd hung up, I said, "Do you know what kind of automobile Johnny Autumn drives?"

Ernie gave me one of his patented eye-rolls. "Yes, damn it. He owns a nineteen twenty-five Pontiac."

"Aha!"

"Aha, my foot. There are lots of 'twenty-five Pontiacs on the streets of L.A."

"Huh. I'm sure that machine belonged to Johnny Autumn, and I'd bet you anything he was involved in Mr. Gossett's death."

"You might well be right, but the police don't have any proof."

"They don't have any proof Calvin Buck shot the man, either, but it doesn't seem to bother them overmuch."

Ernie shook his head. "You're right."

"I wish I'd thought to get a description of Johnny Autumn from Peggy Wickstrom when I had a chance."

"I know what the mug looks like."

"You do?" For some reason his words surprised me.

"Of course, I do. For God's sake, Mercy, I *am* doing my best for the Bucks, you know."

"How could I know that when you never tell me anything?"

"Sheesh."

"May I please have a description? Just in case he comes back and decides to denude the rest of my residence of its property?" Impertinence, thy name was Mercy Allcutt.

Ernie frowned at me, but he condescended to answer my question. "Five-ten. Brown hair and eyes. Wears his hair slicked back. Wears flashy clothes and jewelry."

"Jewelry?" I asked, confused, thinking about necklaces and earrings and brooches and those sorts of thing.

"Cuff links, snappy wristwatches. Pinkie rings. You know."

"Ah. I see."

"He's a flashy customer."

"It's a shame he seems to have led Peggy astray."

"Huh. For all you knew, she was already astray when they met."

I hesitated for a moment before conceding the point. "Perhaps."

"But I guess I owe you ten bucks, huh?"

I held out my hand and smiled. "You do indeed. I'll take you to lunch with my ill-gotten gains."

Handing me a ten, Ernie said, "Cheap at twice the price."

"Thank you." Then, because I really wanted to know, I asked, "Say, Ernie, what's a hood ornament?"

I felt really stupid when he told me.

Mrs. Buck fixed fried chicken, green English peas, biscuits, mashed potatoes and gravy for dinner. For all the unpleasantness we'd gone through recently, I felt fortunate to have my home and my friends and tenants and the Bucks in my life. I was a little worried about Caroline Terry.

"Are you feeling all right, Caroline?" I asked her at the dinner table as we partook of our succulent meal. "I still feel awful for allowing the Wickstrom girl into my house. You and Lulu suffered for my mistake."

"Please don't feel guilty, Mercy. You aren't responsible for the girl's actions." Caroline shook her head mournfully. "It's a shame when people allow the devil to direct their actions. I was fortunate I had parents who taught me right from wrong."

"Good point," said Lulu, pouring gravy over a biscuit. I have to admit, I'd never seen anyone eat a biscuit smothered in gravy before. If I weren't so full by then, I might have tried the same thing myself. "Our parents taught us right from wrong, too, but what parents say doesn't always take. If you know what I mean. I knew a couple of kids I grew up with who were rotten, but their parents tried to keep them on the straight and narrow."

"I remember you telling us about that bully," I murmured, wondering if I might try half a biscuit with some gravy on it. Maybe instead of dessert.

"Oh, Gerald. Yeah, but his folks were rotten, too, so you can't tell anything by him. I'm thinking of Pauline Welch. Her ma and pa seemed to be the salt of the earth, but when she hit seventeen, she ran off with a rambling man who drove through town. Last I heard, she'd had herself a kid and was barely scraping by as a waitress somewhere in Texas."

"Good Lord." The fate of poor Pauline Welch seemed dire. I suppose the rambling man managed to get away with no consequences whatsoever. "Won't her parents help her?"

"They would, but she won't let 'em. I guess she's too ashamed to come back to Enid."

Enid was the town in Oklahoma from whence Lulu and her brother came. I shook my head in sorrow. "That's such a shame."

"How terribly sad," murmured Caroline, who appeared to mean it. I think I even saw tears in her eyes.

"I think so, too. Mind you, Pauline was stupid for running off with a guy who anybody could see was a no-good bum, but still, she isn't the first one, and she won't be the last. What I want to know," continued Lulu, a furrow decorating her brow, "is how come it's always the girl who suffers? The guys always seem to go on about their business as if nothing ever happened."

"Sad," whispered Caroline.

"Exactly what I was wondering," said I, more angry than sad over the injustices rampant in the world. Then I remembered Mrs. Buck was serving apple brown betty for dessert, and I decided to forego half a biscuit with gravy. Another time, perhaps.

"Things like that happened at home, too," said Caroline. "I feel so sorry for girls who get into trouble. I know they ought to have stronger moral fiber, but just one slip can spell the end to all of one's hopes and dreams, can't it? You'd think people would give other people second chances, wouldn't you?"

"Indeed, you would," I said, struck by Caroline's down-to-earth goodness. None of this tossing the baby out with the bath water stuff for her, by gum.

Mrs. Buck had just come into the dining room bearing a tray with individual bowls of apple brown betty, over which she'd poured cream. Although I was full, my mouth started watering again.

And then, darned if somebody didn't bang at the front door. Most unusual.

Mrs. Buck frowned and turned her head, as though she wondered if she should answer the door or serve dessert. I knew the answer to that one.

Rising from my chair, I said, "I'll get the door, Mrs. Buck. Caroline and Lulu, finish your dinners. I'll get rid of whoever's at the door and be right with you."

Famous last words.

If I'd had a single shred of intuition in my nature, I might have predicted evil to come from that rapping on the door. Naturally, being the possessor of a prosaic character, I hadn't a clue to what catastrophe I was headed when I walked to the door. I peered through the window, but didn't see anything even though I'd turned on the electrical outdoor light. *Odd*, thought I to myself. And I opened the door.

"Peggy!" I all but shrieked when Peggy Wickstrom, looking as though she'd been run over by a fleet of trucks or a railroad car, crawled into the house. "What on earth happened to you?"

The girl was a mess. She'd clearly been beaten. Rage rose within me until I very nearly saw red.

"I'm...I'm sorry," whimpered Peggy, hugging herself as if to keep broken ribs together.

"Good Lord. Here. Let me help you into the living room."

"No! I mean...Oh, Mercy, I'm so sorry."

Through clenched teeth, I said, "Did Johnny Autumn do this to you?"

Tears streaked her face when she nodded.

"I *knew* it!" I cried, feeling oddly vindicated my belief in Peggy should have been proved correct so horribly. The ghastly man *had* led her astray, like a little lost lamb. And then he'd beaten the tar out of her, by golly. "Come into the living room."

I took her carefully around the shoulders and guided her

through the archway and into the living room. Buttercup, who had gone to the door with me, sniffed curiously at Peggy's heels. She didn't seem awfully excited to see an old friend. Buttercup, not Peggy, who was in no condition to be excited about anything.

Lulu had decided to investigate the strange scrapings and cries from the front door by this time. As I carefully arranged Peggy in a chair, she walked in from the dining room. "What's— Good glory! Is that Peggy Wickstrom?"

"Yes. That beast, Johnny Autumn, beat her up."

"Wow," said Lulu. "You look pretty awful, Peggy." Then she said, "Serves you right."

"Lulu!"

Caroline, following closely upon Lulu's heels, gasped at the sight of Peggy, all battered and sore.

Mrs. Buck, who trotted along behind Caroline, muttered, "Lord save us, who done that to you, girl?"

"Johnny Autumn," I said, my teeth still clenched. My jaw would ache tomorrow. I didn't know it then, but you have to be careful whilst clenching teeth because you can strain facial muscles if you clench too hard. It's probably not good for your teeth, either.

"Saints alive," said Mrs. Buck. "I'd best go get my medicines." She shook her head. "Mr. Buck done gone to the prayer meeting at church, or he might could go after the brute."

"No!" I said, unclenching my teeth at last. "No, please, Mrs. Buck. Mr. Buck is to do no such thing. Johnny Autumn is a vicious criminal. I suspect he's the one who killed Mr. Gossett and maybe even Mr. Preston. If Mr. Buck did anything to him, I'm sure the police would only arrest Mr. Buck on some stupid charge or another."

"Johnny's not bad!" wailed Peggy.

We all stared at her, dumbfounded, and I wondered if the girl was born stupid or if being in love addled some people's brains. "Well, he's not awfully nice to have done this to you," I said drily.

She whimpered some more.

"I'll go get my stuff," said Mrs. Buck. She turned on her heel and headed back to the kitchen.

"Is she really hurt?" Lulu asked.

My gaze flew to her. "Look at her, Lulu!"

"Yeah. I see. She looks real bad. But is she faking it, or is she really hurt?"

"Oh, Lulu," said Caroline, putting a gentle hand on her arm. "Show some Christian mercy." Pausing to fling a glance my way, she said, "I mean…"

"I know what you mean," said Lulu. "But don't forget what *she* did to *us*."

Peggy began crying again. "I know. I'm so sorry. I didn't want to do it, but…" She stopped speaking, her words sort of trailing off.

"Did that awful man make you do it?" asked Caroline, her soft voice vibrating sympathy.

I could have warned her not to put words in a witness's mouth, but it was too late by then. Anyhow, I was interested in Peggy's answer.

"He…he didn't exactly *make* me," she said, fudging.

"Was drugging the lemonade your idea, then, and not his?"

"Lulu!" I said, more softly but no less intensely.

"Nuts, Mercy. This girl stole money and property from us and drugged Caroline and me. What's more, she put booze into the stupid lemonade. I didn't notice anybody named Johnny Autumn hanging around the house at the time, did you?"

For the life of me, I couldn't think of anything to say to rebut Lulu's statement. Peggy might have done her evil deeds under the influence of her precious Mr. Autumn, but she'd done them of her own free will. No one had held a gun to her head. What's worse was that she'd been cheerful as she did it.

Peggy hung her head. "I'm so sorry. He...he threatened me."

I jumped at her excuse. I know. Silly me. "What did he threaten you with?"

Peggy tried to spread her arms, winced, and subsided into a hunched figure on the chair. "This."

Lulu said, "Hmm."

"Oh, dear," whispered Caroline. "I think I'll go see if Mrs. Buck needs some help."

"Thanks, Caroline."

"And I," said Lulu, "think I'll call the coppers. Maybe Ernie."

"No!" Peggy all but screeched in my ear, which was perilously close to her mouth. "Please don't call anyone! Don't you see? He'll kill me for sure if you call the cops!"

"Too bad. He needs to be locked up for lots of reasons, not the least of which is what he did to you. Stand up and act like a woman, for Pete's sake!"

"Oh, Lulu," Peggy whined. "You don't understand."

"No," said Lulu. "I don't." And she headed to the telephone.

"Blast," whispered Peggy.

"It'll work out all right," I assured her, trying to get her to sit up so I could remove her outer wrappings and see exactly what her so-called lover had done to her. She groaned a good deal when I got her coat off. Her face looked terrible, although that might have had a lot to do with her hair, which was wildly disarranged. She did have a black eye, though, and lots of red slap marks on her cheeks. Her eye was nearly swollen shut.

"He..." Peggy stopped to sniffle. "He kicked me in the ribs. They hurt a lot."

"We'll have to bind them ribs up," said the efficient Mrs. Buck, bustling back into the room with a tray piled with things of a medicinal nature.

"Do we have anything to help her with the pain?" I asked, thinking of laudanum, which was still relatively easily available, although not sold as openly as it once had been.

"Let's see how she be before we let her drink anything," said Mrs. Buck.

"I don't want to drink anything," said Peggy a trifle more forcefully. "If Johnny hadn't been drinking, he'd never have done this to me."

Caroline and I exchanged a glance. Caroline said, "So this is all the fault of demon rum?" I'd never heard her sound so skeptical.

"It's the truth! Johnny loves me!"

"If he loves you, I'd hate to think what he might do to you if he disliked you." Very well, by then even the softhearted Mercy Allcutt was beginning to tire of Peggy's blind faith in a man who could treat her so badly.

"You don't understand," Peggy said, sniffling some more.

"No," I said. "I certainly don't."

At Buttercup's snarl, I looked up from the pathetic heap that was Peggy Wickstrom and was surprised to see Lulu backing into the living room from the office where the telephone was kept. Her arms were bent at the elbows, and she held her hands in the air. Behind her, holding what looked like the biggest gun on the face of the earth, strode a man I'd never seen before, but whose name I could guess with precise accuracy.

Then Peggy said, "No! No! Please, don't let him take me!" and huddled more deeply into her chair.

Johnny Autumn said, "Shut up."

The rest of us could only gasp in horror.

TWENTY

Because I was so shocked—knocked all of a heap, as a maid of ours in Boston used to say—I cried, "How did you get in here?"

"Oh, please," said the outrageous Mr. Autumn. "If you want to keep people out, lock your damned windows. Get up, Peggy. You're coming with me."

Peggy shrank back some more, clutching at me. Hard, darn it. She had fingers like a vise. "No!" she whimpered. She was good at whimpering.

In this case, I didn't blame her. Johnny Autumn looked like a mighty rough customer to me. "It's all right, Peggy. We won't let that terrible man take you back."

"Move over, Miss Allcutt," said Autumn. "Get away from Peggy. Peggy, move your chassis and come along with me."

Peggy stopped whimpering long enough to sigh deeply. She made as if to rise. Appalled, I tried to hold her down. "No! You can't go with him, Peggy! He's the one who did this to you!"

"Cripes," said Autumn. "Is that what she told you?"

"Yes!" Turning to Peggy, I said, "You can't go back to a man who beat you black and blue, Peggy. You'd be nuts!"

"Gotta keep her in line somehow," he said. "She can be a handful. Anyhow, I didn't beat her up. Another john done that because she tried to steal his cash."

I was becoming confused. Were there *two* people named John in Peggy's life? For goodness' sake, the girl was only eighteen years old.

Peggy's head was bowed. To my absolute shock, she said, "I'm sorry, Johnny. I didn't ought to've done that."

"Damned right," said he.

All confusion on my part vanished. However many Johns pervaded Peggy's life, she simply couldn't return to Johnny Autumn's care. Or…what had Ernie called it? His stable? I more or less bellowed, "*What?* You can't possibly mean to say you're going back to this man, Peggy!"

With another heart-wrenching sigh, Peggy said, "But Mercy, I love him."

Lulu muttered something under her breath. I suppose she didn't dare speak aloud, since Autumn still held the gun on her. When I glanced to see what Mrs. Buck and Caroline were doing, I noticed they seemed to have frozen solid in attitudes of shock and dismay. I figured they'd be safe if they stayed that way.

Unfortunately for yours truly, I was too angry to remain still. I jumped to my feet and shrieked, "That man killed Mr. Milton Halsey Gossett! And probably Mr. Gregory Preston too! How can you go back to a *murderer?* Especially one who beats you up?" I wasn't sure about the last part, but I didn't allow confusion stop me. "*Especially* one who shot a man in the back of the head like a dirty coward!" Don't ask me why Mrs. Wallace's description of the murder came out of my mouth just then, because I don't have a clue.

Autumn's lips thinned before he pried them apart far enough to say, "I didn't kill anybody."

Peggy had her hands clasped to her chest and was gazing up at me with what looked almost like religious fervor. "He didn't, Mercy. I already told you he didn't. He didn't kill Mr. Gossett. Or that other guy."

"Well, if he didn't, he still either beat the tar out of you or let someone else do it. You'd be an idiot to go back to him."

Lulu finally managed to pry her mouth open. "Mercy," she said in a grating whisper. "It's probably better not to argue with either one of them. The man's holding a gun, remember."

She'd mentioned a salient point, although I was loath to give up the fight for Peggy's welfare. Therefore, I said, "Please stop pointing the weapon at Miss LaBelle, Mr. Autumn. You're an armed man against a room full of helpless women." I sneered at him. "I'm sure those odds are almost as much to your liking as shooting a full-grown man in the back of the head."

"Oh, no!" said Peggy. "He didn't do it!"

"Dammit," said Autumn. I think he'd have elaborated on his theme, but just then, an apricot-colored streak raced across the floor from the direction of the kitchen, and Buttercup bit him on the back of the leg. He hollered "Damn!" once more, only this time in a pained-sounding voice, and tried to shake her loose. He was off-balance and fell against the doorjamb. This had the happy result of his gun, after discharging once with a hideous boom, falling to the polished wooden floor next to the Persian carpet. I saw later it had nicked the wood, but at the time I was only intent on getting that gun into my own hands.

Buttercup eventually went flying, although she shook herself off and raced back into the fray, aiming for the back of Autumn's other leg this time. He shouted, "Keep your damned dog away from me!"

"Buttercup!" I shouted as I dove for the gun, not, of course, out of consideration for Johnny Autumn, who deserved no consideration, but because I feared he might harm my faithful, *heroic* dog.

To my utter shock and astonishment, someone beat me to the gun. The someone was Peggy Wickstrom and, while her hand shook, she aimed the deadly weapon at me. Me! The person who'd tried to save her from the mad killer, Johnny Autumn.

"Get back, Mercy," she said.

Looking at her black eyes and vicious bruises, I had a hard time believing what was going on in front of my eyes. "But Peggy, he did that to you!" I waved a hand at her. I was sorry I'd done so instantly, when I heard a click that meant she'd pulled the something-or-other back on the gun. I leaped aside.

"Johnny loves me," Peggy said. "And I love him."

"Damn it. That dog bit me!" said the patently unlovable Johnny Autumn.

"Good Buttercup," I said because I couldn't help myself.

"Shoot the damned dog," snarled Autumn.

"No!" I shrieked.

"I don't want to shoot Buttercup," she told me. "But you have to stand aside and let us get out of here."

It was Lulu who spoke next, which was probably just as well, as Peggy's words had rendered me speechless. "Why'd you come here if you're just going to go back to him? Do you like getting beat up?"

"He didn't mean to do it. I deserved it."

"Damn it all, I *didn't* do it," muttered Autumn.

Peggy whimpered some more.

I was really sick of her whimpering by then. "Oh, for goodness sake, go away, both of you," I snapped. "Get out. And don't ever come back. I don't care if he blackens both of your eyes and breaks both your arms and legs. I never want to see you again."

Peggy lifted her chin. "He won't hurt me. He loves me."

The idiocy of the human animal never ceases to amaze me.

The heroic nature of my toy poodle doesn't, either. No sooner had the latest declaration of her brutal lover's adoration left her lips than Peggy screamed, and I looked downward to see Buttercup firmly attached to her calf. Golly, the dog might be small, but she had a grip on her.

Again the gun went flying. Again I dove to get it. I saw it flipping in the air like a sleek, black seal doing tricks and prayed hard Buttercup had rendered both of her targets too badly wounded to react quickly.

She had, but it wasn't I who snabbled the gun. By golly, Caroline Terry rose from the floor, the gun clasped in both of her hands and pointing it at the crippled duet of criminals clutching each other in the hallway leading to the office. Buttercup, barking madly, was doing her best to keep them at bay.

"Tie them up!" I hollered to the room at large.

Fortunately for all of us, neither Lulu nor Mrs. Buck lacked sense. Lulu instantly withdrew the sash to her dress, yanked Peggy out of Johnny Autumn's arms, and tied her arms behind her back. Peggy kicked and bellowed. "Ow! Stop that! You're hurting me!"

Lulu said, "Shut your yap, you idiot!"

Johnny Autumn turned to hightail it out of the house, but Mrs. Buck, a quick-thinker if ever there was one, had managed to get hold of the heavy tray upon which she'd carried her medicaments and bashed him on the head with it. He went down with a thud, and she sat on his back. It was a brilliant move, because as much as he tried, he could only thrash about. Mrs. Buck wasn't fat, but she was a large woman.

I scooped Buttercup up, told her she was a good, brave girl, but she could stop barking now.

Mrs. Buck said, "Go get me a cast-iron skillet. Use it on that one before you give it to me." She jerked her head toward Peggy

Wickstrom, who was giving Lulu a hard time with the tying-up-of-hands maneuver.

I decided to heck with the skillet for the nonce, plucked an ugly statue from the mantel, and conked Peggy on the head with it. The conk stopped her long enough for me to fetch the skillet and some heavy twine Mr. Buck kept in the utility room. I also bethought me of the dirty sheets waiting to be washed in a basket beside the laundry tub and brought those into the living room, too. Whoever said one couldn't improvise when suppressing criminals? Nobody I know of.

By the time we had Peggy and her boyfriend snuggly tied up and unable to move, I went to the telephone and dialed Phil Bigelow's number at the police department. Phil wasn't there, but I told the answering policeman a disturbance had taken place at my home, the nature of the disturbance, and asked him please to send officers with sense to handle the situation. "And I don't mean Sergeant Vincent Croft or Officer Lawrence T. Williamson. I want officers who have a brain cell or two to rub together."

The man on the end of the wire said, "Yes, ma'am," and hung up.

I hoped he'd take my words to heart. Then I dialed Ernie's office number, praying he'd be there. There was no reason for him to be, since it was after hours. If he didn't answer, I'd telephone him at his home.

The office telephone rang twice, and then my heart lifted when I heard Ernie growl into it, "Templeton."

"Oh, Ernie, thank God you're there!"

There was a pause on the end of the wire. Then Ernie said, "Aw, damn it all to hell and back, Mercy, what did you do now?"

While furious with my employer, I was pleased he'd been in his office with Phil. What's more, if I could believe him, they'd been discussing the Gossett and Preston cases when my call came in. They arrived at my home about fifteen minutes after I'd telephoned, and a good deal before the police contingent arrived. I frowned at Ernie when I led him and Phil into the living room.

Mrs. Buck had kindly cleaned, salved and bound the bitten calves of both Johnny Autumn and Peggy Wickstrom. Peggy had whined a good deal about her stockings having been ruined by Buttercup's bite, but I told her to be quiet. "My noble dog saved us from you and your so-called boyfriend, and if you keep blathering about your torn stockings, I'll jolly well hit you again and slap some tape over your mouth."

She would have rubbed her head, but she couldn't move her arms, so she subsided into surly silence instead.

Johnny Autumn didn't say a word. He only sat, bound and bleeding, on a sheet Mrs. Buck had laid out for him and Peggy to sit on. "So they don't get this pretty carpet all messy," she'd said. Made sense to me. Autumn's pant legs were rolled up, and he looked mighty ridiculous sitting there with his hairy legs hanging out of his torn trousers, a pretty white bandage tied around each of his calves and knotted with a bow. He scowled a good deal, but I didn't care.

Lulu and Caroline sat on the sofa. Caroline had carefully set the gun on the mantelpiece, swallowing hard as she did so. I considered her almost as brave as Buttercup.

"There's your killer," I said to Ernie and Phil, pointing at Johnny Autumn. "And there's the weapon. Probably," I added because I wasn't sure he'd used the same gun both to kill both Mr. Gossett and Mr. Preston and to fetch Peggy.

"I didn't kill nobody," Autumn muttered, finally breaking his silence.

"We can check with ballistics to see if the Gossett bullet came from this gun."

I hoped it had.

Ernie glanced around the room, his gaze lingering on each occupant as it lit thereon. "All right. It'll probably kill me to hear it, but will someone please tell me how you all happened to end up here like this?"

Lulu, Caroline and I glanced at each other. Mrs. Buck said, "Miss Mercy ought to tell you."

Ernie allowed his gaze to land on me and remain there. "I should have guessed."

Straightening my shoulders, I said, "Yes, you should have. This is my home, after all."

"Right. Okay, Mercy. Go on."

"We'd better wait for an officer with a notebook, Ernie," said Phil.

Both men had shed their hats and coats in the front hallway. At the moment, Phil scratched his head as he surveyed my living room, which had never been put to such a purpose as this before. Both Johnny Autumn and Peggy Wickstrom looked kind of silly, actually, bundled as they were with bed sheets, strong twine, etc. But I couldn't find any real rope. I'm sure if Mr. Buck had been there, he'd have known just where to locate it.

"How come their legs are bandaged?" asked Phil, not as if he cared much, but because he was curious.

My bosom swelled with pride. "Buttercup bit them both! She knew they were evil, and she took matters into her own hands. Er, teeth, I mean."

"She bit 'em both?" Ernie looked from my face to that of the dog in my arms. Her tail wagged joyously. She loved Ernie.

"Yes. She bit Mr. Autumn when he was holding us at gunpoint, and then she bit him again, and then she bit Peggy when *she* was holding us at gunpoint."

"Good dog," said Ernie absently. "You mean they were in this together?"

"Wait for the policeman with a notebook and pencil, Ernie."

"Right, right," said Ernie. "But you have to admit it's kind of confusing."

"Consider the source," muttered Phil under his breath. I heard him, though, and I resented his remark.

"Is it all right if I make us up some tea?" asked the practical Mrs. Buck. "I think we can all use some."

"Yes, please," I said, realizing as I did so that my knees were becoming somewhat watery. Therefore, I plunked myself onto a chair, still clutching my noble dog.

Eventually the police arrived. Phil answered the door and ushered two uniforms into the living room. To my disgust they were Sergeant Croft and Officer Williamson.

"Why'd they send *you*?" I asked, snarling slightly and reminding myself of Buttercup.

I presume neither man dared act up, what with Phil there and all. Officer Williamson merely said, "We were on duty."

"Well, you'd better *do* your duty this time, and do it right."

"Mercy," Ernie muttered.

"Nuts," said Lulu. "The last time these two morons came here, they were about as useful as tits on a boar-hog." Then she blushed when we all turned to gape at her. She muttered, "Sorry. We used to say that back in Oklahoma."

"No need to apologize," I said stoutly. "It's not only a colorful expression, but it tells the story with truth and precision." I glared at the two new arrivals. "This time, you'd better do your jobs fully and correctly."

I could tell Sergeant Croft really wanted to say something nasty to me, but he didn't dare with Phil there. Good.

Phil made both policemen get down to the business at hand. I told the story in a well-organized, precise manner. Well, as precisely as I could, with only a few detours here and there. I ended with, "He's the person who killed Milton Halsey Gossett and Gregory Preston. Check the…" Drat. I couldn't remember the word. Oh, yes. "Check the ballistics, if you don't believe me."

"He didn't do it!" cried Peggy, still standing by her man, the idiot.

"I didn't do it," said Autumn sullenly.

"Check the ballistics," I repeated.

"We will," said Croft.

I squinted at him. "Be sure you do."

"We *will*," Croft repeated, sounding aggravated. I didn't care.

"Damn it, the ballistics will show that's the gun that shot Gossett and Preston!" Johnny Autumn said at last, as if a dam had burst and he couldn't keep his words contained any longer. "But I didn't kill them!"

"Shut up, Johnny," said Peggy.

"I won't shut up! I told you not to go to either of those places, but would you listen to me? Will you *ever* listen?"

"Shut up, Johnny," Peggy repeated, this time with some menace in her voice.

"You were both at Mrs. Gossett's house the day of the murder," I said to the two of them. "We have a witness."

Johnny muttered, "Shit."

"Stop swearing in my house!" I told him, fed up to the back teeth with him and Peggy both.

"So what if we were there? That doesn't prove anything." Peggy glared at me.

Suddenly I thought I understood, although I could scarcely believe my own idea. What Johnny Autumn had said about a john having beaten Peggy because she tried to steal from him at last made sense. Still, it was difficult to take in the truth.

Staring at Peggy in utter flabbergastation (if that's a word), I said, "It was you, wasn't it? *You're* the one who shot those poor men!"

"Damn it, No! Johnny did it."

"I didn't kill either one of them!" bellowed Johnny Autumn.

"Yeah, you did. You did it because they was going to stiff me!" Peggy cried angrily.

"God damn it, I'm not going to hang for what you did! They both found you rifling through their things. You told me so yourself."

"So when they went to call the police or something, you shot them in the back of the head. Both of them," I ended for Johnny Autumn.

Peggy.

Had murdered two men.

Peggy glowered at me. Then she sneered. Then she said, "What do you know about anything, anyways? You and your prissy, goody-two-shoes act. You don't know what it's like to have to grub for a living or have disgusting men like those Gossett and Preston characters paw you."

"You didn't have to do it, either," I said quietly. "You could have gone into some other line of work."

"Yeah? Well, I did something else. I shot the bastards and got away with hundreds of dollars! *Hundreds*, I tell you!"

"Christ, Peggy," said Johnny Autumn, pleading. "Will you shut up?"

I kicked him in the bandage, making him howl.

"Stop swearing in my house." Then I turned to Croft. "Get these two out of my home. You have a confession." I could barely look at Peggy, but I forced myself. "I've never met anyone truly evil before, Peggy Wickstrom. I think you're a first for me."

"Bitch," said Peggy.

Buttercup growled ferociously at her.

"I think she meant me, sweetie," I told my loyal pooch.

Ernie stifled a chuckle. I glowered at him.

The police escorted Peggy and her erstwhile boyfriend to the police station. Phil was going to accompany them, but I stopped him by putting a firm hand on his arm. "I presume you're going to release Calvin Buck now?"

Phil kicked the carpet with the toe of his shoe. "If the ballistics—"

"*Damn* the ballistics!" I shouted, shocking myself, not to mention Phil, Ernie, and the rest of the members of my household. "You didn't have any ballistics when you *arrested* the boy! You locked him up on the word of a woman who didn't know what she was talking about! You just heard confessions from two people about who did the shooting! Release Calvin Buck this evening, or I'll sue the Los Angeles Police Department and every officer in it!"

"Mercy," Ernie grumbled. "Take it easy."

"I *won't* take it easy! The Los Angeles police arrested Calvin Buck for no better reason than that he's a Negro boy. I talked to Mrs. Wallace yesterday. She didn't even see the face of the man she fingered as Calvin Buck, Phil Bigelow, and you know it! She only said it was Calvin because she saw a Negro man walking on Carroll Street the day of the murder, and the only Negro man whose name she knew was Calvin Buck's! She also saw Johnny Autumn and Peggy Wickstrom at Gossett's house that day, but did the police arrest *them*? Lord, no! They didn't want to arrest a couple of *white* people, did they? Even though the machine Mrs. Wallace described was a nineteen twenty-five Pontiac, and Johnny Autumn drives a nineteen twenty-five Pontiac!"

"Mercy," said Ernie once more, a little louder this time.

But to my surprise, Phil shook his head. "No, Ernie. She's right." Turning to me, he said, "Yes. We'll release Calvin Buck. We'll have to verify the confessions of Autumn and Wickstrom, but if they pan out, and I'm sure they will, one or both of them will be arrested for Milton Halsey Gossett's murder and that of Gregory Preston. Calvin Buck clearly didn't have a thing to do with either crime."

I'd have thanked him, but I was too shocked to do anything but stare at his back as he and Ernie followed the policemen to the station.

TWENTY-ONE

Mr. Buck came home as Ernie and Phil were driving away. He hurried through the back door, looking worried, especially when he saw his wife crying in my arms.

"What happened?" he cried. "What did them policemen want?"

I think he suffered a shock when I looked up from Mrs. Buck's heaving back and gave him a mile-wide smile. "It's all right, Mr. Buck. The police have the real murderers in custody, and they're releasing your son today. This very evening." I frowned. "If Phil Bigelow told me the truth. And if he didn't, the L.A.P.D. is going to have to defend itself against a lawsuit filed by *me*."

Mr. Buck looked blank for a moment. Then Mrs. Buck pulled away from me and hurled herself at her husband. "It's the truth, Em! Miss Mercy found the killer!"

"I...I...I..."

"I didn't really," I said. "It was Buttercup. She saved the day."

Evidently Mr. Buck was too overwhelmed to take in any more

information. Still clutching his wife, he more or less fell into a kitchen chair.

But it all worked out all right. After Caroline made a fresh pot of tea, the entire bunch of us sat at the kitchen table, supplementing the kitchen chairs with chairs nabbed from the hallway, and ate lukewarm apple brown betty with cream and drank tea.

I called the police station after we'd partaken of our delayed dessert, and spoke directly to Phil Bigelow. Not, I must add, without some difficulty and assorted threats of lawsuits, etc. But I finally managed to talk to Phil and ask him when the Bucks could go to the police station and pick up their son.

A heavy sigh came through the telephone wire. "Give me an hour, will you? Jeez, Mercy, there's a lot of paperwork to wade through before we can let a guy out of jail, you know."

"An innocent man who was arrested for no good reason," I reminded him in a steely voice.

"Right. Right. You're right."

"And I want him released this evening."

"He will be." Phil sounded frazzled.

Suddenly a new voice came through the wire. "Quit harassing Phil, Mercy. I'll bring Calvin Buck home as soon as he's released. Will that be all right with your majesty?"

"Don't 'your majesty' me, Ernest Templeton! The police arrested Calvin Buck on the word of a woman who didn't even see him! What's more—"

"*Stop!*"

His voice was so loud, I stopped. Then I snapped, "Well?"

"I'll bring him home in an hour. Will that suit you?"

"I'll ask his parents." My voice was so cold, I'm surprised the telephone wire didn't freeze and crack into pieces.

"Fine." Ernie sighed. I heard him.

So I asked Mr. and Mrs. Buck. Mrs. Buck began crying again.

So did Mr. Buck, but he wiped his eyes and said, "That would be mighty nice of Mr. Ernie."

I said, "Mighty nice, my foot." I was still angry. Nevertheless, I told Ernie to bring Calvin Buck home in an hour. "And it better not be longer than an hour. I have a lawyer at my disposal, you know."

"Why am I not surprised?"

Sometimes being taken for a spoiled rich girl can have its benefits. Not often. For instance, I didn't really know any lawyers in Los Angles, except those who worked with Harvey Nash. But I'm sure I could have called Chloe and Harvey and managed to come up with an attorney in no time flat if I'd had to.

But Ernie was as good as his word. The Bucks, Caroline, Lulu and I were in the living room, nervously waiting and shooting quick glances at the Ormolu clock on the mantelpiece— for some reason, Peggy Wickstrom hadn't taken it—when I heard Ernie's ratty old Studebaker pull into my driveway. We all looked at each other.

Mrs. Buck had her hands folded and pressed to her bosom. She whispered, "Thank God. Thank God."

"Come on, you two. You can meet your son at the door."

They both rose from the sofa and headed toward the kitchen. "Where are you going?" I asked, surprised.

"To the back door," said Mr. Buck as if I should have known as much.

"Nuts." I said. "Ernie will bring him to the front door. Come along with me."

They exchanged a glance. I knew what they were thinking: black folks used the back doors to white folks' houses. Nuts to that nonsense.

I swung the front door wide and, sure enough, Ernie and Calvin Buck were climbing the front porch steps. I instantly forgave Ernie for his many sins.

The reunion was a happy one. More than happy, really. Ecstatic was more like it. Soon, however, the Bucks and Calvin removed to their own quarters, where they could be private and catch up on each other's news. It took them a long time to finish thanking Ernie and me. And Lulu, Caroline and Buttercup, but I finally put my foot down. It's not a very big foot, but it belonged to the owner of the house, so they quit thanking us and carried their son off.

I sat with a plop on the sofa. "Whew! This evening was pretty harrowing for a while there."

"It sure was," said Lulu.

Ernie stood before us shaking his head, then he too sat. "I can't believe Buttercup saved the day."

I eyed my dog with love and approval. "Well, she did." Then the events of the evening rushed back upon me and it was my turn to shake my head. "Peggy Wickstrom. Killed two men. She's only eighteen years old."

"She's bad," said Lulu. "No two ways about it."

"I guess so," I said, discouraged. I'd really and truly hoped my newly established apartment-boarding house operation would be used to give young working women the chance at a good life in this ugly world.

"She's not your fault," said Ernie.

I glanced up at him, wondering how he managed to read my mind with such unsettling regularity. "I suppose not. I'm…disappointed, though."

"You're not to blame," said Caroline Terry, her soft voice ringing with honesty. "You truly tried to help the girl."

"She's right, Mercy. Not everyone can be helped." This profound truth came from a woman clad in a violent yellow kimono with orange flowers embroidered all over it. Lulu, of course.

"And that's a lovely charm bracelet you gave me," said Caroline.

"Maybe," I said, "but it's not the one Peggy stole from you."

"It's all right. My grandmother wrote to tell me she'll replace the charms."

"That's nice of her," said Lulu.

"It is. Mercy was nice when she tried to help Peggy, too," said Caroline.

"True," said Lulu. "Peggy's just a bad egg. Nobody can help her."

"Well...thank you all. I still feel really bad about allowing her into my home, because she stole from you and Caroline, Lulu."

"She stole from you, too, Mercy. She stole your innocence," said Ernie.

I eyed him for a hint of irony, but didn't see any. "I guess so," I said uncertainly. "That's one way to put it."

"Right. But from now on, *I'm* interviewing candidates for tenancy in your house."

"Bother. Ernie Templeton, if you're not—"

The telephone rang just then, interrupting me as I was getting into full-rant mode. Since the Bucks were otherwise occupied, I answered the telephone.

I must have looked a little shaky when I re-entered the living room, because Caroline jumped to her feet. "Mercy! What's wrong?"

Lulu, too, stood and came over to me. "What's the matter, Mercy?"

Then Ernie showed up at my side. "What is it, kiddo? Don't tell me Autumn and Wickstrom escaped from police custody."

I looked at each of my friends in turn. "It's worse than that."

A general gasp met this announcement.

"That was Chloe on the phone. *Mother* is coming to visit for Thanksgiving!"

They all laughed. Which just goes to show that not even friends can be relied upon sometimes.

THANKSGIVING ANGELS

A MERCY ALLCUTT MYSTERY, BOOK 5

"I think it would be a good idea to get Daisy and the rest of the séance attendees into the séance room," said Harold. "Before Lola escapes and busts in on us."

Mrs. Pinkerton giggled. It was an incongruously girlish sound coming from the large green asparagus stalk.

"Yes, that's an excellent idea, Mr. Kincaid. Come along, Mercedes Louise. Clovilla, I expect you to join us, too."

"Yes, Mother," said Chloe, winking at me.

So Mother, Mrs. Majesty, Chloe, Harold, Mr. and Mrs. Pinkerton, Mrs. Bissel—whom I hadn't noticed before—and I all trouped to the breakfast room, which had been set up for the séance. Riki was there, too, stationed at the light switch, ready, I presumed, to turn off the lights when Mrs. Majesty gave the signal.

The table was bare except for one cranberry-glass candle-holder in the middle of the table. The set-up was great. The room already appeared mysterious. I expect Mrs. Majesty had arranged the mood. So far, it seemed Harold was right, and she was a mistress of her art, if art it was and not a true calling. I can't say that I believed in spiritualism myself.

Mrs. Majesty sat at the table's head, and the rest of us parked ourselves in the other chairs. I noticed there were only eight of us at the table. It looked to me as if Mrs. Majesty held firm sway over her domain. I approved. Not that she needed my approval, but it was nice to see that my mother hadn't cowed her into altering her arrangements.

"Everyone, please take hands," she said after we were all seated. I sat between Chloe and Harold. Mother sat next to Mrs. Majesty.

We all took hands.

Mrs. Majesty then smiled at Riki and nodded. The lights went out, and I heard the door to the kitchen close.

"Please be silent," Mrs. Majesty told us.

We obeyed.

Then we sat there in silence for what seemed like forever, but probably wasn't more than a couple of minutes. Then I heard a sigh from the table's head, and the fun began.

It really was fun. Mrs. Majesty conjured up the spirit of a Scottish gent named Raleigh or Rolly or something, and he, her supposed spirit control, told us all sorts of stuff about our dearly departed. Not that I personally had any dearly departeds, but Rolly chatted about Mother's aunt, who'd ruled the social set in Boston during the 'eighties and 'nineties. Then he told us that Mrs. Bissel's late husband was happy on the Other Side and expected Mrs. Bissel to be happy on this one until she joined him naturally. I guess if you're a spiritualist, you have a duty, of sorts, to keep people happy. It would be a shame if someone were so eager to join his or her late relations that he or she decided to commit suicide in order to join them.

Anyway, the séance proceeded apace. Nothing spectacular happened, and I was still unwilling to believe in spirit-conjuring when it came to a conclusion. We knew it was the conclusion when Mrs. Majesty sighed heavily and slumped in her chair.

Someone whispered (I think it was Mrs. Bissel), "We must remain quiet until Mrs. Majesty recovers from her swoon."

"Absolutely." I knew that was Harold, because I sat next to him. "We wouldn't want Daisy floating around in the nether reaches forevermore, would we?"

"Harold," said Mrs. Pinkerton, "that won't happen. Daisy knows what she's doing."

"Of course, Mother." But Harold was smiling; I could tell.

Anyway, we were all quiet for several seconds until Mrs. Majesty "recovered" from her spirit-induced spell, sat up straight in her chair and sighed once more. Then we stood, someone turned on the lights, and the ladies began chatting animatedly with Mrs. Majesty. We left the breakfast room in a clump and walked out into the hall where the great staircase loomed.

And then, reminding me of a fairy, a vision in rose-colored taffeta uttered a shriek of hellacious fright, fluttered over the high balcony, and fell to the parquet floor with a sickening splat.

Available in Paperback and eBook from Your Favorite Bookstore or Online Retailer

ALSO BY ALICE DUNCAN

The Mercy Allcutt Mystery Series

Lost Among the Angels

Angels Flight

Fallen Angels

Angels of Mercy

Thanksgiving Angels

The Daisy Gumm Majesty Mystery Series

Strong Spirits

Fine Spirits

High Spirits

Hungry Spirits

Genteel Spirits

Ancient Spirits

Spirits Revived

Dark Spirits

Spirits Onstage

Unsettled Spirits

Bruised Spirits

Spirits United

Spirits Unearthed

Shaken Spirits

Scarlet Spirits

ABOUT THE AUTHOR

Award-winning author Alice Duncan lives with a herd of wild dachshunds (enriched from time to time with fosterees from New Mexico Dachshund Rescue) in Roswell, New Mexico. She's not a UFO enthusiast; she's in Roswell because her mother's family settled there fifty years before the aliens crashed (and living in Roswell, NM, is cheaper than living in Pasadena, CA, unfortunately). Alice would love to hear from you at alice@aliceduncan.net

www.aliceduncan.net

facebook.com/alice.duncan.925

CPSIA information can be obtained
at www.ICGtesting.com
Printed in the USA
BVHW032326040220
571480BV00001B/7